THE
MONTANA
GOLD MINE

Other books by Tim Piper

Jubilee Walker Series

The Powell Expeditions

The Yellowstone Campaign

The Northern Pacific Railroad

THE
MONTANA GOLD MINE

JUBILEE WALKER SERIES **BOOK 4**

TIM PIPER

Book design by The Book Designers
https://bookdesigners.com/

ISBN 979-8-9884186-9-6 (hardback)
ISBN 979-8-9993084-0-5 (paperback)
ISBN 979-8-9993084-1-2 (ebook)

Library of Congress Number: 2025913128

Published by
Sunshine Parade Publishing
1907 Sinclair Ct.
Bloomington, IL 61704
https://www.sunshineparadepublishing.com

To Lee Piper

CHAPTER 1

On the first day of spring in 1874, Jubilee Walker stepped out of the stagecoach in front of the Metropolitan Hotel in Bozeman, Montana Territory. He disliked travel by stagecoach, but it was faster than horseback, and he was pressed for time. The weather was dry and the temperature above freezing, but Jubil turned the collar up on his parka and pulled his hat down to his eyes—not for warmth but for privacy. He was on a reconnaissance mission and wanted to go unnoticed, if possible.

He stood by as two other passengers exited the stagecoach and the driver began unloading baggage from the boot. Jubil leaned his Henry rifle against the wheel of the stage as the driver handed him his trapper's pack. He slipped his arms into the straps and settled the pack on his back, then picked up his rifle. He hoped to be here no longer than a few days, but he was carrying everything he needed to survive indefinitely.

He had hardly spoken a word to the driver or his fellow travelers, which went against his nature. It took a good amount of discipline now to turn away without saying goodbye to them, but he managed to do it. He set out toward the livery, where he was relieved to find an unfamiliar man working, so he was able to hire a horse without interacting with the livery owner, whom he knew well. He would be out of town and on his way before anyone recognized him.

He chose a young chestnut stallion that reminded him of his own horse, Star. As he saddled the horse and strapped the pack across his haunches, Jubil talked to him to calm him, as was his habit with all horses. "We're hardly going to be together long enough for me to name you," he said. "How about No Name? Would you answer to that?" Jubil rubbed and patted the horse's neck, smiling at his own joke. The name was not as meaningless as it might sound. It had been the name of one of the boats in which he had ridden the Colorado River through the length of the Grand Canyon with Major John Wesley Powell in 1869. The boat had ended up broken in half on the rocks, and he had nearly drowned in the incident. He hoped to avoid such drama on this trip.

He rode south through town and then turned east. In less than an hour, he was passing a group of white buildings to the north—Fort Ellis. He would stop there on the way back from the Crow reservation, which was near the Yellowstone River, about thirty miles away.

Once past the fort, he was able to breathe easy and stop looking over his shoulder. He settled into the ride. The aroma of pine needles filled the air as the trail followed the East Gallatin River over hilly country covered with pine timber on the northern slopes. The ravines and small valleys were still filled with snow, and the icy streams sparkled in the sun. It felt good to be out here on his own in a place that meant so much to him.

Six miles from Fort Ellis, he crossed the Bozeman Pass, a notch in the Gallatin Range forming the apex of two watersheds, one that sloped to the Gallatin River, the other to the Yellowstone. When he reached the top of the pass, he paused to take in the beloved vista of Paradise Valley. All the way to the southern horizon, the Yellowstone River meandered through a valley several miles wide and bounded by snow-capped mountains on either side. Spread across the floor of the valley were thousands of grassy acres dotted with the habitations of settlers. Further south lay the wonderland of Yellowstone National Park.

For a moment, Jubil longed for the incredulous awe he had experienced the first time he had seen the geysers, the falls, the mud pots, and hot springs—and for the innocence and simplicity of his life back then. A lot had happened in the four years since he had first traveled this way. Those four years had been filled with life lessons and increasing responsibility.

Last year, he had barely escaped the loss of his outfitting business and his farm to financier Jay Cooke. He was forced to admit to his wife, Nelly, and his surrogate parents and senior business partners, Abe and Lily Warner, that he had been rash in his involvement with Cooke. They were gracious enough to accept his apologies.

But his original goals remained: He wanted to share the wonders of Yellowstone National Park with adventurous tourists and see it protected from exploitation. His partnership with Jay Cooke over the past two years had promised significant funding and political support for responsible development of the park. But when Cooke's financial empire collapsed, so did Jubil's plans. His dream of seeing the park fulfill its promise had faced a major setback, but he had not lost hope.

To finance his effort, he planned to market Warner and Walker's custom merchandise through new mail-order and wholesale channels, expand his adventure tour business to include Yellowstone Park, and possibly open a store in Bozeman. He was also determined to end the corruption at the Crow Agency supplying the reservation where his friend White Dog lived. He had made some progress in that regard, but the problem persisted.

Now, only six months after Cooke declared bankruptcy and his financial empire collapsed, all those plans and ambitions were threatened by a depressed economy, which many businesses, including Jubil's, were struggling to survive. People weren't spending their money on outdoor gear, and if he did not find another source of income for his store, Warner and Walker Outfitters would have to close its doors.

He had come to Montana to find out who was supplying the Crow Agency now. Opening a store in Bozeman would only be profitable if he could win the supply business for both the fort and the reservation, and whoever was currently doing that would not welcome competition, especially from Jubil.

Jubil and No Name continued down the path beside Trail Creek to the Yellowstone River and then followed the river as it curved to the east. A few miles further on was the ferry crossing where Jubil had nearly lost his life when he crossed the flooded Yellowstone on horseback during the Northern Pacific Railroad survey in 1872. But today the water was low, and he dismounted and led No Name across, his knee-high oiled-leather boots keeping his feet warm and dry. From there it was only a short ride to the reservation.

Dusk was falling as he approached the agency compound, south of which the teepees of the tribe were spread across a wide area. Jubil scanned the settlement for his friend White Dog but didn't see him. Two Crow boys were beginning to close the gates to the stockade fence. They stared at him as he tipped his hat and rode into the compound. Inside was a corral, a mission school, and the agency store. On the porch of the store, a red-haired man about Jubil's age sat in a rocking chair, watching him.

"Sure, and if it isn't Jubilee Walker," the man said with a grin. As Jubil dismounted, he continued, "I assume you'll be spending the night. You can put your pack in the store, and we'll put your horse in the corral." He called to the boys to take No Name.

"Hello, Flynn," Jubil said, climbing the steps to the porch.

The man rocked back in his chair and looked up at him without rising. "I've never known you to pay a social call when it was good news. I hope you're about to surprise me."

"I've come especially to see you," Jubil said, amused and a bit surprised to find himself happy to see Flynn.

"I'm honored," Flynn said sarcastically.

Jubil had first met Flynn seven years ago as one of three Irish teamsters—Murphy, O'Brien, and Flynn—on a Warner and Company supply train while traveling across the Nebraska plains. Murphy and O'Brien had been unpleasant then and eventually proved even more so, but Jubil had always liked Flynn. At first, Jubil had taken him for a good-natured but simple-minded fellow who meekly went along with whatever he was told. But over time, he had come to see him as a crafty survivor, capable of adapting to any situation while staying just outside the danger zone.

Jubil sat down in the rocker next to Flynn's.

"Did you get my letter?" Jubil said.

"I did," Flynn said.

"Why didn't you answer?" Jubil said.

"I'm in a delicate situation here, Walker," Flynn said, giving him the side-eye and shaking his head. "The only place I can mail a letter is through the Bozeman post office. Your name would draw attention, that letter would get read, certain people would get the word, and my goose would be cooked."

"That's why I'm here," Jubil said. "To find out who those 'certain people' are."

Flynn turned his head to meet Jubil's gaze directly. His expression was a mixture of puzzlement and exasperation.

"I last saw you in what—the summer of '72?"

Jubil nodded.

"You were all wound up in the railroad business," Flynn said. "Why are you suddenly so interested in the goings-on out here?"

"We'll get to that," Jubil said, "but first I want to know who is in charge of the operation now that Phineas Black, Murphy, and O'Brien are out of the picture."

Flynn looked away again and rocked in his chair as he considered his response.

When Jubil had first come to Bozeman in 1870 to join the Washburn Expedition, he had been confronted by a local businessman, Phineas Black, who owned the local mercantile, the only one in town, along with a local hotel and various mining interests. Black's mines in Virginia City and Cooke City were financing his growing business interests, and he was determined to remove any resources of value from the Yellowstone Basin.

Jubil informed him that he intended to campaign for government protection of Yellowstone, and Black subsequently hired a man to burn down Jubil's store as a warning to stay out of Black's way. Jubil's business partner and friend, Luke Warner, had died in that fire. Black had then ordered Jubil kidnapped and killed, but White Dog had stepped in and interrupted the plan. In the ensuing showdown, Jubil had killed Phineas Black, and White Dog had killed his henchman, Mr. Murphy.

Jubil had also identified Black as the man responsible for the corruption at the Crow Agency. After Black's death, the situation had continued under another of his men, Mr. O'Brien. When Jubil returned to the area on the Northern Pacific Railroad survey, he was ambushed by O'Brien, who was killed in that battle. But the corruption at the agency continued.

"As I believe I told you the last time we met," Flynn said, "I knew O'Brien wasn't the kingpin of the operation—he was just another toady. There was talk that Black had a partner who helped finance his businesses, but I had no inkling who that person was. And I didn't want to know. Then a few weeks after O'Brien's demise, a fellow showed up in Bozeman who bore a striking resemblance to Phineas Black. He introduced himself as none other than Lucius Black, Phineas's older brother and mysterious business partner."

Jubil leaned back in his rocking chair, taking in this news.

"Well, that's not good," he said. He was surprised to learn that Phineas Black had living family members. He would have expected any family ties to increase the urge for revenge after Phineas's death, but it had been two years since the showdown that had killed him and Murphy. Nor had anyone vowed revenge on Jubil for O'Brien's death over a year ago. Perhaps Lucius Black was not interested in revenge.

"What do you know about him?" Jubil said.

"I know he made his fortune in the California gold fields and moved here from San Francisco," Flynn said. "I rarely see him. Most often I deal with his security man, McTavish. I've learned a fair lot from letting him blow hard about himself and his boss."

Jubil was pleased that Flynn was giving up this information so willingly. He seemed open to working with Jubil, even friendly. But Flynn had always been a cagey one, and Jubil's instincts were telling him to be careful of trusting him completely.

"How do you think Black would take to my presence out here?" Jubil said.

Flynn gave him a suspicious look. "Not kindly, I expect," he said. "But he's a cooler head than his brother. He doesn't wear a gun, but he still gets his way. He's just wilier about it." Flynn studied Jubil. "How long are you staying? What are you up to?"

"I'm only staying a few days," Jubil said, ignoring Flynn's other question. "The supply corruption here at the agency, is that still happening?"

"Sure, you know it is," Flynn said. "Same as it ever was."

Jubil nodded.

"What kind of records do you keep?" Jubil asked. "Do you have all your ledgers, invoices, reports, and the like?"

"Not here," Flynn said. "Black has a man at the mercantile who handles all that."

"They don't trust you with it?" Jubil said.

"They believe I'm too feeble-minded to manage the job,"

Flynn said with a glimmer of humor in his eyes. "I'm not sure where they get that idea, but I don't mind. It's a bother anyway." He narrowed his eyes at Jubil. "Why do you ask?"

"I'm determined to put an end to this ill treatment of the Crow," Jubil said, "and to the defrauding of the government. I've got some meetings in Washington, DC, to visit with government officials. I'm going to bring the situation to their attention. I came to find out who is behind the operation and bring back some hard evidence. But I'm satisfied with just knowing who is accountable—for now anyway."

Jubil's friend Walter Trumbull had arranged two meetings for next month, one with Secretary of the Interior Columbus Delano, the other with General William T. Sherman. With General Sherman's support, Jubil hoped to expand his business arrangements with the US Army. And he hoped Secretary Delano would give him a role in the development of Yellowstone National Park and would be eager to stop the illegal activity at the Crow Agency. The Department of the Interior was responsible for the nation's public lands, mineral resources, and Indian Affairs, so Secretary Delano had authority over both of Jubil's concerns.

"You're inviting a mess of trouble," Flynn said.

"I made White Dog a promise to do whatever I could to stop this," Jubil said. "And I intend to keep that promise. Speaking of White Dog, is he here?"

"No," Flynn said. "He's out scouting for the army. The new fort commander and Lieutenant Doane passed through a couple of days ago leading a patrol. They were headed east to remind the Sioux to keep to themselves."

Jubil's heart sank. "That's too bad," he said. "When you see him next, tell him I'm sorry I missed him."

Jubil was disappointed, not only because he wouldn't have the chance to see White Dog, but also because he wouldn't be able to visit Lieutenant Doane at Fort Ellis. He had hoped

Lieutenant Doane would introduce him to the fort command-er to discuss Jubil's prospects for supplying the fort. His visit would be even shorter than he had planned.

Jubil sat looking at the sky above the agency compound as the red-orange sunset made gray clouds glow like the embers of a dying fire. Flynn had given him the information he came for, and there was nothing to be gained by staying longer. He would start back tomorrow. He studied Flynn in the fading light as he considered not only his own future but Flynn's as well.

"You ought to get out of here," Jubil said, "before the gov-ernment comes down on the place. You look guilty in this job—you *are* guilty. You're complicit, if nothing else."

"Aye," Flynn said, "but don't you think the Bureau of Indi-an Affairs knows what goes on out here? I think they're more interested in feathering their own nests than booting me out of mine. I'll know when it's time to fly—but I appreciate your high-minded concern."

Flynn's scorn stung a bit. Jubil was truly concerned for him, as a friend. Flynn was actually doing the best he could for the Crow people under the circumstances, and White Dog had never expressed any displeasure with him. To Jubil, this said more about Flynn's character than his association with Black did. Flynn's comment about the Bureau being complicit in the corruption triggered a concern.

"Are you sure the Bureau of Indian Affairs knows what Black is up to?" Jubil said.

"Do I have proof?" Flynn asked. "Well, no. But I've got a pretty fair idea how these things work, you know. You can bet Black pays someone for his spot at the trough."

"How far up the chain of government do you think the cor-ruption goes?" Jubil asked.

"At what level of government do your officials suddenly be-come pillars of virtue?" Flynn asked with an air of bemusement.

"Hmm," Jubil said. "Point taken." He might have to tread

more carefully with Delano than he had been expecting to. "You won't mention our visit to your associates, will you?" Jubil said.

"I don't see how that would serve me well," Flynn said.

Jubil nodded. The sky was dark now, and a thin crescent moon shone through a gap in the clouds. He wondered how he might go about finding out if Lucius Black were more reasonable than his brother.

"Let's go inside," Flynn said. "I'll find us some supper."

They walked through the store to a door which opened into Flynn's private quarters. Flynn fetched a chicken from the coop, and while it roasted on a spit in the fireplace, he made an excellent pan of cornbread. The sizzle and smell of the chicken reminded Jubil of his uncle Pete's cabin on the family farm near Bloomington, Illinois, where Jubil had roasted many a chicken and wished for a life of adventure. After the best meal he'd had in a week, he spread his bedroll out near the hearth.

"I'll be on my way early tomorrow," Jubil said. "Thanks for the information and the hospitality. You look out for yourself."

"Sure, and I always do, don't I?" Flynn said, sounding unconcerned.

"Tell White Dog I'll be back, but I don't know exactly when," Jubil said.

"I'm not sure that's good news," Flynn said glibly. "But I'll tell him."

Jubil was on his way in the morning before Flynn awoke. The next stage to Corinne would not leave until the following day, so he had time on his hands. It was tempting to get a room at the Guy House and pump the proprietor, whom he knew well, for information about Lucius Black. Instead, he found a spot outside Bozeman and set up camp there. In the morning, he packed up and rode to the livery, where he returned No Name.

The stage depot was the Metropolitan Hotel, formerly owned by Phineas Black and now, apparently, owned by his brother. He had a voucher for his return that he had purchased in Corinne, so he would not need to see the desk clerk inside. Jubil assumed that Black lived in the hotel, as his brother had, so he was reluctant to go in and chance being recognized. Instead, he stood in the alley between the hotel and the building next door and watched as the stage pulled up.

A middle-aged couple and a younger couple stepped out of the hotel, each carrying a travel bag—which meant the stage was full. As the passengers debated their seating arrangement, the driver took their bags and arranged them on the boot. Jubil stepped out of the alley, showed the driver his voucher, and asked him how he would feel about Jubil riding with him up top, which the driver agreed to. Jubil handed over his pack to be stowed with the luggage, and the driver finished arranging the bags, covered them with a sheet of canvas, and lashed them down tight. As Jubil stood admiring the driver's technique, a man coming out of the hotel caught his eye.

He was dressed in a cream-colored suit and had gray shoulder-length hair and a well-trimmed mustache. The resemblance to Phineas Black was unmistakable, although this man was at least ten years older. He lit a cigar and leaned against the wall of the hotel. Jubil watched from under the brim of his hat as the man and some of the passersby exchanged greetings.

"Mr. Walker?"

A jolt shook Jubil as he heard someone call his name.

"Is that you?"

It was John Mendenhall, the local sheriff, standing on the boardwalk between Jubil and Lucius Black. Mendenhall's voice had attracted Black's attention. To Jubil's dismay, the sheriff, grinning, stepped off the boardwalk and came to shake his hand.

"I'm pleased to see you looking so fit," Mendenhall said. "Last time I saw you, you were laid up with a hole in your shoulder, courtesy of Phineas Black. What brings you to town?"

"I had some business at the fort," Jubil fabricated. "I'm just passing through."

"I see," the sheriff said. He turned to spit tobacco juice.

Out of the corner of his eye, Jubil saw the man in the cream-colored suit approaching them. So much for anonymity.

"Introduce me to your friend, Sheriff," the gray-haired man said, looking Jubil in the eye. His eyes were a pale gray that gave him the look of a wolf.

Jubil decided to take the initiative, now that his presence was known. "Jubilee Walker," he said and extended his hand.

"Lucius Black," the man said.

Black's grip was firm, but his hands were soft, clearly not those of an outdoorsman.

The sheriff looked back and forth between the two men with wary anticipation as he explained Jubil's presence to Black.

"I'm fortunate to have encountered you then," Black said, finally releasing his grip on Jubil's hand. He smiled with his mouth but not his eyes. "You have business with the army?"

"Yes, but it's preliminary," Jubil said. He decided to be as straightforward as he could with Black, which was truer to his nature than sneaking around. "Look, that situation with your brother—" he began.

"You needn't say another word," Black said, holding up his hands, palms out. "Phineas was always a hothead. The sheriff looked into the matter and was satisfied. That's good enough for me. Whatever differences my brother had with you, that was no way to go about resolving them."

Jubil wanted to believe Black was sincere, but his instincts were telling him otherwise. What would Black be saying if the sheriff were not standing here?

"I'm glad to hear that's how you see it," Jubil said. "I regret that it had to come to that."

"I followed your involvement with Jay Cooke with interest," Black said. "Too bad it all collapsed. Are you still determined to promote Yellowstone? Sounds like you're considering doing business out here."

"Well, like I said," Jubil said, "my plans are tentative right now."

"Yes, terrible climate for business these days," Black said. "I'm sure you feel it too. Well, if you decide to do business out here, you'll find me very competitive—" Black turned to address the sheriff with a jovial smile "—within the bounds of the law, of course."

Black's tone was light, even comedic.

Mendenhall looked at Black skeptically and spit again. "Yes, well, you make sure that's true, Mr. Black. Good to see you, Walker."

As the sheriff walked away, the stage driver called out to Jubil.

"Excuse me gents, but the stage is ready to roll."

With the sheriff out of earshot, Jubil could not resist testing Black's congeniality.

"Speaking of the bounds of the law," Jubil said conspiratorially, "a friend at the reservation told me about some irregularities with the supplies. You might want to check on that before word gets out."

Black frowned, his friendly facade slipping. "I wouldn't know anything about that," he said. "I've got a man at the mercantile who handles that business. I understand the agent out there is an Irishman. Who knows what he's up to?"

This comment told Jubil everything he needed to know about Black. Nothing he had said could be trusted.

"Good day, Mr. Black," Jubil said. Without a handshake, he walked past Black and climbed onto the seat beside the stage driver. The driver snapped the reins, and the coach lurched forward toward Corinne.

A week later, Jubil arrived by train in Council Bluffs, Iowa, took up his pack, and walked up Lower Broadway to Warner and Walker Outfitters, where he found one of his partners, Ike Boswell, straightening the stock on a shelf. There were no customers in the store. Ike turned around as Jubil opened the door.

"Welcome back," Ike said.

"Thanks," Jubil said. "Has business been this slow since I left?"

Ike nodded.

As Jubil took his pack off and leaned it against the wall, his other partner, Eli Boswell, walked out of the storeroom.

"What are you doing here?" Jubil asked Eli. They had decided before Jubil left for the Crow Reservation that Eli would go on the road to try to drum up wholesale business.

"I work here. Remember?" Eli said sarcastically.

Ike and Eli were his wife Nelly's younger twin brothers. They had helped Jubil and Luke build their store in Bloomington and then worked for them once it opened. After Luke died, Abe and Lily Warner had moved back to Nantucket, and the boys became Jubil's partners in operating the Council Bluffs store. Although they were identical twins, they were easy to tell apart. Ike was the tidy, organized one, Eli the rumpled, rowdy one. Still, they shared the deep bond that seemed typical of twins.

"I asked him to come back," Ike said. "We weren't generating enough sales to even cover his travel. Store owners don't want to take on new products in this slow market. Plus, I need him here—Caleb quit. His father can't afford a hired hand anymore, so Caleb is needed on the farm. This month I wasn't able to make payroll, even without you drawing your usual salary. I paid Caleb in full, and Eli and I took a partial salary. We can't keep this up for long."

"No, we can't," Jubil said. "But I want you and Eli to get paid. I have reserves we can draw on. Don't worry about me, I'll manage." Jubil had not drawn his usual salary since December. He was living on money from the inheritance his parents had left him, and he still had enough left to support himself for a while. But if he started using it to cover all the store's operating expenses, it wouldn't last long. Technically, he was heir to the Warner estate, but that was money he did not have access to without going to Abe, which he did not want to do routinely.

"Sorry the wholesale venture wasn't working out, Eli," Jubil said.

"That's all right," Eli said. "I wasn't enjoying it as much as I had hoped. I think we should just make up the revenue shortfall by doing more adventure tours."

"We'll need a better turnout than we've gotten so far for our July trip," Jubil said.

He and Eli would be leading their first adventure tour this summer, taking a group of tourists along the same route in Colorado that Jubil had traveled with Major Powell in 1868, the year they summited Longs Peak. Jubil was disappointed that only eight people had signed up. He had expected at least twice as many. More tour revenue would have helped keep the store afloat, but that prospect was not looking good.

"Did we hear back from Mr. Ward?" Jubil said to Ike.

They had been trying to arrange a meeting with Aaron Montgomery Ward to discuss the status of their new mail-order business partnership.

"No," Ike said, "but I'll try contacting him again while you're in Washington."

"Good," Jubil said. "Thanks."

"What did you find out in Montana?" Ike said.

Jubil described his visit with Flynn and his unexpected meeting with Lucius Black. The twins exchanged a long look. Jubil found these silent conversations of theirs somewhat eerie.

"Don't you think Black is dangerous?" Ike asked.

"I don't think he's to be trusted," Jubil said. "But he's had plenty of time to come after me if he was interested in revenge. I think there's plenty of trade out there for both of us."

"I agree with Jubil," Eli said. "Bozeman's growing. There's plenty of room for another store. Black can't stop us from doing business out there if we want to."

Ike looked unconvinced, but he kept his thoughts to himself. Jubil fixed his gaze on Ike.

"I owe it to Luke, and to all of us, to keep this business going," Jubil said patiently, "and besides, there's more at stake here than just business. I made a vow to White Dog that I intend to keep. Black is taking advantage of the Crow and the government, and if he won't do the job right, then I will. I can't control how Black responds to that, but I'll defend myself if necessary."

Ike held Jubil's gaze, then nodded.

"Do you think Abe's going to support this?" Ike said.

"I'd like to have his support," Jubil said, "but this is my decision. He's agreed to my idea to try to win the supply contract at Fort Ellis. He knows we've got limited opportunities to make a profit in this economy. I wrote and told him that I was making a trip to Bozeman to look into our prospects for doing business there. After my meetings in Washington next week, Nelly and I are going to visit Abe and Lily, and I'll go through the details with them."

"I don't see how we can afford to open another store," Ike said, "when this one isn't even making a profit."

"I've got some ideas," Jubil said, "but let's not worry about that until I get back." He was not happy with the current situation, but he wasn't deterred either. Neither a weak economy nor Lucius Black was going to stop him from building his business.

"Who would run a store for us out there"? Eli said.

"I was thinking I might—for a while," Jubil said. "Or maybe you."

Eli's eyebrows went up.

"But we're getting ahead of ourselves," Jubil said. "I'm going on up to the house to get cleaned up and pack. I'll be on my way to Washington tomorrow, and we'll soon know which direction we're going."

Jubil and the boys lived in the Warners' home in Council Bluffs, where their long-time staff, Mr. and Mrs. Garcia, continued to maintain the house and property. What had once seemed like a luxurious estate to Jubil had come to feel like home.

Before leaving Council Bluffs the next morning, Jubil stopped by the post office, where he was excited to find a letter from his friend Nathaniel Langford. He had last seen Langford in 1872 in Bozeman. Langford was in the area to scout a route for a railroad spur up from Corinne to enter Yellowstone from the west. He had just been named park superintendent, and Jubil told him of his partnership with Cooke. Langford's congratulations had seemed strangely subdued, and Jubil wondered if Langford had been hoping that Cooke would offer him such a partnership.

Jubil had written to Langford since then—once to invite him to his and Nelly's wedding and once after the collapse of Cooke's business to reiterate his interest in developing the park—but Langford had not replied. At first, Jubil assumed Langford's government positions were keeping him so busy that he couldn't respond right away, but as the months passed, he worried that he had somehow offended his friend.

Once Walter had scheduled a meeting with Secretary Delano, Jubil shook off his uneasiness and wrote to Langford again, this time to say that he would prefer to have Langford's support before talking to Delano about developing the park. He also mentioned the urgency he felt about the Crow Agency situation and his hope that he would find an ally in Delano.

My Dear Mr. Walker, Langford's letter began:

I apologize profusely for my bad manners in having delayed so long in responding to your letters. I offer the thin excuse of an unreliable system of forwarding and holding my mail, which delayed my receipt of them, but now having them in hand, I hasten to reply.

First, please accept my congratulations on your marriage! I'm sure it was a delightful event and regret my absence. Please offer your bride my congratulations, and extend my best wishes.

With regard to your situation following the collapse of Cooke's financial empire, my sincerest condolences. At our last meeting, I did not feel it was my place to express my concerns over your financial entanglement with Cooke, but I am pleased to hear you escaped relatively unscathed. I find Cooke to be fundamentally a good man, but his failures are as monumental as his successes. It can be dangerous to be caught up in such grand schemes.

I am pleased to hear that, following your disappointment with Cooke, your dedication to seeing the park meet its potential is still alive. I hate to deepen your disappointment, but I am not in favor of developing amenities for tourists in the park until adequate funding from Congress has been allotted to see to its proper administration and protection. I have made this position abundantly clear to Secretary Delano.

I understand completely your desire to move forward in the face of my unresponsiveness by arranging a meeting with the secretary. You may feel free to tell him you have my support for being involved in the further development of the park, under the condition that you reiterate that Congressional funding is para-mount before any such activity begins in earnest. Perhaps add-ing your voice to the call for funding will have some benefit. I wish you the best of luck in the matter of the Crow Agency.

My bank examiner duties are satisfying, and my circle of business associates has grown considerably, but my heart yearns to spend my days in the service of protecting and enhancing the wonderland of Yellowstone National Park. Alas, I find little time to be there.

I look forward to the occasion of our next meeting. Should one not occur soon by chance, we should arrange one by design.

Your friend,

Nathaniel P. Langford

The letter was a great relief. Jubil would gladly offer to support the lobbying effort to get funding for the park. Walter had recruited him to lobby for passage of the park bill, and he had enjoyed it more than he had expected to. He left Council Bluffs feeling confident about his plans.

CHAPTER 2

Jubil arrived at the National Hotel in Washington, DC, in the late afternoon. He was looking forward to a relaxed and, he hoped, profitable visit with his friend General William T. Sherman, but he did not dare to hope that his meeting with Secretary Delano would be as comfortable. He was always a bit intimidated before meeting important people, but he knew he would be fine once the conversation got underway. Knowing that didn't soothe his jittery nerves.

He checked into the hotel, and the desk clerk informed him that Walter Trumbull was waiting for him in the dining room. Jubil tipped the bellman to take his bag to his room and went to join his friend. The dining room was large and open with windows facing Pennsylvania Avenue, and it buzzed with the conversations of two hundred or more diners and the activity of dozens of waiters and busboys.

Across the room he saw Walter, tall and lanky, stand to greet him. Jubil had met Walter, the son of now-retired Illinois Senator Lyman Trumbull, on the Washburn Expedition to Yellowstone in 1870.

"Welcome back," Walter said with a hearty handshake, a smile creasing his long clean-shaven face.

They took their seats, and Walter hailed a waiter. Walter ordered another glass of wine, and Jubil ordered one for himself.

"It's good to see you," Jubil said to Walter. "I appreciate the time you've put in to help me with this."

"What good is a friend in Washington if he can't help you make a deal?" Walter said, waving off the compliment.

The waiter brought their drinks and took their supper order.

"I've got some news," Jubil said. He told Walter about Langford's letter.

"That's excellent," Walter said. "It strengthens your position."

"Yes," Jubil said, "but it changes the nature of our visit a bit. Rather than petitioning Delano for his support, we've come to offer ours—to lobby for park funding."

"Good," Walter nodded. "This is good."

"Yes," Jubil said, "Now what can you tell me about Secretary Delano? Do you think he'll take my concerns seriously?"

"Well . . . he's a lawyer, rancher, banker, former congressman from Ohio. An independent and opinionated sort. Grant appointed him, but they don't see eye to eye on everything—and we might not either," Walter said, pointing a finger at Jubil for dramatic effect.

"He's a great champion of Yellowstone National Park. He approved government funding for the Hayden survey in '71; helped get the park bill passed; appointed our friend Nathaniel Langford as the park's first superintendent; and he's pushing a bill to fund enforcement of park policy and make improvements.

"But," Walter said, pausing for effect, "he is no friend to native tribes. He stops short of advocating for their elimination, but that's mostly to humor Grant and his Peace Policy. He's very vocal, however, about the need to confine them to smaller and smaller tracts of unproductive land. And he advocates openly for the extinction of the bison herds as a means to force them to adapt or die. We're not likely to get any sympathy from him regarding the situation at the Crow reservation."

Jubil remembered how General Sherman had described Grant's Peace Policy: The army was not to exterminate the Indians but to subdue them. As Jubil saw it, the final blow would be to let them die from neglect.

"Another thing that won't help our cause," Walter continued, "is that he apparently feels comfortable ignoring the legal guidelines of the Civil Service Commission, which Grant himself put into place to make sure federal government employees are hired on merit rather than through cronyism. I'm not sure why Grant is letting him get away with it, but we're not likely to get much sympathy regarding how contracts are awarded by agents at the reservations."

"I spoke with Flynn at the Crow Agency," Jubil said. "He thinks the Bureau of Indian Affairs is complicit in the corruption. He thinks it may go up the chain of command. Do you?"

Walter looked uneasy. "I don't know," he said. "There are always rumors in Washington. I think you should talk mainly about developing Yellowstone, your tours, and opening a store in Bozeman." Walter leaned in conspiratorially. "Once you have some agreement about Yellowstone, then slip in a mention of the problems with the agency—offer to help clean up the operation there. Convince him you're the better-connected man who can deliver higher-level favors and influence."

Jubil sat back in his chair and stared at his friend. "You went too far there, Walter," Jubil said. "I won't pretend to be part of his schemes."

"All right, all right," Walter said, shaking his head at Jubil's concerns. "But whatever you do, don't lecture him."

The waiter brought their food. The aroma wafting from the stuffed loin of veal on Jubil's plate reminded him of how long it had been since lunch.

"I'll discuss Yellowstone first," Jubil said. "But I won't leave without a clear idea of what Delano is going to do about the Crow Agency."

"Of course," Walter said, with a note of doubt in his voice that planted a small seed of irritation in Jubil's mind.

In the morning, Walter and Jubil set out in a hired carriage for the short trip up Pennsylvania Avenue to Secretary Delano's home on Fifteenth Street. Several of the president's cabinet lived near the White House, within walking distance in decent weather.

The housekeeper escorted them into Delano's office. Every surface of hardwood was burnished to a shine, and the room smelled of lemon oil and leather. Jubil rubbed his hands together to warm them and to occupy his jittery nerves. He looked at the sets of matching books that filled the bookcases and wondered whether anyone had ever read them.

When Delano came in, Walter said, "Thank you for meeting with us, Mr. Secretary." He gave a small bow. "I'd like you to meet Jubilee Walker."

Delano and Jubil shook hands. The secretary was tall and thin, with a clean-shaven upper lip and a salt-and-pepper beard that contrasted with his head of dark hair. His bushy eyebrows stood out like ledges over sparkling deep-set eyes that belied an otherwise stern demeanor.

"Mr. Walker," Delano said, his voice deep and resonant but soft. "How do you do? I understand you are one of the few to participate in both the 1870 and the 1871 Yellowstone expeditions?"

"Yes, sir," Jubil said. "Second Lieutenant Cheyney Doane and I share that distinction."

"I understand you've also adventured with Major John Wesley Powell," Delano said.

"Yes, sir," Jubil said. "The major is a family friend. He allowed me to join him in '68 and '69." These had been Jubil's first expeditions, and Jubil was a bit surprised that Delano knew about them. While adventuring with Powell, Jubil had been one of the first to summit Longs Peak in the Colorado Rockies and run the length of the Colorado River through the Grand Canyon.

Secretary Delano took a seat behind his desk and invited them to sit down in the chairs facing him while the house-keeper came in to serve coffee.

"I have heard that the two of you met on the 1870 expedition with General Washburn," Delano said to them both.

"Yes, sir," Walter said. "I was assistant to Truman Everts, and Jubil was there at the invitation of General Sheridan."

"Was that the trip during which you almost lost Mr. Everts?" Delano asked with a troubled expression.

"Yes, sir. That was a dreadful experience—having to go on without him. It seemed a miracle he survived."

Walter's friend Truman Everts had gotten separated from the expedition party in the heavy woods and rough terrain on the southern end of Yellowstone Lake. The men scoured the area for several days looking for him, but an early winter forced them to abandon their search. Remarkably, Everts managed to survive a month alone before being rescued by Jack Baronett, who operated a toll bridge on the Yellowstone River.

"Yes, I'm sure," Delano said sympathetically. "How is Truman these days?"

"Feisty as ever," Walter said with a grin.

"You both became well acquainted with Mr. Langford on that expedition then?"

"Yes, my friend here made a particularly strong first impression on him," Walter said, glancing at Jubil.

"I suppose that's true," Jubil said, the conversation having put him completely at ease. He told the story of how one of the mules spooked and ran; how Langford's hand was tangled in the lead rope and he was dragged behind; how, after a collision with a log, he was knocked unconscious before Jubil ran the mule down and stopped it. Thankfully, Langford was not badly hurt.

Delano laughed at the images as Jubil described them. "I can see how Mr. Langford would decide you were a handy fellow to have along," Delano said. "It must be a wonderful place—the Yellowstone Basin. I'd love to see it myself one day."

"I'd love to show you around, sir," Jubil said.

Delano nodded agreeably. "Well, I'm sure you and Mr. Trumbull could regale me for hours with tales of Yellowstone, but I suppose you're not here to relive your adventures. Mr. Trumbull mentioned that you would like to discuss the development of the park. I'm surprised you still have an appetite for it, considering your recent experience with Jay Cooke."

Jubil felt his brow furrowing. It wasn't a criticism, but it wasn't a compliment either.

"My interest in Yellowstone began during my first visit there, sir, so it predates my involvement with Mr. Cooke," Jubil said carefully. "My ideas may not be as grand as his, but they have the advantage of being achievable."

"That summarizes Cooke neatly," Delano said with a grin. "You're no longer involved in business affairs with him then?"

"No, sir," Jubil said. "We parted on decent terms, but we haven't been in touch."

"I see," Delano said, gazing out at Jubil from beneath the ledges of his brows. "Your interests are your own. I'm curious to hear your proposal."

"I don't see the Northern Pacific Railroad continuing west from Bismarck anytime soon," Jubil said. "I believe the route to Bozeman and into the park from the north will remain pretty remote for several years to come. When I last saw Mr. Langford, he was thinking about bringing people in through the west side of the park instead. I don't know why the Union Pacific hasn't built a spur up from Corinne, Utah, to Bozeman and Helena, but I'm not going to make railroad routes my mission anymore. I'm thinking of building customized stage-coaches to make a comfortable trip north from Corinne to a nice inn by the Madison River, then follow the river into the park from the west."

"That's a sound plan," Delano said with a nod. "But you don't need anything from me to do that."

"No, I don't expect the government to bring people to the park," Jubil said, "but once they've arrived, they need access. No private investor can afford to build roads and trails. Without those, the park will never be enjoyed by great numbers of people, and it will eventually be despoiled by people who would exploit its resources."

"I've made Jubil aware of the funding bill," Walter said. "We're willing to assist in that lobbying effort if you approve of our involvement."

"I believe we have the votes we'll need," Delano said, "but your offer is appreciated. I'll be in touch if things change. I can't guarantee that the funds will go toward building roads. The decisions about how to apply the funding will be the responsibility of Mr. Langford, as the superintendent of the park. I make it a practice not to meddle in the business of those I put in positions of responsibility."

"He has an excellent plan for constructing a loop of roads to reach the major attractions," Jubil said, "and I'm interested in building and operating hotels or cabins to house people during their visit. That would give me some influence over the degree of comfort they could expect during their adventure, from beginning to end."

"I see," Delano said, steepling his fingers. "There is a gentleman already operating a facility of some sort at Soda Mountain, and another who operates a toll bridge that leads up to the gold mines and Cooke City. Mr. Langford will be bound to give them some preference in further developments. Perhaps you know them as well?"

"Yes," Jubil said. "Mr. McCartney runs the bathhouse at Soda Mountain, and Mr. Baronett owns the bridge. I think they'd both gladly partner with me."

"Interesting," Delano said, studying Jubil.

"I've corresponded with Mr. Langford," Jubil said, "and he supports my plans. But only on the condition that funding for the administration and protection of the park is forthcoming. We've come mainly to offer our help in making that happen."

Walter said, "We just wanted to meet with you to offer our help with lobbying—and so you'd be comfortable when Jubil's name comes up in the conversation about Yellowstone."

Jubil frowned at Walter for overdoing it, but Walter ignored him.

"Yes, well I have no objection to you being involved, Mr. Walker, in developing the park," Delano said, leaning back in his chair, "if Mr. Langford and others see fit. As to the matter of funding, as I said, I believe we have that matter in hand."

Only one funding bill had come up for a vote in Congress since the park had been established, and it failed, so Jubil was surprised that Delano was so confident about the passage of this one. He also wanted to know when the bill might come up for a vote, but he did not feel comfortable questioning Delano about the specifics. He would ask Walter about it later.

"Thank you, sir," Walter said, smiling as he finally turned to Jubil.

"Yes," Jubil said, "thank you. I appreciate the vote of confidence and the opportunity."

"You're welcome. Is there anything else?" Delano asked.

Jubil could feel Walter willing him to quit the conversation there, but he could not. Delano had been surprisingly friendly and open to his ideas, and he was leery of spoiling the positive atmosphere. But while he had this opportunity, he had to address the business at the Crow Agency, or he would forever regret missing the chance.

"There is one other matter," Jubil said. "I'm going to visit General Sherman later today to discuss increasing the level of business my outfitting company does with the army. If I'm successful, my plan is to open a store in Bozeman to supply Fort Ellis."

"That's very enterprising," Delano said.

Jubil nodded, considering how to phrase his next request.

"I mention it because I believe my store could also be of service to the Indian Agency at the Crow reservation. I'd like your support to get the contract to supply the agency. I believe my operation could save the government a significant amount of money."

Delano frowned. Jubil met his suddenly stony gaze, his eyebrows raised with disingenuous innocence.

"Well, that would be a matter for you to take up with the local agent," Delano said, as he looked around at the materials on his desk. He found a ledger and paged through it. "That would be a Mr. Shawn Flynn. He is the agent of record there."

"I know Flynn," Jubil said, realizing with surprise that he had not known Flynn's Christian name until now, "and I think he would be happy to work with us. Do I just take up the details with him directly? If he does agree to our offer, I assume he'll just switch the contract from the current supplier to Warner and Walker?"

Delano stared at Jubil over his steepled fingers with the calculating gaze of a predator sizing up its prey. "Considering the issue further, Mr. Walker, I wonder if you're the right person for this particular job. While I'm impressed by the success of your explorations and your outfitting business," Delano said, "you have some troubling history associated with the Crow Agency."

Jubil knew where Delano was going, and he could tell by Walter's sidelong glance that he did as well. Jubil fought back his growing anger.

"You have been involved in the deaths of three men who previously supplied the Crow reservation," Delano said. "Have you not?"

"I defended myself during more than one ambush," Jubil said, struggling to maintain a calm tone of voice. "No charges were ever filed against me or my friends, because we did nothing wrong."

"Hmm," Delano said. "It still seems of questionable propriety for me to endorse a man for a job who shot the previous holders of it . . . Wouldn't you agree?"

"I don't believe anyone will look at it that way, sir," Walter said in Jubil's defense.

"Oh, really?" Delano said. "How long have you lived among politicians?"

Walter's silence confirmed the truth of what Delano said.

Jubil knew that politics were as much about appearance as fact, and maybe more so. But having his own future subject to that superficiality did not sit well with him.

"Sir, my contacts on the reservation report continued irregularities with the supplies that threaten the well-being of the people living there. Surely you understand my concern. Will you at least order an investigation of the Crow Agency to root out these persistent problems?" Jubil asked Delano. "Whether I get the contract or not, the people on the reservation deserve the supplies they are due, and the government is owed honest dealings."

Delano scowled. "Certainly not! I do not see why you insist on laying this at my door. I'm sure Mr. Flynn would have the full support of Commissioner Smith and the Bureau of Indian Affairs were he to bring his situation to light with them."

Jubil knew full well that these officials had no jurisdiction over the agency supply. He could see there was no way to continue the conversation without endangering Flynn, but Delano had not finished with him.

"Your inflammatory charges are a troubling harbinger of

the turmoil your involvement would bring to the development of the park. I'm concerned your presence would only inflame the situation, and I intend to tell Mr. Langford as much."

Jubil and Walter exchanged a glance and simultaneously stood to leave. Jubil was so angry, it was all he could do to keep his wits about him—an invaluable piece of advice given to him before he first went West.

"I'm disappointed that you've taken this position," Walter said to the secretary. "We'll show ourselves out." With that, Walter turned toward the door of the office.

Jubil made eye contact with Delano one last time and couldn't help speaking his mind: "Sir, I'm aware of your feelings, or lack of them, toward the native tribes. I believe you know exactly what's going on out there. I don't know how you can sleep at night." He turned and followed Walter out the door.

"Did I lecture him?" Jubil asked as they left the residence.

"Your parting comment was harsh," Walter said, "but I suppose he deserved it."

"Well, as long as he's in office," Jubil said. "I won't have any friends in the Department of the Interior."

They climbed into their hired carriage and set off for the hotel. Jubil was disappointed by the outcome of the conversation, but he was not ready to give up yet.

"I suppose that leaves President Grant as our final court of appeal?" Jubil asked.

Walter's eyes widened. "That's a long shot," he said. But then the idea seemed to take root. "We might be able to get his attention. After all, you're a celebrated constituent from Illinois. I'll see what I can do."

Later that day, Jubil presented himself at the War Department offices of General William T. Sherman. He had known General

Sherman for years. Jubil's first trip West had been in 1867, on a Warner supply wagon train escorted by General Sherman and his young Pawnee scout, White Dog. Their group had been attacked by a band of Tall Bull's Dog Soldiers, and, in the skirmish, Jubil had saved White Dog's life. White Dog had shown his appreciation by making a gift to Jubil of his medicine bag and its collection of spirit tokens that protected his life. They had been friends ever since.

As Jubil was escorted into the general's office, Sherman rose from his chair to greet him. A pleasant smile showed through his scraggly reddish-brown facial hair, softening his normally stern, rough-complected countenance.

"Jubilee Walker," General Sherman said, offering a hearty handshake. "It's good to see you, my friend."

"Good to see you too, sir," Jubil said.

Jubil was truly grateful for his relationship with General Sherman. Of all the people Jubil had met since he left home, he admired Sherman the most. From the first day his friend Lew Keplinger had introduced them, Sherman had been helpful to him, and he set an example of leadership that Jubil aspired to. Not only had he met White Dog through him, Sherman had recommended Jubil to General Sheridan for the 1870 Washburn Expedition and later hired him to guide the Barlow Expedition in 1871. More recently, he had helped Jubil understand what he was getting into with the Northern Pacific Railroad surveys.

"What brings you to Washington?" Sherman asked.

"I've come to discuss my chances of picking up more business for Warner and Walker Outfitters as a supplier to the military."

"Have you now!" Sherman said, giving his desktop a little slap. "Well, that catches me by surprise. I thought your business these days was all about supplying fashionable travelers and adventurers."

"Yes sir, it was—it is," Jubil said. "But my business is suffering the consequences of this economy."

"Ah," Sherman said, "folks are clutching their purse strings."

"Yes," Jubil said. "Our Council Bluffs store had the lowest holiday sales ever this past Christmas. I've got to find another source of income to keep my store open. I came here to see if you think I might win more business with the army, and, if so, to ask how I should go about it."

"Yes, of course," Sherman said. "I normally don't make those decisions. The division and fort commanders have control over their own logistics. But you can use me as a reference when you deal with them. Just this morning I received a telegram from General Sheridan saying that he's having problems finding a supplier for some additional equipment needed for a mission your friend Lieutenant Colonel Custer is being sent on this summer. Custer has a new command at the new army fort at Mandan, in the Dakota Territory—Fort Abraham Lincoln."

"Good for him," Jubil said. "I'd be honored to help outfit them, if I can. When does he need the supplies?"

"In May," Sherman said. "He'll be setting out June first."

"I can manage that," Jubil said. "I'll deliver the supplies myself. I'd enjoy seeing our new fort commander." The possibility of supplying Custer's expedition made the visit more fruitful than Jubil had hoped for.

"Good," Sherman said. "I'll send General Sheridan a telegram and tell him we spoke. You're on good terms with him. I imagine he'll be relieved to have this off his mind."

"Thank you, sir," Jubil said. "I'll stop in Chicago and see him, on my way back to Council Bluffs. What is Custer's mission this summer, if I may ask?"

"He's leading a group of soldiers and scientists into the Black Hills to determine if stories of gold deposits there are credible," Sherman said, "and whether more government protection is warranted. We're currently in the curious and likely untenable position of defending Sitting Bull and his supporters from white prospectors who are poaching their gold. According to the 1868 Treaty of Laramie, that land belongs to the Sioux Nation. You could probably go along with Custer, if you move smartly."

Jubil felt a familiar thrill at the invitation, followed seconds later by a deep sense of disappointment. "No, I'd best not," Jubil said. "I can't run off looking for gold while my business is suffering. But I appreciate your advice and support."

"Certainly," Sherman said. "It's always good to see you, Mr. Walker."

"I'd like your thoughts on another matter, if it's not too much trouble," Jubil said. "I met with Secretary Delano this morning, and it did not go in my favor. I wonder if you have any suggestions about how to handle the matter?"

Sherman nodded encouragingly, and Jubil recounted the details of the meeting.

Sherman shook his head in disgust. "Do you recall the counsel I once gave you about the Washington bureaucracy?" he asked.

"Yes, sir," Jubil said with a smile. Sherman had once told him that his past policy of shooting the bad guys in Montana was likely far more effective than waiting for help from Washington, DC. Sherman had delivered this observation in a joking manner, but he had not been joking.

"I applaud your efforts," Sherman said, "but Delano is notoriously good to his friends and hard on his enemies. I myself am neither to him, so, I don't believe I can be of much assistance to you with that situation, I'm sorry to say."

"That's all right. I appreciate your candor," Jubil said. He mentioned that Walter might be able to secure an audience with President Grant.

"I can put in a word for you with him, if that will help," Sherman said. "He listens to my advice on military matters, but not much on government policy. I admire him greatly as a commander-in-chief, but I'm disappointed in him as a president. He allows his virtues to become his worst flaws—he believes most people are honest, and he's too trusting and loyal to many people who don't deserve it. I'm not sure where he will stand on your issue."

"A word from you would be much appreciated," Jubil said. "Thank you, General."

In his hotel room that evening, Jubil wondered when the political wind might blow Delano out of office and, he hoped, supplant him with someone more sympathetic to his position. For now, he pinned his hopes on Walter getting an audience with Grant, who, in the best-case scenario, would overrule Delano.

If he did get the chance to make his case with Grant, Jubil would need actual evidence of corruption at the Crow Agency that did not involve betraying Flynn's confidence. Another trip to Bozeman might be necessary to see if he could get the records kept by Black's clerk at the mercantile. The most direct route to justice at the agency would be persuading Flynn to testify against Black, but the success of that option seemed highly unlikely. As Jubil lay down to sleep, Delano's words were still echoing in his mind—*I'm concerned your presence would only inflame matters out there*. All of the important decisions Jubil had made since his mother died were based on what he felt in his heart was right and on being bold enough to follow that path. His heart was telling him now that nothing should stop him from being part of the responsible development of his beloved Yellowstone Park. Nothing should stop him from setting things right for White Dog and his people.

CHAPTER 3

The day before Jubil left Washington, he sent a telegram to Nelly, telling her he would arrive in New York City the following afternoon. From Grand Central Station, he took the trolley down Park Avenue, then walked down Eighteenth Street to his and Nelly's apartment. The place was quiet as he removed his boots and hung his coat in the foyer. Nelly would be home soon from *Scientific American* magazine, where she worked as an editor. In the meantime, he would unpack his bag.

The apartment was warm, comfortable, and familiar, but it was really Nelly's apartment. She and Jubil lived together as often as they could, but his business and expeditions often kept him away for months at a time. He hadn't been in New York since February. These separate living arrangements worked well for them—although the idea had taken some getting used to for Nelly's parents.

Jubil jokingly referred to himself as nomadic. He lived in the New York apartment with Nelly when he could; he lived in the Warner's house in Council Bluffs when he was minding the store there; and he had a cabin on his family farm in Bloomington, Illinois. He also spent a good amount of time in the wilderness. The old adage *home is where the heart is* rang true to him.

He was in the kitchen, scouting for supper, when he heard her come in.

"Are you here?" she called from the foyer. "I'm home early."

"I am," he said, stepping out of the kitchen to greet her. He watched appreciatively as she removed her coat and unpinned her long black hair. He never tired of appreciating how beautiful she was.

"Welcome home," she said, reaching out to him, her blue eyes sparkling, while they shared a warm kiss and a long embrace.

"Can I help you with your boots?" he asked, breathing in the citrusy aroma of her hair.

"Thank you," she said, and took a seat. "How did your meetings go?"

Jubil knelt before her and unlaced her boots—the best wool-lined oiled-leather calf-high women's boots that Warner and Walker Outfitters sold.

"Pretty much a bust with Secretary Delano," he said. He explained how the meeting had gone from encouraging to disappointing. "But I can't let matters stand as they are," he said.

"I know," she said, bending to kiss him on the forehead. She slipped on a pair of beaded moccasins Jubil had brought back after one of his adventures.

They went into the parlor and settled on the sofa in front of the fireplace.

"My scouting trip out to Bozeman turned up some unexpected news," Jubil said. He had written to tell her he was going. He shared the details of his conversation with Flynn and his chance encounter with Lucius Black.

"That's unsettling," Nelly said with a frown. "Do you think you can resolve the situation out there without violence?"

"I certainly hope to," he said. "He seems like a more reasonable person than his brother."

"You're an optimist, Jubilee Walker," she said, reaching over to cover Jubil's hand with hers. "Be careful."

He patted her hand and nodded. He was grateful Nelly had learned to accept the dangers inherent in the life he had chosen to lead. The advantage was that she was able to live with the kind of independence she had always longed for.

"Things went very well with General Sherman," he continued. He explained about his contract to supply Custer, and his plan to make the delivery in May.

"That's wonderful," Nelly said, looking into his eyes. "Do you think I might be able to go along?"

He was surprised by her question. She had never asked to travel with him before.

"Can you get the time away from your job?" Jubil asked.

"Actually, I want to talk to you about that," she said.

"What is it?"

"I love working at the magazine," she said, furrowing her brow in a way that belied her words. "I'm fortunate to have gained the professional experience and to have made so many good contacts. The daily environment is stimulating, and I love New York—" She paused and smoothed the lap of her dress. "I hate to sound ungrateful. . . but I'm growing restless."

Nelly had been in her position as an editorial assistant for a year and a half. Her main responsibility was proofreading, which she had described to Jubil as a critical job that entailed reading fascinating subject matter.

"I find myself growing bored with doing largely the same thing every day," she said.

"I don't see you as ungrateful," Jubil said. "You told me long ago that you expected to come at your literary career from more than one angle. Are you looking for another job?"

"Yes, in a manner of speaking," she said. "I have been pleased by readers' reactions to my journal entries."

Nelly had kept a journal during their Colorado honeymoon trip, and a friend of Jubil's, William Byers, had published selected entries in his newspaper, the *Rocky Mountain News*.

Byers then helped get the journal entries syndicated by the Associated Press. More recently, Nelly had been writing essays on suffrage, and publicist Sam Wilkeson had placed them in various newspapers. Jubil knew Wilkeson as Jay Cooke's publicity man, and Nelly knew him as the brother-in-law of her friend and mentor Mrs. Elizabeth Cady Stanton.

"I'd like to write enough entries for a book. I checked with the publisher to be sure they're still interested in such a book, and they are."

"You're leaning toward writing then, rather than working in publishing?" Jubil asked.

"Yes, exactly," she said.

"Well, that's exciting," he said. It was not hard to imagine Nelly's writing becoming very popular. She had always had a talent for homing in on the heart of a matter.

"Thank you," she said, touching his cheek affectionately. "I've already written Mr. Byers. He will take me on as a columnist for the *Rocky Mountain News* and pay me a salary of twenty-five dollars a week, starting whenever I am available. That will give me the freedom I want and the income I need to feel I'm making my own way."

"Well, that's settled then," he said. Other husbands might have disapproved of their wives taking such initiative, but Jubil didn't. He was proud of her for it.

"And, since I can write from anywhere, I've been thinking about the possibilities that presents. I'd like to travel with you—as much as possible."

"Really?" Jubil looked at her with disbelief. "Well, I'm thrilled you'd like us to spend more time together, but what exactly do you mean?"

"I'd like to be a part of your adventure tour business," she said. "I'd like to go along on the tours themselves."

He stared at her and wondered how someone he knew so well could surprise him so.

"Our honeymoon trip to Colorado opened my eyes in a number of ways," Nelly said. "I enjoyed living rough more than I expected to. I appreciate the pains you and Eli took to make me comfortable, but I believe I could manage without quite so much coddling. I'd like to have more outdoor experiences to inspire my writing, and I just enjoyed being with you—seeing you in your element. I'm convinced I can be useful in some way."

He smiled at her offer. It was the same pledge he had made to Major Powell when he first asked to join his expeditions. "I have to admit, I'm surprised," Jubil said. "I'm also pleased . . . but mainly surprised."

What he didn't admit was that a shadow of doubt had begun to creep into his peripheral view. What if Nelly decided she wanted to go on his expeditions as well as the adventure tours? Major Powell's wife occasionally accompanied Powell on his expeditions, but, unlike Mrs. Powell, Nelly didn't take kindly to being told what she could and couldn't do. Could too much togetherness ultimately be bad for both Jubil's professional life and their marriage?

"Are you sure you agree?" she asked, reading him closely.

She had been the one to propose a number of things that had changed their lives: the strategy that first won Jubil a place on Major Powell's expeditions; her decision to attend Vassar College; proposing that they live independently after they were married; and now this. If her instincts were telling her this was a good idea, Jubil felt he should trust her.

"I'm sure," he said, deciding to stop overthinking the matter. "We'll make it work."

"Good," she said, kissing him lightly on the cheek.

"What about the rest of the time, between adventure tours?" he asked. "Will you live with me in Council Bluffs?"

"Yes," she said, "most of the time. I'll probably want to travel to New York, to see friends and tend to literary business while you're away on your expeditions. Maybe visit Mama and Papa in Bloomington, or the Warners on Nantucket."

He was relieved to hear she did not expect to travel with him on his expeditions.

"You'll give up the apartment?" he asked.

"I hate to," she admitted. "But it's too expensive to keep."

It was true, and Jubil nodded.

"Then, if we are in agreement, I'm going to give notice of my resignation from the magazine, and travel with you in May to visit Custer, and then in July—our first Warner and Walker Outfitters adventure tour in Colorado."

"We are in agreement," he said with a smile, moving to take her in his arms.

Later, once they had had their fill of each other and eaten a light meal of toast and scrambled eggs, Nelly said, "I have a confession to make. There was one aspect of our honeymoon trip that I was uncomfortable with. I didn't want to complain and spoil everything, and there was nothing to be done about it, so I kept quiet. It's about my attire while we're on tour—actually, anytime I'm on horseback. I don't want to ride sidesaddle, and I don't want to wear skirts. I want a Western saddle, and I'm going to wear trousers."

Jubil conjured an image of Nelly in a pair of baggy men's pants and laughed. Nelly narrowed her gaze at him.

"You're serious?" he said, suppressing the urge to gulp.

"I certainly am," she said. "And I don't mean bloomers or Turkish pants or women's riding pants—they're too fancy. I mean the same pants you sell to men in your store. A man's size small will fit me—I've tried them on. Ike helped me."

It was becoming clear to Jubil that Nelly had been thinking about this issue for some time—and that she had discussed it with her brother Ike. The more Jubil considered the implications of this idea, the more questions occurred to him.

"Do you plan to wear them when we visit Custer?" he asked.

"No!" Nelly said. "I'll dress like a proper lady then. I'll only wear them when I expect to be on horseback extensively."

He could see her mind was already made up.

"You know," Jubil said, warming to the idea, "I don't really mind at all. It makes good sense to me, and I would think most women would agree. But you know that people are going to have strong opinions about it. It'll likely cause a stir among our clients."

"Would you rather I not risk upsetting clients?" Nelly asked.

"To be honest, I'd rather not give people something else to complain about," he said, "but if it's important to you, then they'll just have to take it or leave it. We'll be dealing with people who don't like the food or the sleeping arrangements, or who find the route too difficult. This will just be one more complaint to listen to."

"You don't sound very enthused about the prospects for the tour," Nelly said.

"I'm just being realistic," he said. "I've traveled with people enough to know that they complain. Some of our clients will, and I'm going to have to deal with it. That's a chore I won't enjoy, but it comes with the territory."

"Well then, thank you for allowing me to add to your burden," she said.

"Oh, the benefits of your company will far outweigh the burden," he said.

"You hold onto that thought," she said with a grin.

Before they set off to visit Abe and Lily on Nantucket, Jubil wrote Ike and Eli a letter explaining how his meetings had gone with Delano and Sherman. He hoped they would find the news about the contract for Custer's expedition encouraging. He would plan his trip home around Ike getting a meeting date set with Ward in Chicago, and he would then try to see General Sheridan that same day. He also told them about

Nelly's decision. He knew Ike would have no problem accepting the news, but Eli was another matter. He and his sister had not always gotten along.

The Warners had moved to Nantucket Island two years ago, after their son Luke died in the spring of 1871. It was Lily's childhood home, and Abe had gotten his start there as an outfitter. Abe had acquired some rental properties since they had moved back, which kept him busy and brought in some income, and Lily occupied her time painting and selling her work to tourists. Jubil loved the natural beauty and bustling energy of the island, even though his prairie upbringing left him feeling somewhat out of place.

The crossing from Hyannis to Nantucket Island on the side-wheeler steamship *River Queen* was windy, cold, and choppy; they spent the whole trip huddled in the crowded indoor cabin. The weather on the island was more temperate than on the mainland, a fact Jubil still found surprising. He hired a carriage to take them to the Warner house, which stood on a hill overlooking the town of Nantucket and the harbor. It was a plainly elegant two-story white house with tall red shutters and a red front door. Two small outbuildings with red eaves and doors and a matching stable stood nearby.

Jubil paid the carriage driver, and as he and Nelly started toward the house, Abe stepped out.

"Welcome," he said, waving and coming to greet them. He wore a flannel shirt but no coat, and he looked hearty and healthy for his fifty-some years. Lily stood in the open doorway with a shawl wrapped around her shoulders, her salt-and-pepper hair pinned up in a pile. Something about her struck Jubil as unsettling. Her normally smiling face looked sad and distracted, as if she were watching them leave rather than arrive. He glanced at Nelly—her concerned expression told him she had noticed it too.

"Here let me help," Abe said, taking one of the suitcases from Jubil. "Come in and warm up! The fire is stoked, and Lily made chowder."

"It sounds delightful," Nelly said, taking Abe's arm and beaming a smile at him. Nelly loved the Warners as much as Jubil did, especially Lily. Lily was Nelly's most trusted advisor after her mother. It was Lily who had made arrangements with her sister, Professor Maria Mitchell, for Nelly to live with her in Poughkeepsie and attend Vassar College, which had changed Nelly's life.

As Jubil and Nelly neared the house, Lily seemed to come out of her reverie. She greeted each of them with a hug and a smile. The house was warm and filled with the aroma of freshly baked bread.

"It's so good to have you here again," Lily said, as she helped Nelly remove her coat. "I've been thinking of you both a great deal lately."

Jubil studied Lily for a moment and then looked at Abe quizzically. He gave Jubil an uncomfortable twitch of a smile, then looked away.

As they enjoyed the meal of chowder and bread, the main topic of conversation was Nelly's decision to give up her position at the magazine and develop her writing. Lily was thrilled for her and began to seem her usual self again. The more controversial part of Nelly's plan was her desire to join Jubil on his guided adventure tours. Abe teased them both about too much togetherness, which struck a nerve with Jubil, since he had been thinking along the same lines, but he did not say so. Lily was surprised to hear that Nelly had found living outdoors so enjoyable, but, as usual, she encouraged her to follow her instincts.

After lunch they all joined in to clean up the dishes and

stow the leftovers, and then they went into the parlor, where Abe turned the conversation to Jubil's affairs.

"We got your letter. I'm sorry to hear about the store's disappointing holiday sales," Abe said. "How are Ike and Eli handling the downturn?"

"Ike's not taking it well," Jubil said. "He knows we won't be able to keep the store open for long under these circumstances. We're going to meet with Ward about our prospects, but we're giving up on the wholesale business—no takers."

"That's a shame," Abe said. "It's still a good idea—the timing is just bad. I'm not sure what to think about the mail-order business. I'll be interested to hear what Ward has to say."

Jubil nodded and glanced at Lily. She sat studying him, fidgeting with a handkerchief she held in her lap. She looked troubled again.

"And your tour attendance isn't what you'd hoped for either," Abe said, shaking his head.

"I'll admit I'm disappointed," Jubil said. "I thought there'd be more folks with the money and desire for these trips. Maybe they just don't want to travel with me." In the aftermath of Jay Cooke's financial collapse, Jubil was concerned about how his association with Cooke might have damaged his reputation.

"Now, now," Lily said, scolding him mildly. "I'm sure it's nothing personal—it's just the financial panic. You'll see."

"I hope you're right," Jubil said, giving Lily a weak smile. He couldn't help but wonder how many people saw his two-year promotion of Yellowstone National Park and of Jay Cooke's Northern Pacific Railroad as a means to fleece unsuspecting investors.

"Lily and I have lived through hard times before," Abe said. "We had to cut every possible corner to make it through the Civil War years, but we managed. This downturn will pass. You'll see."

"I'm sure you're right," Jubil said. He wasn't as certain as

Abe and Lily were that Warner and Walker would survive, but he appreciated their good intentions.

"We're anxious to hear about your trip to Washington," Abe said.

"The meeting with Secretary Delano was unproductive," Jubil, said, minimizing the situation, "but General Sherman was very helpful, as always."

He described how Sherman had helped him land the contract to supply Custer's expedition, and Abe praised Jubil's initiative.

"There's a new commander at Fort Ellis," Jubil said. "If I open a store, I think we can win the contract to supply the fort. Folks know me out there, and I think we can pick up some of the local Bozeman trade as well. I also have other ideas."

"Would those other ideas involve supplying the Crow reservation?" Lily said.

Jubil was surprised that it was Lily who brought this up. He had thought Abe might.

"Yes," Jubil said evenly. "I still intend to correct the situation out there—or at least try."

"You said the meeting with Secretary Delano was unproductive," Abe said. "He's not willing to address your concerns?"

"He thinks I should take it up with Indian Affairs," Jubil said dismissively, "even after I told him they're part of the problem."

"What about the law?" Abe said. "Can't they put a stop to it?"

"Not unless they have hard evidence of illegal activity," Jubil said. "Which I have not been able to gather."

Both Abe and Lily looked worried. Nelly looked at him with sympathetic concern.

"Jubil, we know you are well-intentioned," Abe said, lowering his voice, "but we don't think you should open a store there until the authorities have resolved that situation. This obsession of yours with trying to save those people is futile, and you are going to get yourself killed. You almost have . . . twice! Why do you see this as your problem?"

"Whose problem is it then, if not mine, Abe?" Jubil said, his frustration showing in his tone. "I want to see justice done for them. The Crow can't rise up against it, or they'll be slaughtered. Local law enforcement and citizens allow it because they're either paid off or terrorized. White Dog is my friend, and I promised to do what I can to put a stop to it—and I intend to keep that promise."

Abe studied Jubil and sighed deeply.

"Your commitment is admirable," Abe said. "But sometimes you act as though you are invincible. Even if you aren't concerned for your own safety, you should give more consideration to the feelings of the people who care about you."

As Abe expressed his concerns, Jubil remembered feeling similarly about his friend Lew Keplinger. Lew had followed General Sherman through every campaign of the war without ever being wounded. His fearlessness in the wilderness was admirable but had occasionally put Jubil's own safety at risk. But he was not convinced that Abe's point was relevant now.

"Nelly has no concerns," Jubil said, looking at her for confirmation. She raised her eyebrows but did not protest. "Well . . . she understands anyway. I don't see why you should be more concerned than she is."

"I'm not talking about myself," Abe said gently.

Jubil looked at Lily, whose face had once again taken on the haunted expression they had noticed on their arrival. His heart sank.

"I'm very worried about your involvement with the Crow reservation," Lily said, clutching her handkerchief against her chest. "Those men want you dead, and I don't believe they'll stop until they've succeeded in killing you."

Jubil frowned. "They won't succeed in killing me, Lily. I can look out for myself, you know I can. You've never worried about me like this before."

"No, I haven't," she said. "And that's why I have to mention it. I have a very bad feeling about this situation, a terrible sense of dread."

Lily was obviously experiencing a high level of discomfort, but Jubil wasn't sure it was his plans that had stirred her feelings.

"It's something I have to do, Lily" he said calmly. He wouldn't change his plans to tamp down Lily's worries. Her fragility after her older son Sam's death was what had kept Luke from striking out on his own—until he met Jubil. Lily had been understandably devastated by Luke's death—they all had been—but she had managed better in the subsequent months than Abe feared. Jubil thought she had been getting stronger and stronger since returning to Nantucket. He wondered what might be causing this setback.

"I don't know what I'd do if we lost you," she said, tearing up. "First Sam . . . then Luke . . . It would be more than I can bear to lose you too."

"Now, Lily," he said, kneeling in front of her and taking her hands. "You can't think that way. This is not like you. I'll be fine. You know me. I can take care of myself. You just have to believe that."

With a panicked expression, she searched his face.

"Since we're being very frank about our concerns," Jubil said, glancing at Abe, "I think I have to say that when I first met Luke, he had some bold ideas about transforming the outfitting business to fit the world of the transcontinental railroad. But Abe was reluctant to change his store, because he felt the risk was too great. He encouraged Luke to try them out in a store of his own, but that would have meant moving away from you, and he wouldn't do that."

Lily wiped her eyes with her handkerchief.

"As much as you both loved him, you held him back. I'm

not Luke, but I know you care about me too. But I have to be true to who I am. You know that. And I can't let anyone—however much I love them—hold me back."

Lily leaned over to embrace Jubil. Nelly and Abe were both wiping tears from their eyes. Jubil stood, still holding Lily's hands.

"These plans of mine are just that—plans," Jubil said, squeezing Lily's hands. "We may never end up opening a store out there anyway. First, I need to win the contract to supply Fort Ellis, and the new commander wasn't available while I was there. I've got other business to attend to before I can even get back out there."

Jubil was trying to find a way out of this awkward moment. He had also left out any mention of his meeting with Lucius Black, but he couldn't possibly bring that up now.

Lily sighed and seemed to relax somewhat as Jubil returned to his chair. Abe glanced at him with a look of melancholy, then looked away.

Later, after Jubil and Nelly had retired to their bedroom for the night, they discussed the evening's events.

"Do you think bringing up Luke was too harsh?" Jubil asked.

"No," Nelly said. "You were right—and it needed to be said."

He nodded.

"I feel dishonest not mentioning Lucius Black or admitting how poorly the meeting went with Secretary Delano. Do you think that was wrong of me?"

Nelly considered the question. "Sometimes too much honesty is not helpful," she said. "I do think Lily was overreacting and that Abe was reacting more to her distress than to your actual plans. I wonder if Lily is too isolated here. In Council Bluffs, she ran a busy household with people around her all the time. They have a social life here too, but maybe she has too much time on her hands, and she's become fixated on you."

"Maybe," Jubil said with a shrug.

During the week Jubil and Nelly spent with the Warners on Nantucket, Jubil received a telegram from Ike with news of the meeting date with Mr. Ward. Jubil also telegraphed General Sheridan to arrange a visit with him. He was pleased that Sheridan could see him but disappointed that he was only available at the same time as the meeting Ike had set up with Ward. Ike would have to attend that meeting on his own.

Jubil and Nelly tried to make the rest of their stay with the Warners pleasant by bringing up lively topics of conversation and avoiding any further discussion of Jubil's plans, but the mood remained reserved. When the week ended, he and Nelly were ready to return to New York.

CHAPTER 4

On Friday, April 10th, Jubil arrived in Chicago, where he was to meet Ike at the Tremont House. They would spend the night there before their meetings the following morning. It was Jubil's first time seeing the hotel in its new incarnation after the original had burned to the ground in the Great Chicago Fire of 1871, and he was not disappointed. The new hotel, which the builders claimed was fireproof, was a graceful six-story edifice of buff-colored sandstone with arched windows and a mansard roof.

Ike had left a message at the desk with his room number on the fourth floor.

"Welcome to Chicago," he said as he opened the door. He looked dapper in his three-piece suit, his shoulder-length wavy blonde hair neatly combed back. Jubil stepped into the bright room, where the windows looked down onto Dearborn Street.

"I'm sorry I can't come to the meeting with Mr. Ward," Jubil said.

"I don't mind talking to him on my own," Ike said unenthusiastically. "There's not much to say. People are buying less, and they want cheaper products."

Jubil found himself irritated by Ike's attitude. He didn't disagree with Abe that he was somewhat responsible for keeping Ike happy in his position at Warner and Walker, but he wished that Ike would show more drive. Luke would never have let circumstances dictate his attitude toward the job. He would have found some way to make the best of the bad situation they were in. But Ike wasn't Luke, and neither was Jubil.

The following morning was unseasonably warm, as if Mother Nature were as anxious to get on with spring as Jubil was. Chicago had done an admirable job of rising from the ashes of the fire and creating a better version of itself, which inspired him to square his shoulders and face his own challenges anew.

At Court House Square, he went to the office of the US Army Military Division of the Missouri. A soldier at the desk in the waiting room went to report his arrival to General Sheridan.

"I'm sorry, sir," the soldier said when he returned, "but the general needs a few minutes. Please be seated, and he'll be with you shortly."

Jubil waited . . . and waited. He looked around for something to read or otherwise occupy his time and found nothing. Waiting was not Jubil's strong suit. About the time he had run out of patience, the door opened, and General Sheridan stepped out.

"I am sorry, Mr. Walker," Sheridan said, coming to shake Jubil's hand. "I'm afraid our time together has been unavoidably preempted. I can only spare a few minutes today. Or we can reschedule."

"That's all right, General," Jubil said. In a way, he was relieved. He had never found the easy rapport with Sheridan that he shared with General Sherman, though they had developed a mutual respect. General Sheridan's unapologetically harsh position on Indian policy meant there was no point in Jubil wasting time petitioning him for any support in dealing with the Crow Agency situation. "I understand you need a supplier for Lieutenant Colonel Custer's mission."

"Yes, I was pleased to receive General Sherman's telegram that you could handle the situation," Sheridan said. "My apologies for not contacting you myself. I thought this would be too far afield for you."

"I understand," Jubil said. "I'm trying to expand my business. That's why I was visiting with General Sherman. What kind of gear do you need?"

Sheridan fetched the manifest, and Jubil looked it over. Small tents, blankets, mess kits, rope—probably camping gear for the civilian scientists—nothing difficult for him to come by.

"He's leaving June first," Sheridan said, "so you have a few weeks yet to fill the order, but the sooner the better. Can you manage that?"

"Yes, sir," Jubil said. "I'll deliver the supplies myself."

"Good," Sheridan said. "Sorry to rush you, but if that's all—"

"Actually, there is one other thing," Jubil said. "What are my chances of picking up some business with Fort Ellis? I understand there's a new commander there. Would you be willing to put in a recommendation for me?"

The previous commander, Colonel Baker, would not have had any interest in working with Jubil. Baker had led the escort during the 1872 survey for the Northern Pacific Railroad with Colonel Haydon, and he had conducted himself very badly. In the midst of an attack by Sitting Bull and his warriors, he was stupefied drunk, and he subsequently refused to continue following the survey crew. Haydon abandoned the survey, and this setback was a major contributor to the eventual collapse of Jay Cooke's financial empire.

"Certainly," Sheridan said. "The commander's name is Major N. B. Sweitzer. He's a good man. Fort Ellis is a bit distant from your base in Council Bluffs, isn't it?"

"It is," Jubil agreed, "but we're considering opening another store in Bozeman."

"Well, good luck with that," Sheridan said sincerely.

Jubil left Sheridan's office in good spirits and was back at the hotel within an hour of having left. He hoped to catch Ike on his way to meet with Ward, but Ike had already left. Rather than interrupt them, Jubil decided to leave the meeting to Ike. Jubil had to admit that he didn't have much to say to Ward about their situation either.

The morning dragged on as Jubil bided his time. Lunchtime came and went, and finally Jubil decided he was hungrier than he was patient. As he opened his door and stepped into the hallway, Ike was coming toward him.

"There you are," Jubil said. "That must have been quite a conversation."

"Sorry," Ike said. "We lost track of time."

Jubil ushered Ike into his room. "How did it go?"

Ike took a seat in one of the chairs by the window. Jubil sat down across from him and watched as Ike straightened his lapels and fussed with his tie.

"You all right?" Jubil said. "You seem jumpy."

"I'm fine," Ike said, finally looking Jubil in the eye. "I'm afraid I don't have good news though. Of course, the panic has reduced sales of everything, but Mr. Ward predicts sales of our brand are going to suffer even more from some new competition. He says there is a new product outselling all its competitors and setting new standards for quality and price."

"What is it?" Jubil asked.

"Pants," Ike said. "Men's work pants, or travel pants, or any kind of wear really. They're made from a durable blue denim, and the pocket stitching at the corners is held in place by rivets. Ward says they stand up to any abuse, and they cost less than any competitor's product—including ours. They're manufactured in San Francisco by a man named Levi Strauss."

"Well, we sell more than men's pants," Jubil said.

"Yes, but we sell quite a lot of them," Ike said. "Or we had been anyway. Our prices are higher than average now."

"Our quality is higher than average," Jubil said defensively. Ike shrugged.

"Is Ward still willing to handle our products?" Jubil asked.

"Yes, if they sell," Ike said. "Otherwise, he'll want the catalog space for something else."

"Hmm," Jubil said, wishing Luke were there to handle the issue. He would have had ideas that would never occur to Jubil. "Do you have any suggestions?"

"Lower our prices?" Ike said, tentatively.

"We'd best be careful about that," Jubil said. "I'm not sure what the cost of making them is. Before we drop the price, we ought to know how much our price can come down and still make a profit." Jubil had no intuition for matters of this sort, unlike Luke, who always seemed able to feel the right way forward. Jubil could feel his way forward in the wilderness, but in the business world, he often felt he was groping in the dark.

Ike nodded.

"You interested in lunch?" Jubil asked.

"Sure, but I have something else to tell you first," Ike said, nervously rubbing his hands together. "Mr. Ward made me an offer. He's been very complimentary of my sketches, and today he offered me a job illustrating for his catalog."

Jubil was shocked. "As a sideline?"

"Full time," Ike said. "I'd have to move to Chicago to meet with clients and the printers."

Jubil struggled to temper his reaction. He felt like he had been climbing a steep slope since his ordeal with Cooke, and now loose talus was sliding out from under his feet. Losing Ike would have a huge impact on Warner and Walker, and he couldn't believe Ike would abandon the store.

"Is that what you want?" Jubil asked carefully. He could

imagine how exciting this chance must be for Ike, and how rewarding he would find the work.

Ike nodded. It wouldn't be fair to deny him such an opportunity, one that fit his talents and, apparently, his dreams so perfectly. Jubil had neither the power nor the right to do so.

"It might help you out with the store," Ike said apologetically. "It would relieve the burden of paying my salary."

"And put an end to us designing any new products," Jubil said flatly, without considering the hurt his words might cause.

"They're not selling anyway," Ike said, his voice rising defensively. "But if you have any product ideas, or if I do, I'll draw them for you. You don't even have to pay me."

"Don't go making promises like that, Ike," Jubil said. "You should always know your worth." His mind raced as he tried to decide whether to try to talk Ike out of taking the job or to congratulate him.

"I honestly don't know how I'll get along without you," Jubil said. "But I won't try to stand in your way. Whatever you decide, I'll support you."

Ike's eyes filled with tears. He reached into his pocket for a handkerchief. "Thank you," he said. "I'd like to be the one to tell Eli."

"Of course," Jubil said. The twins had been separated on a couple of occasions for weeks at a time, but their lives had never gone off in separate directions entirely. Despite this, Jubil knew Eli would never interfere with Ike's happiness.

"Let's go have some lunch," Jubil said.

In the hotel dining room, they lapsed into an awkward silence. Jubil's thoughts became more and more worried as he considered how he would replace Ike, how Ike's decision would affect Eli's decisions about his own future, and how Nelly would feel about it.

"You can count on Eli to run the store," Ike said. "He pays more attention to how things are done than he lets on. As long as I'm around to do whatever it is, he lets me do the work. But he knows how—for the most part anyway. The main thing I do for the store that he can't do is draw."

"I think you're being generous toward your brother and miserly toward yourself," Jubil said, "but I take your point. It's more a matter with him whether he wants to or not. Sometimes I'm not sure what he wants. Sometimes I'm not sure *he* knows what he wants."

"I'm sorry about this," Ike said with a tortured expression. "I walked around the block about ten times before coming back here, because I didn't want to tell you about Ward's offer. But I have to do it. I know I agreed to be your partner after Luke died, and I know you don't trust Eli as much—"

"It's all right, Ike," Jubil said sincerely. "Things change. You have an opportunity here that you can't pass up. Eli and I will manage—if he wants to."

"I'll talk to him," Ike said.

"When are you planning to move?" Jubil said.

"Ward wants me to start the first of May," Ike said.

"All right," Jubil said. "That gives me a few weeks to get organized."

This turn of events created two new concerns for Jubil: He needed to deliver supplies to Custer in May, which meant that Eli would have to operate the store without him, which he had never done. Also, Nelly was planning on making the trip to visit Custer, and Eli was not going to like being excluded. If Eli did not like this new arrangement and also quit, Jubil's situation would go from bad to worse quickly. He was going to upset either Nelly or Eli, and he wasn't sure yet which would be worse.

An idea occurred to him. "You go on back to Council Bluffs this afternoon without me. That will give you and Eli a day to talk things over without me underfoot. Sheridan gave me the manifest for Custer's expedition, and I can use the time to talk to one of our suppliers here and see if I can get the order placed."

Ike thought about this for a moment and nodded.

After breakfast, Jubil walked north to the offices and warehouse of Smith and Company Wholesale and Distribution, located at the corner of Dearborn and South Water Street, hoping to speak to the owner, Robert Smith. Smith supplied most of the camping equipment they sold at Warner and Walker Outfitters, as well as most of the luggage and travel bags. Years ago, Abe Warner had bought a partnership interest in Smith's business to help him expand his operation. Abe still drew returns on his investment, though he was rarely involved in Smith's operations.

Jubil had met Smith once before, several years ago, when he had first come up with the idea of offering guided adventure tours. He and Luke had signed up a full roster of clients for the first trip, and Smith, who had heard about Jubil's exploits in the Grand Canyon from Abe Warner, was among them. When Jubil was offered the chance to join an expedition to Yellowstone and cancelled his adventure tour, he returned Smith's money and apologized in person. Smith had asked Jubil to keep him in mind when he offered another tour, and Jubil was surprised that, after all this time, Smith was still interested in joining the Colorado tour. Not only did Smith sign up, but he was bringing his wife as well. Jubil had been a little concerned about that, but with Nelly joining them, he knew Smith's wife would be more at ease.

He entered the busy warehouse, where he was directed up a flight of stairs to an office that looked out over the operation.

"How do you do, Mr. Smith?" he said.

"Jubilee Walker!" Smith said, coming to shake Jubil's hand. "What brings you here? Not coming to return my money again, I hope."

Based on the length of time Smith and Abe had been partners, Jubil figured he had to be in his forties. But he looked fit and vigorous.

"No, sir," Jubil said with a smile. "Our Colorado adventure is still on. I'm looking forward to it."

"Good, good," Smith said. "I can't overstate how enthused my wife and I are to be going West with you."

"Tell your wife she'll not be the only woman on the trip," Jubil said, explaining that Nelly would be traveling with them.

"Oh, she'll be thrilled to meet your wife," Smith said.

Jubil had no doubt Mrs. Smith would enjoy meeting Nelly. He just hoped she would feel the same after she saw Nelly ready to ride.

"Last I heard from Abe, he seemed to be weathering the financial panic," Smith said.

"His rental homes are idle more than he'd like," Jubil said, "but he's holding onto them."

"Give him my regards," Smith said. "What can I do for you today?"

Jubil explained his contract to supply Custer's expedition and showed the manifest to Smith.

"I'd like to come back in a few weeks," Jubil said, "and oversee the loading of the order onto the train. I plan to deliver it to Custer myself."

Smith nodded. "Give me a set date," he said. "And I'll have it all here ready for you. I have most of what you need in stock. I'll send you a wire if I hit a snag."

"Excellent," Jubil said. "Thank you."

Back at the hotel, he sent Nelly a letter telling her that the trip to supply Custer's expedition was confirmed for May. He also shared Ike's decision to work for Mr. Ward's catalog company and admitted how nervous he was that Eli would quit in protest.

On the train from Chicago to Council Bluffs, Jubil mulled over what Warner and Walker Outfitters would become without

Ike's artistic talent. Were they destined to return to Abe's original utilitarian operation? This and related questions kept him up much of the night, and he was wide awake as the train pulled into Council Bluffs early in the morning. He walked up Lower Broadway to the store and looked in the window. Ike and Eli were standing near the cash register, having their morning coffee, as usual. He imagined Luke and Abe standing there with them, and he longed for good times like those, which never seemed to last long. Soon, Ike and Eli running the store together would be just another memory.

"Morning, gentlemen," Jubil said, as he opened the door.

"Welcome back," Ike said. "How did your business go?"

"Very well," Jubil said, and gave a brief account of his meeting with Smith.

Eli hadn't spoken and had barely looked at Jubil since he had come in. Now he glared directly at him.

"Nelly is quitting her job and going on the adventure tour?" Eli said accusingly. "If I have to mind the store while she goes on the tour, I swear I'll quit."

"That is not going to happen," Jubil said, struggling to maintain his calm. "I need you on our tours. There's too much work for me alone."

"She's planning to wear men's pants and ride astride?" Eli said incredulously.

"That's her plan."

"Why?" Eli asked. "She'll just stir people up! She's so selfish! She's also going with you to visit Custer?" Eli said.

"Yes," Jubil said.

"While I stay here and mind the store?" Eli said, gripping the edge of the counter in his agitation.

"Well, I hadn't planned it that way, but yes," Jubil said. "When I agreed that Nelly could visit Custer with me, I didn't know that Caleb had quit."

"But she gets to go in favor of me?" Eli said.

"You're assuming I would have invited you."

"You wouldn't have?" Eli said, offended.

"Are you honestly asking me whether I favor Nelly over you?" Jubil said. "She's my wife, Eli. Of course, I do!" Jubil was trying to rein in his aggravation with Eli and barely succeeding. It wasn't just this current jealous behavior that riled him; it was a lifetime of Eli feeling this sense of competition with Nelly. Jubil's patience with it had worn thin. "I knew you'd take issue with this whole arrangement, but I didn't expect you to be this troublesome about it."

"I'll not have it, Jubil," Eli said angrily. "I'll not have her privileged over me. I've put up with it my whole life, and I'll not have it any longer!"

"Let's step into the office," Jubil said.

Ike looked at Jubil apologetically as Jubil followed Eli into the office and closed the door. Jubil sat at the desk, and Eli slumped in the chair across from him, stewing.

"I'm very disappointed in you, Eli," Jubil said. "I thought you had made amends with Nelly after coming to our wedding and being so helpful on our honeymoon trip. Was that all just an act?"

Eli silently chewed his lip and would not make eye contact with Jubil.

"I've watched you do this with her your whole life," Jubil said. "I've always thought it was petty of you, but I never felt it was any of my business to call you out on it. Well, I do now—you're my brother-in-law and my business partner. I need you here. And you need to get over your issues with your sister. I know you want adventure, but this store is what affords us those opportunities. With Ike leaving, you and I are going to have to be partners and look out for each other, or it's not going to work. I've got to be able to trust you completely out in the wilderness to look out for Nelly—and all our guests. To that point, if you're harboring any misgivings about defending our party with your life against anything we encounter, you best quit now. I can't be worrying about you out there."

Eli finally met Jubil's eyes but remained silent.

"I want you to give this serious thought while Nelly and I are away," Jubil said. "Do we have an understanding?"

Eli nodded and looked away.

"Now," Jubil said, rising from his chair, "we have a business to run."

Out in the store, Ike was unnecessarily straightening some stock on a shelf. He and Eli locked gazes, and Jubil knew no words needed to be spoken about what had just happened. He didn't regret lecturing Eli; he felt relieved. It was overdue. Eli's father had not tolerated his jealous behavior either, but Eli still harbored it and revealed his resentment when his father wasn't watching—but often, Jubil was. Jubil wouldn't tolerate it any longer.

"Sorry the situation is going require you to mind the store alone, Eli," Ike said. Without waiting for a response, Ike addressed Jubil, "How are you going to manage the store when you go to Colorado?"

"I'm not sure," Jubil said, "but I'll figure it out."

"Maybe you could just close it while you're gone," Ike said.

"If I do, we may not have much success reopening it," Jubil said. "People may find what they need elsewhere and not come back. Especially if we make a routine of closing and reopening."

"Maybe it's time to admit the store's not pulling its weight and just close it," Eli said, still somewhat in a huff. "We could just do tours all the time."

Jubil took note that Eli was indicating they had a future together.

"There isn't enough of a market for that right now," Jubil said. "I don't know if there will ever be. Besides, I'm not prepared to close the store. It's important to my plans for the future. Abe believes—and I agree with him—that we can weather this panic and come out stronger on the other side. We have to take the long view. I'm going to make this store work, and I'm going to open another one in Bozeman."

"And who's going to run it?" Eli asked.

"I'm not sure yet," Jubil said. "I was thinking of asking you."

"Really?" Eli said, looking surprised.

"That was before Ike decided to take the job with Ward and Caleb quit and you blew up about Nelly," Jubil said. "I'm still considering it, but it's more complicated now." Jubil met Eli's gaze, but Eli quickly looked away.

"At least this outfitting contract for Custer will keep us afloat for a while," Ike said.

"Yes," Jubil said. "And we might be able to get more business out that way. I'm thinking of making another trip to Fort Ellis after we get back from Colorado, to visit with the new fort commander."

"Can I go on that trip?" Eli said.

"If we can find somebody to operate the store," Jubil said.

Ike stayed on in Council Bluffs until the end of April and helped Eli learn the tasks in the store that he had always left to his brother—mostly recordkeeping. Jubil felt some sympathy for Eli. He had always been the most boisterously confident and outgoing among his siblings. And yet truthfully, when tested, he was meeker and less intellectually talented than his sister or brother. The insecurities and fearfulness he had hidden from everyone, including himself, had almost gotten him killed when he traveled with Jubil during the 1872 railroad survey. He had seemed to recover from those experiences—though he hadn't faced any real danger since. He had made amends with his sister on the honeymoon trip, but apparently, he had not taken their reconciliation fully to heart. Jubil could see that Eli was deeply upset watching his brother and sister move on in life, while he felt stuck and aimless.

Jubil cared for him like a brother, but if he created problems during the adventure tour, they would have to part company, regardless of the impact on the store.

CHAPTER 5

Jubil waited in the lobby of the Tremont Hotel in Chicago for Nelly. At the end of April, she had gone to Bloomington to visit her parents, and then she had come to Chicago to help Ike settle into his apartment and prepare for his new life. Today, she and Jubil would set off for Bismarck to make the delivery to Custer. Eli, who had begrudgingly accepted the situation, was in Council Bluffs minding the store.

Jubil scanned the busy lobby. Their meeting time had arrived, but he saw no sign of Nelly. Suddenly, he had the sensation that someone was watching him.

Scanning the room again, he met the gaze of a man sitting on the opposite side of the lobby. He wore a brown bowler hat and a three-piece suit. Did Jubil know him? The man lifted the newspaper to cover his face. Just then, Nelly entered the lobby, and as Jubil went to greet her, he walked past the man in the bowler hat. The man did not look away from his newspaper. Jubil wondered if the man recognized him from the publicity surrounding the campaign to make Yellowstone a national park.

"I'm sorry I'm late," Nelly said. "The traffic . . ."

"We have plenty of time," he said. "You look beautiful, as always." She looked sophisticated in a smart suit and boots, her long black hair plaited into a coil at the nape of her neck.

"Thank you," she said warmly. "I told the driver to wait—are you ready?"

"Yes," Jubil said, shouldering his bag and following Nelly to the carriage. He gave the driver the address of Mr. Smith's business, and they set off.

"Did you get your brother settled?" Jubil asked.

"Yes, poor Ike," Nelly said, making a little pout. "He is so conflicted—elated and distraught all at once. He feels terrible about leaving you in the lurch, but on the other hand, he's ecstatic about his new job—and living here in the city. He's worried about Eli and how hard this will be on him. He feels elated at finally being his own person, then he feels evil for feeling that way. I'm so happy for him. It will be a wonderful experience."

She took his arm and snuggled close. "I'm so excited. It may be a business trip for you, but it's an adventure for me."

He smiled at her childlike joy. "It will be a pleasure having you along," he said. "It's a bit of an adventure for me as well. Seeing Custer is never a dull experience."

The carriage pulled up in front of Smith's business on South Water Street. Jubil and Nelly went inside to confirm the receipt of two flatbed freight wagons packed with supplies that would be loaded on the train bound for Duluth. Nelly and Mr. Smith enjoyed meeting one another and chatted about the trip to Colorado in July.

The drivers steered the wagons out of the warehouse as Nelly and Jubil climbed back into their waiting carriage. As they pulled away to follow the freight wagons to the train depot, Jubil noticed a man watching them from across the street—a man wearing a brown bowler hat and a three-piece suit. Jubil started to ask Nelly if it was the same man who had been in the hotel lobby, but he realized he hadn't pointed the man out to her. Was it merely someone dressed similarly? Either way, it was probably nothing more than coincidence.

Jubil shepherded Custer's supplies onto the freight car he

had arranged, and then he and Nelly found their compartment. They were on their way to Duluth. After lunch in the dining car, they returned to their compartment and settled in on the sofa.

"How was the visit with your parents?" Jubil asked.

"Quite pleasant," Nelly said. "I was fully prepared for Papa to lecture me about giving up my position at the magazine, but he didn't. Mama is excited for me, of course. They were more critical of Ike's decision than mine. They're worried for him. And for Eli too—how he'll manage without Ike."

"It might be good for him, don't you think?" Jubil said, and Nelly nodded pensively. "I've been giving some thought," Jubil continued, "to who can mind the store while the three of us are in Colorado. I wonder if Abe would mind doing it. Do you think that would be asking too much?"

"I don't think it's a bad idea to ask," Nelly said, "but Abe is going to consider what's best for Lily, not what's best for the business. If she doesn't mind coming back to Council Bluffs for a while, he might do it. But he won't leave Lily alone on Nantucket. Lily has to be the one to decide."

The Warners had only been back to Council Bluffs once since Luke died—for Christmas in 1871, two and a half years ago.

"Do you think I should ask her first, instead of Abe?"

"No," Nelly said. "I think you should make your request to both of them, with equal concern for their feelings."

Jubil reached over and took Nelly's hand. "I'm going to benefit greatly by having your counsel on a more regular basis."

"Remember that," she said, "the next time you disagree with my opinion."

Jubil laughed.

Nelly spent the afternoon reading, while Jubil alternated between watching the scenery roll by and working on a letter to Abe and Lily. That evening, their train arrived in Duluth.

"I need to find the conductor," Jubil said, "and supervise the detachment of our freight car onto a siding where it can be connected to our train to Bismarck tomorrow. Do you mind hiring a carriage and asking about a hotel? I'll be along shortly."

"All right," Nelly said.

The conductor introduced Jubil to a yardman for the railroad, who directed the efforts to move his car. Once it was parked, Jubil checked the padlock on the door one last time. Finding it secure, he turned to walk back to the main terminal and spotted a man in a brown bowler hat walking away.

Was his imagination playing tricks on him, or had this man followed him from Chicago? He considered confronting him, but on second thought, it wasn't impossible that they had both been in Chicago enroute to Duluth. As he made his way through the crowd to find Nelly, he spotted the man again, waiting in line to board a train. Jubil walked toward the train to get a better look at the man's face, but he stepped onto the train without looking in Jubil's direction. A porter passed him, pushing a cart of luggage.

"Excuse me," Jubil said to the porter. "Can you tell where this train is headed?"

"It's the night train to Bismarck," the porter said. "There's another one out in the morning."

Jubil walked alongside the train, looking through the windows to see if he could spot the man again, but he could not. He stood watching the train until the conductor called out for final boarding. If the man was indeed following him to Bismarck, why would he take the earlier train? Jubil could not shake the feeling that something was amiss. He suddenly felt concerned that he had left Nelly on her own. If she was going to travel with him frequently, he could not let other matters distract him from thinking of her safety.

He was relieved to find Nelly in front of the station, waiting with a carriage to take them to the hotel. Since he had nothing to go on but an uneasy feeling, he decided not to worry her needlessly with any mention of the man in the bowler hat. At least one of them would sleep well tonight.

Jubil was up before dawn to make sure the freight load was connected to their westbound train. He returned to the hotel to find Nelly packed and anxiously awaiting their departure.

"You're raring to go," he said.

"We're going to ride the Northern Pacific Railroad and meet General Custer!" she said.

"Lieutenant Colonel Custer," he said, correcting her with a grin. He was pleased by the level of her enthusiasm.

"Oh yes," Nelly said. "Why do I insist on making him a general?"

"He was breveted a general in the war," Jubil said. "But he took leave after the war, and then came back as a Lieutenant Colonel. Most of the men still call him General—he doesn't mind. Especially if there are other generals around."

"He's expecting us then?" Nelly asked.

"Yes, but we'll arrive late. We won't see him tonight," Jubil said. "I asked him to send some men with freight wagons to collect the load and take it to the fort. We'll stay in Bismarck tonight, then go to the fort tomorrow to meet with him."

As they left the hotel, Jubil posted his letter to Abe and Lily. He hoped by the time he and Nelly returned to Council Bluffs, there would be a reply waiting. Jubil hired a carriage to the depot, then they found their compartment on the train.

"This is very nice," Nelly said, admiring the plush red velvet sofa.

"Yes, Jay Cooke spared no expense on his railroad," Jubil said. "You see where that got him."

Nelly grinned as she retrieved a journal and fountain pen from her bag, and found a comfortable spot on the sofa. He went to the dining car to fetch them some coffee, and then he joined her on the sofa. As the morning passed and the landscape rolled by, Nelly alternated between gazing out the window and writing in her journal.

"This is beautiful country," she said. "It's easy to see why they call it the land of ten thousand lakes. I wonder if there really are that many? Minnesota is surely an Indian word—I wonder what it means? How in the world did the railroad ever find a straight stretch of dry land to build on?" She stopped and looked at Jubil. "I'm prattling, aren't I?"

"I don't mind," he said with a smile. "I don't know the answer to your first two questions, but I do know that surveying and building this stretch was a big mess. Mr. Rosser and his men were hired to correct years of incompetence, buck passing, and dishonesty. But he did it." He knew Thomas Rosser from the 1873 railroad survey. Rosser, in an act of staggering compassion, had saved Jubil from losing his farm and store when Jay Cooke's business collapsed.

In the afternoon, Nelly's wonderment with the landscape continued as the terrain gradually rose from low-lying wetlands to the arid plains of the Dakota Territory. Some people might have described it as desolate, but Jubil found it magnificent. The train flew straight west the whole distance across to Bismarck, unimpeded. Nelly commented occasionally, but for the most part, she was absorbed with her writing. Jubil did not mind, though he was having trouble staying interested in his book. Nelly had suggested James Fenimore Cooper's *Leatherstocking Tales*, but it was slow going—Cooper seemed determined to describe everything in great detail, whether it was important to the story or not. Jubil would have preferred one of his dime novels.

About an hour after sunset, the train pulled into Bismarck.

In preparation to disembark, Jubil opened his bag and removed his pistol and White Dog's medicine bag.

"I'll be wearing these while we're out here," Jubil said to Nelly as he strapped on his holster then slung the medicine bag strap over his head and settled the pouch on his right hip.

"You expect to need those?" she asked.

"No," he said, "but I'd regret not having them if I did."

Nelly nodded in agreement.

Though Jubil was not generally superstitious, he wore the medicine bag every time he came out West, out of respect for his friend and to avail himself of any power the spirit tokens had to protect his life.

He carried their bags across the main street to the Sheridan Hotel and got Nelly settled in their room.

"Will you be all right here without me?" he asked. "I'm not sure how long it will take to unload the supplies."

"I'll be fine," Nelly said. "Bismarck looks very civilized. After having conquered New York City, I feel capable of anything."

"I'm going to ask you to stay here in our room until I get back," Jubil said, dropping the pretense he had constructed to keep her from worrying until absolutely necessary.

"Why?" she said, looking at him with shocked surprise.

He described his sightings of the man in the brown bowler. "I don't know why anyone would be following me, and it might just be my imagination, but better safe than sorry."

Nelly stared at him with concern, but she did not protest, just nodded. He was relieved that she was handling the matter calmly, without arguing. If they were going to travel together out here, he needed to be able to be honest with her about the dangers in any situation. Keeping her ignorant of danger was no protection against it.

He left the hotel and enlisted the yardman to help with his freight car. Once it was secure, he went in search of the soldiers Custer had sent to meet him.

On the platform outside the station, he studied the crowd of people. At the end of the platform, three uniformed soldiers stood huddled together, smoking and laughing. Jubil saw two empty freight wagons nearby. He approached them.

"Evening, gentlemen," Jubil said. "Would you, by chance, be here to pick up a load of supplies for Lieutenant Colonel Custer?"

The soldiers went silent as they looked at Jubil. He got an awkward feeling—as if he had caught them at something.

"My name is Jubilee Walker. I'm helping outfit Custer's expedition."

"Yep, we're your men, all right," the apparent leader said. "I'm Corporal Jones, and this here is Private Smith and Private Johnson. We've got orders to haul your gear back to the fort."

Jubil was surprised by the soldier's informal manner, but even more so by the group's motley appearance. The corporal wore brown work boots rather than army issue footwear. Neither of the privates wore caps. These were not Custer's typical sharp and disciplined men—something was wrong here. Rather than confront them immediately, he decided to bide his time. He needed to get his freight off the train.

"The freight car is parked on a siding in the rail yard," Jubil said. "Let's pull the wagons down there." The corporal took the reins of one wagon, and Jubil joined him. The two privates drove the other wagon.

The siding was about a hundred feet past the platform, dimly lit by the streetlamps at the front of the station. Jubil unlocked the padlock on the freight car, and the four of them set to work. Jubil instructed the men on how to unload the supplies and stack them on the freight wagons, and soon they had the wagons loaded, covered, and lashed down.

While they worked, Jubil came up with a theory about what might be happening—these men were most likely planning to steal his freight. When he went back to the hotel, they might just drive off with Custer's supplies and never be seen again. He also came up with an idea about how to flush them out.

"I believe I'll ride along to the fort with you boys," Jubil said. "Are we ready?"

The soldiers exchanged a glance, and Jubil could see his theory was correct. He had spoiled their plan. His instincts shifted into high alert.

"We was told you'd be staying in town with your missus," the corporal said, sounding suspicious.

"I changed my mind," Jubil said. "I'll ride back once the freight is safely unloaded."

The soldiers exchanged another glance.

"Suit yourself," the corporal said.

The corporal went to the front of the wagon to mount up, and Jubil walked around to the other side. As he rounded the rear of the wagon, he sensed something behind him. He glanced over his right shoulder to see the tall soldier rushing toward him with a short club in his right hand. *Keep your wits about you*, he told himself as the world went into slow motion.

He shoved his coat behind his holster and spun around to face his assailant. The taller private drew his club back, but as he brought it around, aiming for Jubil's head, Jubil ducked his roundhouse swing. As the soldier stumbled forward, off balance from missing his target, Jubil grabbed him by the shoulders and slammed his head into the side of the wagon. The soldier fell in an unconscious heap.

The shorter private stepped out from behind the wagon, assessing the situation and raising his rifle. Jubil drew his pistol, took rapid aim to wound him, and fired. The shot took the private in the left shoulder and sent him flying backward, as the rifle clattered to the ground. Jubil spun to check his back and found the corporal standing behind him watching, his hands in the air and his rifle lying in the dirt beside him.

"I didn't sign up for killin' nobody," the corporal said. "This ain't worth that."

Jubil counted himself lucky he had not been shot in the back—the corporal was either a coward or had a conscience.

"Step away from the rifle," Jubil said, gesturing with his pistol.

The tall soldier had come around but still lay on the ground, holding his head.

Jubil kept his weapon trained on the men as he collected their rifles and tossed them under the wagon seat. He directed the corporal to attend to his wounded companion.

"Move over near your partners," Jubil ordered the tall soldier.

"You just clipped Johnson's arm," the corporal said, "but he needs the doc."

"Get him up," Jubil said unsympathetically. "The lot of you—walk back over to the station."

The damaged men gathered themselves up and stumbled toward the station. Jubil followed behind, his pistol trained on them.

"You weren't sent by Custer. Who are you?" Jubil asked the corporal.

"We was hired by a fella we met in the saloon," the corporal said, looking over his shoulder at Jubil. "We was to make off with the load, turn the wagons over to him out east of town, get paid, and walk away."

"What was his name?" Jubil asked. "This man who hired you."

"We wasn't introduced," the corporal said. "Looked like a proper gentleman, not a working man—fancy suit and hat."

The man in the bowler hat. But why? Why would anyone go to such an effort to rob him of these supplies for Custer? The load was not valuable enough to be worth the effort and danger required to steal it. It made no sense.

"What did you do with Custer's men?" Jubil asked.

"We got the best of them," the imposter corporal said. "Hog-tied them and put them in that equipment shed over yonder." He pointed across the rail yard at a small outbuilding.

"You better hope they're still alive," Jubil said.

As Jubil and his prisoners neared the front of the station they drew the attention of people milling about on the platform.

"Hold up right here," Jubil said to his prisoners, deciding to keep them at a distance from the station, in case they tried to run and he was forced to shoot. He called out to the small crowd, "I need some help here! Get me a lawman and a doctor!"

One of the men in the crowd spoke to a young boy, who then went running off, returning a few minutes later with a young man wearing a pair of pistols, who announced himself as the sheriff's deputy. Jubil explained the situation and pointed out the equipment shed holding Custer's men. The deputy sent some bystanders to liberate the soldiers, who staggered out of the shed. They stood around awkwardly in their red union suits, having lost their uniforms to their assailants.

The deputy took custody of Jubil's assailants and took them to retrieve their own clothing from the shed just as the doctor arrived in his carriage, which was then used to transport the men to jail for treatment and incarceration. The soldiers then drove Jubil's loaded wagons to the jail to retrieve their stolen uniforms. Jubil told the deputy about the men's plan, and the deputy said he would send a man to watch outside of town for the man who had hired them.

It was well past midnight by the time Jubil walked back to the hotel. He gently knocked on the door of their room, and within seconds, Nelly opened it, wrapped in a heavy robe and wearing her beaded moccasins.

"I couldn't sleep," she said. "You're so late. Is everything all right?"

"More or less," he said with a shrug. "Let's sit down." He looked up and down the hallway—the man in the bowler hat was very likely still around—but seeing no one, he entered the room and locked the door. "I had a bit of a run-in," he said as he took off his hat, coat, and boots. Nelly listened intently as he explained what had happened.

"You think they weren't really after the supplies?" she asked. "That they did it just to harm you or your business?"

"It's the only thing that makes sense to me," he said. "Otherwise, it's a lot of trouble for very little reward. We'll need to be extra cautious from here on out and watch for the man in the bowler hat."

"I hope he's considerate enough to keep wearing it," Nelly said wryly, "so we can recognize him."

She was right. Jubil had not managed to get a clear look at the man. All he had to go on was that he was a clean-shaven middle-aged white man; otherwise, he had noticed no memorable features. If the man was wearing a different hat and clothes, Jubil wouldn't be able to pick him out of a crowd.

"Who do you think is behind it?" Nelly asked.

Jubil had a feeling she already knew. "Lucius Black would be my first guess," he said.

She nodded.

"What do we do now?" she said.

"What can we do?" Jubil said. "Go on about our business—very carefully."

CHAPTER 6

In the morning, the deputy came to the hotel to tell Jubil there had been no sign of a man waiting to meet the thieves outside of town last night. Jubil and Nelly saw no sign of a man with a bowler hat along the route to the ferry across the Missouri River to Mandan, where Fort Lincoln was located.

As their hired carriage drove off the ferry, Jubil saw that Mandan had become something entirely different from the sleepy village he remembered from a year ago. West of the Mandan Indian village along the river, where last year the military escort and survey crews for the Northern Pacific Railroad had camped, there were now several dozen wood-frame buildings of various shapes and sizes set roughly in a circle, leaving a large parade ground in the center. Among the buildings was a modest white house with a yard enclosed by a picket fence. Standing on the porch was Custer, a woman Jubil did not know, and a young soldier. As the carriage drew to a stop, Custer sent the soldier to meet it. He helped Nelly down and then took their bags. Nelly struggled to contain her glee.

"He looks exactly as I thought he would," she whispered as Custer descended the stairs of the porch.

"Wait till you see him in full regalia," Jubil said with a smile. Custer had on his uniform pants, with their wide yellow stripe down the leg, and a casual white shirt. His only hint of extravagance was the red bandana he wore tied around his neck.

"Welcome to Fort Lincoln, Mr. Walker," Custer said, meeting them as they came into the yard. "I was pleased to learn we were doing business together again."

"Thank you, sir," Jubil said, shaking hands with him. "Congratulations on your new command. I'd like you to meet my wife, Nelly."

"It is a pleasure to make your acquaintance, ma'am," Custer said with a small bow. "I hope you enjoy your visit. Come along and meet my wife." He led them onto the porch and introduced them to Libbie Custer, whom Jubil estimated to be in her early thirties. She had a pleasant face, auburn hair, and blue-gray eyes.

"How do you do, Mr. Walker, Mrs. Walker?" Mrs. Custer said. "Welcome to our home. I must apologize for the humble setting, but it is comfortable. We suffered a terrible loss this winter when the beautiful house we had designed ourselves burned down."

"What a tragedy," Nelly said sympathetically. "I'm very sorry."

"Thank you, dear," Libbie said, reaching out to take Nelly's hand. "I was very pleased when Autie told me you were coming. We get so few refined guests. I understand you are a graduate of Vassar College and a journalist. I'm anxious for our conversation."

"How kind," Nelly said, graciously allowing Libbie to hold her hand.

Jubil had never heard anyone refer to Custer as Autie before. Custer directed the soldier to take their bags to the guest room, and they all went into the house.

"Perhaps I could give you a brief tour," Libbie said to Nelly, "and we'll have tea while the men talk."

"How lovely," Nelly said, and she took Libbie's arm, smiling at Jubil as they walked away.

Custer led Jubil into his office and offered him a chair by

the fireplace. Two mounted antelope heads adorned the upper corners of the wall above the desk. A large framed map of western America leaned against the wall, and directly above it hung portraits of Libbie and Custer. In one corner was his gunrack, in the other, a small bookcase.

"Some mighty embarrassed soldiers rode back into camp last night following your arrival," Custer said. "My apologies. Those boys will be digging latrines to atone for the poor defensive showing they made. I hear you tamed all three of the scoundrels who accosted you. Bravo!"

"They weren't very bright," Jubil said dismissively. "The thieves, I mean—but I suppose your boys weren't either."

Custer laughed.

"Do you know who was behind it?" Custer asked.

"I have a suspicion," Jubil said and gave Custer a brief history of his dealings with Lucius Black.

"Hmm," Custer said. "How do you plan to deal with him?"

"I've been considering it, but I haven't come to any conclusions yet," Jubil said.

"Well, watch your back in the meantime," Custer said, and changed the subject. "I imagine your arrangement with Jay Cooke did not end as you'd hoped."

Custer and his Seventh Cavalry had been part of the military escort guarding Thomas Rosser's Northern Pacific Railroad survey crew. Jubil had ridden with him last year on the survey between Mandan and Pompey's Pillar.

"No," Jubil said. "His bankruptcy prevented him from making the agreed investment in my business, and the financial panic has set me back further yet. I'm trying to make up our retail shortfall by doing more army business."

"Are you planning to open a store in Bismarck?" Custer said.

"No," Jubil said, "that wasn't my plan. I thought I could manage from Council Bluffs."

"I suppose that could work," Custer said. "But you should know, there is a new mercantile in Bismarck that has been handling some of my business. When he couldn't supply everything that I needed this summer, my logistics request went up the ranks. Apparently, someone thought of you."

"General Sherman," Jubil said. "I had gone to visit him about doing more business with the army, and I happened to be in the right place at the right time."

"Well, I'm glad you were," Custer said. "Perhaps on some basis we can work together, but I feel obligated to carry on business with this local merchant. He's a good man, and he's working to expand his suppliers and capabilities."

Jubil was disappointed in Custer's outlook for their business prospects, but he supposed he shouldn't be. He had said all along that to supply Fort Ellis, he would need a store in Bozeman as a base of operations. Why had he thought supplying Fort Lincoln would be any different? He had hoped he could operate from Council Bluffs and that Custer would be anxious to work with him, despite some inconvenience.

"I understand your point about a store," Jubil said, "but it's a hard financial climate for opening new stores. Otherwise, I'd give your local merchant some competition." I've been thinking about opening one in Bozeman, though, as a base for my adventure tours into Yellowstone."

"That's the business you and Cooke would have partnered on?" Custer asked.

"Yes," Jubil said. "I still have ambitions to see the park developed to accommodate tourists." He told the story of his visit with Secretary Delano and the outcome of their meeting.

"He was in favor of you helping develop Yellowstone until you pointed out corruption at the Crow Agency?" Custer asked.

"Exactly," Jubil said. "He said my presence in the area would be disruptive."

"He's probably right about that," Custer said with a grin.

"That's not the point," Jubil said, taking Custer's jibe with a smile.

"Well, that reservation is not the only one that suffers from corruption," Custer said. "The Red Cloud Agency near Fort Laramie does too—or so I've heard tell from one of the scientists going with me this summer—Mr. Grinnell, a paleontologist. His superior at Yale, Professor Othniel Charles Marsh, is working in that area and is all fired up about the situation there. You can ask him about it yourself if you want to—I'll send my aide to see if he's around."

"If you're sure he wouldn't mind the interruption," Jubil said.

"He won't mind," Custer said. "He's a very congenial fellow." Custer left the room to give his orders to his aide and then returned.

"General Sherman told me you're in the unusual position of defending Indians against white prospectors," Jubil said, "but he said your mission is to verify rumors of gold in the Black Hills. How is that supposed to help the situation?"

"We hope to avoid the army being stuck in a war between the gold prospectors and the Indians," Custer said. "If the rumors of gold in the hills continue to build, or if someone makes a strike, there's going to be a rush. That's bound to lead to a fight, and the army will have to take sides. If the government knows for certain what's coming, it will give us time to make a plan to, we hope, avoid the worst. If we only find traces of gold and nothing that indicates a lode might be hidden somewhere, maybe we can convince prospectors not to even bother coming. The joint military and civilian nature of the expedition is intended to lend credibility to the army reports."

"What if you do hit the motherlode?" Jubil asked. He was beginning to more fully understand the explosive situation developing in the region.

"The government would have to do some fancy dancing,"

Custer said. "Washington would be hotly debating the terms of the 1868 Treaty of Laramie."

"They wouldn't break that treaty, would they?" Jubil asked incredulously. "That would start a war for sure."

Jubil recalled General Sherman once saying that if the Indians ever consolidated their forces against the army, then the army would have to bring its full force against them. It seemed to Jubil that government was making this inevitable. Breaking their treaties and forcing the tribes onto smaller and ever more useless tracts of land was giving them every reason to unite and resist.

Custer shrugged. "They haven't been shy about taking back Indian land they've already given away—especially if they find value in it."

"This whole area is going to blow up one of these days," Jubil said.

"Very possibly so," Custer said, nodding.

Jubil wondered if there was anything to be done to stop it. The solution seemed simple to him—follow the Golden Rule. But he wasn't naïve enough to believe that philosophy would ever prevail.

"There's no doubt there's placer gold to be had," Custer said, "but the Indians have made it difficult for a prospector to live long enough to dig. The geologists traveling with us have mixed opinions about what we'll find. They don't feel the area will be as rich as California, but it might be substantial."

"I think I'll just stick to my line of work," Jubil said. "Outfitters generally make more money selling to prospectors than most prospectors make hunting gold."

"Maybe you can set up shop here," Custer said. "Or maybe your store in Bozeman will profit from a rush. I've heard reports of deposits around Cooke City."

"That doesn't amount to much, does it?" Jubil asked. Jack Baronett had built a toll bridge over the Yellowstone River to make a living from the traffic to and from the Cooke City mines, but Jubil had never heard reports of any great riches being extracted there.

"Depends on who you talk to," Custer said. "There's clearly a fairly rich deposit, but there's debate about whether it's playing out or hiding something richer."

Phineas Black had had mining operations in Cooke City, which O'Brien had managed until he took over Murphy's job. For the first time, it occurred to Jubil that Lucius Black was probably operating those mines, now that Phineas Black, Murphy, and O'Brien were all out of the picture.

Custer's aide stepped into the room, ushering in a tall thin man with a bushy mustache groomed to fine-tipped points.

"Excuse me, sir," the aide said, "Mr. Grinnell is here."

Custer and Jubil stood, and Custer introduced Jubil and George Bird Grinnell. As the three men took a seat, Custer described Jubil's interests in the area and invited him to describe the conditions at the Crow reservation.

"I understand you and Professor Marsh have witnessed similar conditions at the Red Cloud Agency," Jubil said to Grinnell.

"Appalling," Grinnell said, frowning and shaking his head. "Simply appalling. Putrid pork, inferior flour, rotten tobacco, and all manner of other shoddy goods foisted on the tribes. Emaciated cattle delivered along with moldy fodder for them. Shameful . . . just shameful."

"Were you able to gather any evidence of corruption," Jubil asked, "other than your personal witness to it? Anything that might hold up in a court of law—falsified records, inflated prices, that sort of thing?"

"Not as yet," Grinnell said. "Professor Marsh has paleontology field work to finish while the weather permits, but then he intends to make a thorough investigation of the Red Cloud situation and document his findings. He plans to petition President Grant to intervene."

"That's encouraging. I'm trying to do the same," Jubil said. "I wonder if he would include a letter from me that outlines my experiences. Perhaps if the president saw a display of outrage from both of us, the issue would be more likely to garner his attention. The professor may not know me, but I could produce character references from respectable sources," he said, looking to Custer.

Custer nodded.

"I'll mention our conversation to him in my next letter," Grinnell said. "You can address your letter to him at the library, and they will see that he gets it."

"Excellent," Jubil said. "Thank you." He was very pleased with this unexpected turn of events. It might even help him and Walter gain an audience with President Grant.

"Before you go, Mr. Grinnell," Custer said, "What do you and your colleagues think of the potential for gold near Cooke City in Montana Territory? Are the rumors about the mines true?"

"Your mission is to look for gold, while mine is to look for bones," Grinnell said pointedly. "However, I have heard Mr. Winchell, the geologist in our party, express the opinion that the mountains around Cooke City have greater prospects than have been delivered on, to date."

"Why do you suppose that is?" Jubil asked.

"Either no one has found a lode," Grinnell said, shrugging, "or they have, and they don't want anyone to know. If you want a better opinion, ask Winchell."

"Don't want anyone to know? That's an interesting notion," Jubil said. "I won't bother Mr. Winchell. Like you, I'm not really looking for gold."

"And the government shouldn't be either," Grinnell said, looking at Custer. "Especially not here."

Jubil did not disagree. Custer looked unconcerned about Grinnell's opinion.

Grinnell rose.

"It's a pleasure to meet you," Jubil said. "You've been very helpful."

"You're welcome," Grinnell said. "Good luck."

Grinnell shook hands with Jubil and Custer, then took his leave.

"I'm impressed by your resistance to the lure of the gold fields," Custer said.

"I wouldn't mind striking it rich," Jubil said, "to put an end to the financial pressure of making a living, but digging in the dirt seems a dull way to go about life."

"You should go along with me this summer," Custer said. "We'll have an adventure exploring the Black Hills, while the scientists dig in the dirt."

Jubil felt his scalp tingle at the suggestion. There had been a time when he would have jumped at such a chance, but that was before he had so many other people counting on him. He wasn't sure he fully approved of this change in his priorities.

"That is a very appealing offer," Jubil said. "But I've got business to attend to."

That evening, Jubil and Nelly had supper with the Custers—a delightful meal of roast pheasant and potatoes prepared by one of the army cooks. After supper, Libbie Custer entertained them by playing piano quite capably.

When Jubil and Nelly retired for the evening, he was pleased to hear that she had enjoyed Libbie's company. She admired Libbie's devotion to her husband and her willingness to live with some hardship, and she found Libbie intelligent and intellectually curious. Libbie had been very keen to hear of Nelly's time at Vassar, her involvement in woman suffrage, and her career and experiences in New York. They had found themselves to be kindred spirits.

In the morning, Jubil made a final pitch to Custer about keeping Warner and Walker Outfitters top of mind for his supply needs. Custer assured him he would but gave him nothing definite. Libbie and Nelly vowed to keep in touch.

Custer's aide delivered them to the train depot and carried their bags as they found their compartment. Once the soldier had left, Jubil unstrapped his holster and started to put his sidearm in his bag.

"You don't want to keep that handy?" Nelly said.

"Did you see someone in a brown bowler hat?" Jubil asked.

"No," she said. "Did you?"

"No," he said. "We'll keep it in my bag, right on top, and I'll leave the bag unlatched."

She nodded.

CHAPTER 7

When Jubil and Nelly arrived in Council Bluffs, they found Eli in good spirits. He and Nelly went into the house, and Jubil went with Mr. Garcia to the stables. He missed his horses when he was away—Star, his beautiful chestnut mare that had been his father's horse; Apollo, the handsome brown-and-white pinto stallion he had ridden during his Yellowstone expeditions; and the newest member of the stable, Comet, Star's colt foal from Apollo, born last October. The colt was a pinto like his sire but with chestnut markings like Star's rather than rich brown like Apollo's. Jubil wanted to take Apollo to Colorado for the adventure tour, but he was reluctant to do so. Having a strong and trustworthy horse in the wilderness was important, but he felt guilty about the prospect of pulling the little equine family apart.

The fourth horse in the stable was Rocky, the muscular gray carriage horse. The army had issued Rocky to Jubil on his first trip west and then discharged him to the care of the Warners.

After tending the animals, Jubil went into the house, where Nelly was helping Mrs. Garcia set the table for lunch.

"Eli is in the office," Nelly said.

Eli was sitting in one of the reading chairs, looking over the Sunday newspaper. "There's a letter from Abe on the desk," he said.

Jubil opened the message from Abe and read aloud.

Jubil,

I do not want to make this a regular occurrence, but Lily and I have decided to return to Council Bluffs mid-June to mind the store while you are in Colorado. Lily claims to be fine, but if she proves to be unsettled by being there, I'll close the store and return to Nantucket. If this is acceptable, we'll see you soon.

Abe

"That's very good news," Eli said.

Jubil told Eli what had happened in Bismarck.

"Are you going to try to hunt down the man in the bowler hat?" Eli asked.

"We'll watch our backs for a while," Jubil said. "When he tips his hand again, I'll be ready. Just keep your wits about you—remember?"

Eli nodded.

"We've got to get ready for Colorado," Jubil said. "Have you made peace with the idea of spending several weeks in your sister's company?"

"I have," Eli said, "but I'd appreciate it if you would remind her, I take orders from you, not from her."

"Duly noted, my dear brother," Nelly said from the doorway. "What did Abe's message say?" she asked.

Jubil shared Abe and Lily's plan.

"Will you tell them what happened in Bismarck?" Nelly asked.

"Do you think I should?"

"Probably," she said without conviction. "We'd have a lot of explaining to do if anything were to happen while they're here."

"I'll write to Abe and tell him, and he can decide whether to tell Lily," Jubil said. "If they then decide not to come, we'll just have to close the store while we're gone."

"I hope it doesn't come to that," Nelly said.

"I don't know what other choice we would have," Jubil said.

Life returned to a slower pace in June as they waited for the Warners to arrive and prepared for the tour. Jubil sent a letter along to Professor Marsh at Yale, detailing his knowledge of the corruption at the Crow Agency. He also contacted Walter Trumbull to see whether he had made any progress in getting a meeting with President Grant. Walter had been told that a meeting might be arranged, if it could be worked conveniently into the president's schedule—but so far, that had not happened. Jubil took heart from the fact his request had not been rejected outright.

Business at the store was slow but steady; they were still losing money but at a slower rate. Eli had done a good job running things without Ike while Jubil and Nelly were away, and Jubil told him so. He was also impressed by Eli's meticulous planning for the adventure tour. He had been concerned that Eli's irritation with Nelly might make him careless, but Eli's attitude toward his sister had calmed considerably since Jubil's pointed discussion with him.

Ike had written with an update on how he was adjusting to his new situation. He was enjoying the work but finding city life a bit exhausting. Nelly thought he sounded lonely. Eli had no comment.

Before Eli contacted the livery in Denver to make sure the stock would be available, Jubil confirmed he would not be taking Apollo on the tour. Not only did he not want to separate Star's family, it would be expensive to transport him. And it didn't seem right for him to have his own horse while Nelly and Eli rode livery horses.

Nelly passed the time in Council Bluffs writing an article

for the *Rocky Mountain News* about the trip to visit the Custers, which Jubil enjoyed greatly.

Recently, Nelly wrote, *it was my pleasure to accompany my husband on a business trip to Mandan, Dakota Territory. We rode the Northern Pacific Railroad along its westernmost leg, crossing Minnesota with its abundance of jeweled lakes and moving at dawn onto the plains of Dakota Territory, an arid land of muted browns and greens, dotted with spires of stone that have been worn by wind and water.*

Our arrival at Bismarck was inconvenienced when my husband was required to get the better of a trio of dim-witted ruffians who tried to make off with his cargo. The men posed as soldiers sent to pick up the load but put on such a poor performance that his suspicions were aroused. The who, what, and why of this episode are beyond the scope of this article; suffice to say my husband prevailed, and the materials were delivered to the post as planned that evening.

We had come to visit General G. A. Custer, the new commander at Fort Lincoln. I am aware of Custer's actual rank, but I find the title by which he is most commonly known more fitting.

Custer was as dashing and congenial a host as one might expect. Displaying nothing of the proud and haughty persona for which he is famed, he introduced us to his charming wife, Libbie, who brought an air of sophistication and culture to this remote outpost. While the men talked business, Mrs. Custer and I deepened our acquaintance. She took great interest in my literary career and advocacy for woman suffrage. Later, after a fine supper prepared by a talented army cook, Mrs. Custer gave a most artful piano performance of "Grandfather's Clock" and "Carry Me Back to Old Virginny."

The purpose of General Custer's expedition this summer is to provide safe escort for a group of civilian scientists charged with assessing the potential gold yield of the Black Hills region. The US government finds it necessary to do so in order to set their strategy for benevolently protecting society thereabouts, though it is not entirely clear whose society they are protecting.

The land that they will be entering is the property of the Sioux people, set aside for them by the 1868 Treaty of Fort Laramie. The US Army has found itself in the curious position of defending the Sioux tribes from violent white men illegally prospecting for gold on their land. Expecting that position to become untenable if a major gold strike should occur, the government hopes to get ahead of the situation.

Though no one has asked my opinion on the likely outcome of these circumstances, I have no reservations about offering it: If the US Government finds significant evidence of gold in the Black Hills, the Sioux people are about as likely to be granted the right to hold onto their land and their gold as women have of being granted the right to vote in the next presidential election.

Myself, I hope that General Custer's expedition finds the Black Hills to have a paucity of gold. Otherwise, I fear that my new friends, General George and Libbie Custer, are perched atop a powder keg on the Western frontier.

Jubil complimented Nelly on her entertaining travelogue and observed that her closing editorial was daring. Nelly took that as a compliment.

The Associated Press circulated the article, which they now did with anything Nelly published. Mr. Byers had written saying that he had some literary business to discuss with her and that he was hoping to meet her and Jubil at the hotel in Denver, before they left on their tour. Nelly was excited by the prospect. Jubil hoped it was good news.

He was also hopeful that the Warners would enjoy returning to their old routines in Council Bluffs. He had received no response to his letter regarding the incident in Bismarck and was encouraged they had not cancelled because of it.

Late in the afternoon on June fifteenth, Jubil and Nelly took the surrey to the train depot to pick up Abe and Lily. As the train arrived and the passengers disembarked, Nelly suddenly clutched Jubil's arm.

"Look there!" she said, whispering dramatically and pointed toward her target in the bustling crowd.

Jubil scanned the crowd and spotted him. The man wore a three-piece suit and a brown bowler hat. He carried a travel bag and walked briskly through the crowd toward the front of the platform.

"Is it him?" Nelly asked.

"I can't be certain," Jubil said. "He's too far away, and I'm not sure about his features."

"Quite a coincidence though," Nelly said. "Don't you think?"

"I don't know," Jubil said. "Our man is not the only one in the country to wear a brown bowler hat."

Nelly looked around, then at Jubil skeptically. "Do you see another?"

"Not at the moment," he said.

As they watched, the man made his way through the crowd to a waiting carriage and stepped in without speaking to the driver. He had not looked their way or taken any interest in the crowd. Jubil watched his carriage pull away, turn up Lower Broadway, and head downtown.

"Should we follow him?" Nelly asked.

Jubil hesitated for a moment, then handed the reins of the surrey to Nelly.

"Collect Abe and Lily and go on up to the house," Jubil said. "I'll be along shortly."

She nodded. "Be careful."

He jumped out of the surrey and ran to the queue of coachmen waiting for a fare. He stopped at the first one he came to.

"You see that carriage with the man in the bowler hat," Jubil said, pointing out his target, "I need to follow him."

The driver hitched his thumb toward the passenger area, and Jubil jumped in. The man did an admirable job of maneuvering his rig through the crowded loading area and turned up Lower Broadway. His target was several carriages ahead, moving along in the steady stream of traffic. As they passed Warner and Walker Outfitters, Jubil turned to see if Eli happened to be looking out the window, but he was not. When the other carriage reached Pearl Street, it turned and pulled up in front of the Ogden Hotel. Jubil watched the man in the bowler hat pay his driver and go into the hotel. Jubil was still fifty yards or more from the hotel when traffic stopped, as carriages waited to turn.

"Pull up to the Ogden Hotel when you can," Jubil said to his driver. "I'll only be a minute inside, and then I'll come back to pay you." Not waiting for the driver's reply, Jubil jumped out and ran up Lower Broadway to the Ogden Hotel. He was only two or three minutes behind his target as he stepped inside.

The lobby was busy with travelers. Jubil scanned the room for bowler hats. Across the room he spotted one, but it was black and on the head of a short portly man. Another man held a bowler hat as he waited to be seated in the dining room, but he was also carrying a fancy cane. Checking in at the front desk was a man in a brown suit, but he was not wearing a bowler hat. He was of average height and build, like the man Jubil had seen, but so were many of the other men in the lobby. On the floor beside him was a tweed carpetbag. Was this his man? Had he hidden his hat in his bag? Had he spotted Jubil following him?

If Jubil were sure that it was the same man he had seen in Chicago and Bismarck, he would confront him, just to put him on notice that he would not tolerate harassment without responding. But he was not sure.

He left the hotel in frustration and found his driver waiting. He asked him to take him back to the Warner house on the north edge of town.

Everyone was gathered in the dining room, having coffee, awaiting his arrival.

"Was it the same man you saw in Bismarck?" Abe asked, remaining seated. He seemed concerned but not angry.

"I can't be sure," Jubil said. "If it is, he's staying at the Ogden Hotel."

Lily regarded him anxiously, and this time, there was a legitimate cause.

"I might have been overzealous in following him," Jubil said, mainly to Lily. "Maybe an abundance of caution. I'm sorry if I worried you. Are you going to be all right here?"

Lily looked at him for a moment, then turned to Abe.

"We'll be fine," Abe said. "It's you we're concerned about."

"I'll be fine," Jubil said. "Thank you."

Mrs. Garcia was in the process of preparing a supper fit for royalty, and Lily and Nelly went about the business of setting the table and helping put the finishing touches on the meal. Jubil was encouraged by how Lily lit up when interacting with her longtime friend and housekeeper. Abe went to take a short nap to recover from the trip, and Jubil took the opportunity to go out to the stable to visit with Mr. Garcia and check on his horses. When Eli returned from work at the store, the whole group gathered for supper. Jubil had expected some awkwardness after their delicate conversation in Nantucket, but so far there had been none. After supper, Lily and Nelly went to Lily's studio to visit. Lily was anxious to hear Nelly's stories about the trip to Bismarck and how Ike was doing. Jubil, Eli, and Abe went into the office.

Abe walked straight to the bar cart and poured himself a short glass of whiskey. He held the bottle up toward Jubil and Eli, but Jubil shook his head—he did not like the taste. Eli declined also. Abe stood in front of the large windows and took in the panoramic view of the Missouri River Valley to the west, the town of Council Bluffs to the south, and the town's namesake hills to the east. The last time he and Lily had been there was the Christmas after Luke had died. At that time, the memories had been too much for Lily to bear.

"I miss it here sometimes," Abe said, with his back to Jubil and Eli. "Actually, part of the reason I was reluctant to come back is that I may enjoy it too much. I don't believe Lily will share my enthusiasm."

Jubil had conflicting feelings about Abe's admission. It was gratifying to have his suspicions confirmed that Abe might enjoy running the store again, but that was a melancholy victory considering Lily's fragility.

"How has she been doing since Nelly and I visited?" Jubil asked.

Abe took a sip of his drink. "We had a long conversation after you left. We agreed that we were probably overprotective of Luke, as you said. We're going to make an effort not to do the same to you."

"I appreciate that very much," Jubil said, relieved that they hadn't taken offense. "I'll do the best I can not to take any unnecessary risks. But I have to be true to myself."

"I know," Abe said. "But I can't help but wonder who have you made such an enemy of? Does this have something to do with the Crow reservation situation?"

"Lucius Black is the only person I know who has any cause to take issue with me," Jubil said.

"Why would he have waited until now to come after you?" Abe asked.

"Maybe my trip out there stirred him up," Jubil said. "Or maybe word about my visit with Delano got back to him and he knows I'm serious about putting an end to this corruption."

"What do you plan to do?" Abe said.

"What can I do?" Jubil said. "If I go out there and face him, he'll just deny everything. I've got to focus on this adventure tour to keep our business afloat."

Abe finished his drink in silence. Then he said, "I'm tired. I'm going to bed. We'll sort it out tomorrow."

"Good night, Abe," Eli said, who had listened quietly to their conversation. "I guess I'll go to bed too," he said to Jubil.

"I think I'll stay up and keep watch on the house for a while," Jubil said.

"Want me to help?" Eli asked. "I can take a shift later."

"Thanks," Jubil said. "I'll wake you if I need a break."

Eli nodded and studied Jubil. "You think he'd do something to the house?"

"Probably not," Jubil said, less confident than he sounded. "I'm just not sleepy."

"Wake me if you want a break," Eli shrugged, and went to his room.

Jubil went to see if Nelly and Lily were still visiting in her studio but found it empty. Upstairs in their bedroom, he found Nelly was fast asleep. Without waking her, he retrieved his jacket and rifle and slipped out of the bedroom. Downstairs, he put his jacket on and stepped out the front door of the house.

The world outside was lit by the silver glow of a full moon. Jubil walked to the gazebo and turned one of the rocking chairs to face the house. He took a seat, placed his rifle across the arms of the chair, rested his arms on the rifle, and settled in to his watch.

If the same man that had followed them to Bismarck had come to Council Bluffs, what was he planning—and what could Jubil do to prepare for it? Concern for the safety of everyone in the house was weighing on him heavily. Was his determination to achieve his goals putting everyone he loved in danger?

Every hour or so, he got up and strolled around the house and barn to make sure no one was lurking in the shadows. All the while, going over the same questions in his mind and finding no new answers. The moon moved across the sky, and the dim glow of first light appeared. He was relieved nothing had happened overnight.

After breakfast he, Abe, and Eli, would open the store. It would feel good to be there with Abe again.

Then something shifted in Jubil's thinking—the store. If someone wanted to hurt him and his business, they might target the store.

He went inside to tell Nelly he was going into town. As he sat down on the bed beside her, she awoke and propped herself up on one elbow.

"Why are you up so early?" she said. "Is everything all right?"

"Yes, everything is fine," he said. "I just had an urge to go check on the store—I'll be back shortly."

He kissed her on the forehead, picked up his rifle, and headed for the stable. He greeted Star, Comet, and Rocky, saddled Apollo, and rode into town. He put Apollo in the stable behind the store and fished in his pocket for the key as he approached the back door—which he was shocked to see was already ajar. As he pushed it open, he beheld a mess that stunned him.

The storeroom had been ransacked, clothing pulled down from shelves and strewn about, shoes and boots dumped from their boxes, and whitewash poured over it all. A dozen empty buckets were strewn about the floor. The store showroom had been given the same treatment. All the products had been pulled off the shelves; the standing displays had been knocked over; whitewash had been splashed over all the goods, as well as the shelves, cash register, and front window. Empty buckets lay everywhere.

"Damn you!" Jubil raged, cursing whoever had done this.

He stared at the ruins of his store—Abe and Luke Warner's store, where they had welcomed him and treated him like family. Between waves of anger and despair, he wondered what purpose such destruction was supposed to serve. He left the store, rode to the sheriff's office, and brought him to survey the damage for himself. The sheriff and Jubil went to question the clerk at the Ogden Hotel about a suspicious man in a bowler hat, but he claimed to have no recollection of such a person. The sheriff promised to file a report, and Jubil rode back to the Warner's house.

Everyone was having breakfast. They all turned to look as he stood in the doorway of the dining room.

"Someone vandalized the store," he said.

Lily covered her mouth with her hand as the rest of them stared in shocked silence.

"Are the Garcias here?" Jubil said. He opened the door between the dining room and kitchen and found them at their table having coffee. "Join us, please," Jubil said. "You need to know what's going on too."

As Jubil described what had happened, Lily broke into tears, and Nelly made an effort to comfort her, but Jubil could sense that she was steaming with anger. Eli made a blustering comment about teaching the vandals a lesson, but he went silent when Jubil did not respond. Abe sat frowning, pondering the situation.

"I'm kicking myself for not staying at the store last night," Jubil said. "I was more worried about protecting the house, and you all." He turned to Abe and Lily. "And I'm sorry to have asked you to come. I think you should go back to Nantucket. I'm not sure it's safe here."

"What about the store?" Abe said.

"I'm going to close it," Jubil said. "At least until we get back from Colorado. I'm not letting anything stop me from conducting this tour."

Nelly nodded with a look of determination.

"We can stay," Abe said, "until you leave. We can help you clean up the store."

"I'd feel better if you just went on home," Jubil said. "I'll deal with it." He turned to the Garcias. "I wouldn't blame you if you wanted to leave too, but I think it will be safe when I'm gone. I'd sure appreciate it if you'd look out for the place while we're away—and take care of my horses. But if you don't want to, I'll understand and make other arrangements."

"We are not going anywhere," Mrs. Garcia said, without consulting her husband. Jubil looked his way and got a confirming nod.

"Thank you, Rosie," he said to Mrs. Garcia.

Lily, who was sitting next to Mrs. Garcia, reached over to cover her hand with her own. Lily looked at Jubil. "You need to get to the bottom of this," Lily said, looking deep into his eyes. "You have to find out who's doing this and why. Going off to Colorado is just going to delay that, and it may put the people you're traveling with at risk."

That brought Jubil up short. He glanced over at Nelly, who raised her eyebrows as if to say, *she has a point*. He leaned back in his chair, breathing deeply as he considered what to do. When he couldn't decide quickly, he did what he always had done—turned to his heart.

"You may well be right, Lily," he said. "But I've got to complete this tour. There are people going that I cancelled on once before, and I'm not doing that again. Why would anyone ever risk traveling with me in the future if I have that kind of reputation? I was lucky to find as many people as I did this time. I'm not letting them down, especially on such short notice. I have to do this. Plus, I need the money—we all need the money. We can't draw on our assets endlessly."

"Right," Eli said. "Some of us don't have assets to draw on. Are we going to open the store again, after we get back? I don't have any other source of income."

"We're going to do our best," Jubil said to Eli. "But I can't guarantee how much business we'll draw."

Eli frowned and nodded.

"What if that's exactly what Lucius Black's counting on?"

Nelly said. "What if he's doing all this to put you out of business? Preventing your delivery to Custer; damaging your store; forcing you cancel your tour. It all seems aimed to hurt your business more than to hurt you. I mean, if he wanted to kill you, he could have had you ambushed and thrown into the Chicago River or shot you dead in Bismarck or burned the house to the ground last night . . ." Nelly stopped, seeming to realize she was veering into melodrama. "Well . . . you get my point."

"I do," Jubil said. "And it's a good one. But it still leaves me with the same strategy we talked about in Bismarck."

"Wait until he shows himself?" Nelly said.

"Yes," he said. "What else can we do? We still have no evidence Black is responsible."

No one seemed to have anything further to add to the discussion.

"Nelly," Jubil said, "I want you to consider going with Lily and Abe to Nantucket."

Nelly made a scoffing sound.

"At least consider it," Jubil said. He rose from the table. He didn't feel like eating breakfast. "I'm going to go back to the store and start cleaning up."

Despite Jubil's urging, Abe and Lily stayed in Council Bluffs for a week to help clean up the store. Abe made arrangements to replace the front window, but he and Jubil had a minor disagreement over who should pay for it. They compromised by agreeing that they would each pay half. Abe offered further financial support to bring the Council Bluffs store back to life and keep it operating, which Jubil appreciated but declined. He had gotten himself into this situation, and he intended to get himself out of it.

Jubil and Eli removed the damaged merchandise from the store and hauled it into the hills to set it ablaze. Whatever was salvageable, which wasn't much, they organized in the storeroom. The shelving and floor in the front of the store was damaged beyond repair and would have to be replaced. Jubil found a carpenter to do the work, but the expense would wipe out his remaining inheritance. He decided to wait until he returned, when he and Eli, and possibly his father-in-law, Mr. Boswell, could do the job themselves, paying only for materials. That would keep the store closed even longer, but he wasn't ready to bet the last of his savings on a business that could no longer pay for itself.

Lily and Abe set off for Nantucket—without Nelly, who could not be deterred from making the trip by either Jubil's appeals or Lily's entreaties. Over the next few days, Jubil, Nelly, and Eli made their final preparations with a certain grim resolve.

As they set off for Colorado, Jubil was leaving Council Bluffs with no guaranteed source of income when he returned. He had expected to use the profits from the tour to make up for the store's shortfall, but now that money would have to be spent just to repair it.

If Nelly was right and Black was trying to put him out of business, Jubil was determined to prove that he had failed.

CHAPTER 8

On July 1, the Colorado Central Railroad delivered Jubil, Nelly, and Eli to the Denver station on time, and Mr. Byers of the *Rocky Mountain News* was there with a driver and carriage to meet them. Since leaving Council Bluffs, they had been on the lookout for a man in a bowler hat and had spotted a few but none that Jubil recognized as their suspect.

It was a short ride to the hotel where they would meet their adventure tour guests—Portico's Delmonico of the West on Larimar Street, a three-story brick-and-stone building with a wrought iron canopy and modest but well-appointed rooms. Mr. Ritchie, the proprietor of the hotel, met them as they entered the lobby.

"Welcome back," Mr. Ritchie said, shaking hands with each of them. They had stayed there on Jubil and Nelly's honeymoon trip last spring, with Eli as their outfitter. At that time, Eli had impressed Jubil by making a deal with Mr. Ritchie for a special rate for their adventure tour. "It's a pleasure to have you and your clients as my guests. As they arrive today, I'll inform them of your supper meeting at six o'clock in our private dining room. I'll have your things taken to your rooms. Here are your keys. Anything you need, just ask at the desk."

"Thank you," Jubil said. "There is one thing—tonight, could you make sure that no one is allowed into the dining room but my clients? I'd like to attend to my guests and not be tied to watching the door."

"Most certainly," Mr. Ritchie said. "I'll attend to it myself."

"I'm going to walk to the livery," Eli said to Jubil after Mr. Ritchie had given them their keys and excused himself. "I'll make sure everything is set for the tour."

"Good," Jubil said. "I'd go with you, but I think I should keep an eye on things here. Be careful. If you think you see our man, come back and get me—don't confront him. But maybe you'd better strap on your pistol just in case."

"All right," Eli said.

Jubil and Nelly joined Mr. Byers, who had been waiting in the comfortable seating available near the large stone fireplace, in which a cozy fire was burning, even though it was July.

"I'm dying to hear your ideas," Nelly said to Byers.

Byers leaned in to address Nelly, elbows on his knees and hands clasped. "You are developing quite a following," he said with a conspiratorial glimmer in his eyes.

Nelly smiled with delight. Jubil had always thought she was beautiful, but at that moment, she was radiant. Her enthusiasm and joy inspired him, and he lingered as long as he could in that moment.

"The article you wrote about your visit with the Custers brought in more mail than anything I can recall in the past year, at least—both praise and criticism."

"Criticism?" Nelly said with a frown.

"At your 'misguided social conscience'—one of your critic's words, not mine," Byers said. "Your opinion that the Indians have no more chance of retaining their land and the gold found on it than women have of getting the vote. But you also got strong praise for pointing out that truth in such an entertaining fashion."

Jubil watched Nelly puzzle over Byers's message.

"I want you to write more of that," Byers said. "You're

entertaining people and hitting nerves at the same time. You're a publisher's dream. Your articles on social justice in the form of woman suffrage are excellent, but anyone uninterested in the subject matter can easily avoid them. But if your reader is captivated by a spritely travel piece and you slip social justice into your rousing story, you may change more opinions than you can imagine. You know the saying—*the pen is mightier than the sword*. Your pen may be mightier than you imagined."

"I appreciate your encouragement," Nelly said. "I'm not sure I can carry the weight of your request, but I'll do my best."

"Send me articles whenever you can," Byers said, "and I'll help you reach your audience. We'll change the world, one opinion at a time."

"Thank you," Nelly said, seeming a bit flustered.

Jubil smiled at her and patted her hand. He was very proud of her. She was making the most of her fearlessly opinionated personality, and she was just getting started.

"And Mr. Walker," Byers said, "how does it feel to be on the brink of your first adventure tour?"

"As you can imagine, it's exciting and daunting at the same time," Jubil said. He gave a brief explanation of events in Bismarck and Council Bluffs.

Byers's expression grew serious. "That's unfortunate," he said.

"I wonder," Jubil said, "if you know of anyone here in Denver who could scout for us. I need somebody with a good eye and the ability to track if necessary."

"Well, the man who comes to mind," Byers said, "is Jack Sumner."

Sumner was Byers's son-in-law and a longtime acquaintance of Jubil's.

"But he's not here in Denver—he's at the Hot Sulphur Springs trading post," Byers said. "Other than that, I know some good outdoorsmen around here, but they're not really scouts. I know a few that are not around here, if you have the time to wait for someone."

"I don't," Jubil said. "I know a few myself, but I didn't have time to make arrangements. I'm glad Jack will be at the trading post." Who he really wished for was White Dog. With him along, Jubil would have slept soundly at night. He would have to do his own scouting until they reached Hot Sulphur Springs. After that, he hoped Jack would be willing to accompany them for the rest of the tour.

Jubil, Nelly, and Eli waited in the private dining room for their clients to arrive for supper. Jubil was pleased with the setup. The wood paneled room held a table set with fine china, silver tableware, and linen napkins. A headwaiter was assigned to conduct the service, and two waiters stood ready to serve champagne to the clients as they arrived, courtesy of Mr. Ritchie, who was minding the door. Jubil and Eli wore their Sunday best, but he doubted anyone would notice how they were dressed—all eyes would be on Nelly. She looked stunning in her handsome tan suit decorated with hand-tooled brown leather lapels, cuffs, and belt. It had a Western feel accented by her brown Western-style boots. Ike had designed the outfit to sell exclusively at Warner and Walker Outfitters. Jubil wished he had a photograph of Nelly to send to Ike—Jubil was sure he would feel proud seeing his work in action.

Jubil straightened his lapels as the first of their clients arrived—the Smiths from Chicago.

"Ready?" he said to Nelly.

"Yes," she said with a smile. "It's exciting!"

He looked to Eli, who held up his glass of champagne, toasting Jubil.

Together, they greeted their clients.

"Mr. Smith," Jubil said, offering a handshake. "It's good to see you. You've met my wife, Nelly. This is her brother, my partner, Eli Boswell. Eli, Mr. Smith is one of our premier suppliers. He sourced everything we needed for the Custer expedition."

"How do you do?" Smith said to Nelly and Eli. "I'd like you to meet my wife, Gala."

She was near Mr. Smith's age, somewhere in her forties, and a bit on the portly side. Jubil hoped she would be able to keep up with the rigors of the tour.

His impulse was to tell Smith about the incident in Bismarck with Custer's supplies, but then he realized that it would be unsettling for the Smiths to hear that Jubil was being pursued by parties unknown.

As they stood chatting, more clients arrived. Mr. Norris was a loan officer at the Council Bluffs Savings Bank, Abe's local bank. Jubil had met him, but he did not know him well. Mr. Norris was accompanied by his son, Darrell, who, at fifteen years of age stood even with Jubil's six-foot stature and was taller than his father. Jubil was impressed with Darrell. He was well-mannered and seemed easygoing, but he was very shy when introduced to Nelly.

The next guests to arrive were Mr. White, an attorney from Springfield, and his son, Francis. Mr. White was in his mid-thirties, tall and thin. Francis was about the same age as Mr. Norris's son, but their manner couldn't have been more different. As Jubil made introductions, Francis hardly spoke a word to anyone. Mr. White's manner toward his fellow travelers was formal and stilted, which Jubil found off-putting.

The last to arrive were Nick and Mark Laur, twin brothers from Chicago. Like Ike and Eli, they looked similar but were easy to tell apart. Mark had a beard while Nick did not. They went straight for the champagne before greeting anyone, and they both had obviously had a few drinks before joining the group for supper. They were loud and overly familiar, slapping the men on the back or shoulder as they met and kissing the women on the hand like courtiers. Jubil did not like the way the clean-shaven Nick looked at Nelly. If they disturbed anyone, he would deal with them immediately.

Jubil found himself standing alone for a moment as the group mingled and enjoyed their champagne. Eli was engaged in conversation with Mr. Norris and his son Darrell, who looked like they were going to be pleasant company. Mr. Smith would be too. He seemed to be getting along with the gregarious Laur brothers, so that was good. Nelly and Mrs. Smith were chatting, but Mrs. Smith appeared to be doing most of the talking. Mr. White spoke to the Laur brothers and to Mr. Norris, but he didn't seem fully engaged in either conversation. He eyed Nelly and Mrs. Smith with a frown of disapproval. Jubil hoped he was simply slow to warm up.

In fact, as Jubil sipped his champagne, he wasn't sure what to make of the group. After all these years of planning to lead adventure tours, these were the clients he had attracted for his first outing. They weren't exactly what he had expected, but he was at a loss to say exactly what he had expected—more rugged individuals, perhaps? These were just normal people. He hoped they were up to the challenges of living rough. He and Eli had done their best to plan for their comfort, but this was a wilderness trip.

He was especially concerned about the women. Mr. Smith's wife was the first woman he had booked on the tour, and he had thought long and hard about whether to do it. He was not only concerned about her physical stamina but also her tolerance for sanitary conditions—both toilet and bath—and her safety when tending to these needs. Such affairs were conducted alone, and, out there, being out of sight of everyone else could be dangerous. But this was equally true for the men. And Nelly would never tolerate tours for men only.

As though feeling his gaze, Nelly looked away from her

conversation and made eye contact with him. She excused herself and came to join him.

"A penny for your thoughts, Mr. Walker," she said.

"Just thinking about what I've gotten myself into," he said with a smile.

"They seem a pleasant enough group," she said, "and a diverse one."

"Yes," he said. "That they are."

"Should we allow the Laur brothers more champagne?" she said with a grin. "Or should we feed them?"

"Good idea," he said. "I'll see about getting supper underway."

After checking with the headwaiter, Jubil announced that supper was ready. He and Nelly took their places at either end of the table as the other members of the group milled about and chose their seats. Jubil remained standing until everyone was settled. As he turned to the headwaiter to nod that service could begin, the dining room door opened and Mr. Ritchie entered the room.

"Could I have a word with you, Mr. Walker?" Ritchie said.

"Excuse me for a moment folks," Jubil said, following Mr. Ritchie. "Go ahead with supper," Jubil said to the headwaiter. Nelly and Eli looked at him questioningly, but he held his hand up to keep them seated. He followed Mr. Ritchie to the door.

"I'm sorry to bother you," Ritchie said, "but there is a man outside who insists that he needs to speak to you, but he won't give his name. He says it's an important business matter."

Jubil felt a tingle rushing through his body and warming his face. He signaled Nelly and Eli to join him and told them what was happening.

"I'll be back in a few minutes," Jubil said. "Go on with supper."

In a corner of the lobby, a man wearing a brown three-piece suit and a bowler hat waited for him—the same man he had seen on the way to Bismarck and in Council Bluffs. Jubil's body tensed up, and he took a breath to calm himself.

"Thank you for your assistance, Mr. Ritchie," Jubil said. "No need to watch the door any longer."

Mr. Ritchie looked back and forth between Jubil and the man. "Yes sir, Mr. Walker," he said, and went on his way.

Jubil approached the man in the bowler hat. He was white, clean-shaven, late thirties or early forties, medium build, about Jubil's height—average in every way. That appearance probably served him well in his line of work.

"I'm Jubilee Walker," he said. "You wanted to see me?" Jubil had almost called the man McTavish, but showing that he knew him as Lucius Black's henchman would surely implicate Flynn.

"Yes," the man said. His voice was deep and soft. "I have some information for you—important information. My name is Mr. McTavish. I'm the security chief for Mr. Lucius Black. I believe you have made his acquaintance."

"I don't suppose you'd know anything," Jubil said, looking McTavish steadily in the eye, "about some misfortune I've had lately? Like the attempted theft of two wagonloads of gear in Bismarck? Or the vandalizing of my store in Council Bluffs?"

"I don't know anything about those matters," McTavish said, barely hiding a smile of pleasure.

"Say your piece," Jubil said flatly, somehow resisting the urge to throttle this man who was obviously enjoying taunting him.

"It has come to Mr. Black's attention that you've been trying to get the government to sanction your profiting from Yellowstone, while you try to run him out of business with the Crow Agency. He wants you to stop all your efforts in those regards. You are to stay out of Bozeman, Yellowstone, and the Crow Agency."

Flynn might have been right—maybe the whole Bureau of Indian Affairs was complicit in the corruption. Black's information could only have come from Delano—or someone near to him. Now it all made sense. If Black could run him out of business, his problems with Jubil would be solved without resorting to his younger brother's tactics—trying to shoot him.

"Lucius Black will not keep me out of Yellowstone," Jubil said, resisting the urge to clench his fists. "As for the Crow Agency, what he is doing there is not only immoral, it's illegal. It isn't my job to bring him to justice, it's the law's. I'm just encouraging them to do their job."

"You heard his message," McTavish said. "Don't meddle."

"If he just follows the law with the Crow," Jubil said, "we'll have no quarrel. Yellowstone is big enough for both of us."

"I'm not sure that's true," McTavish said.

"You tell him he'd best remember what happened when his brother pushed me too far."

McTavish seemed to be fighting back a grin. "Good luck with your tour," he said with a tip of his hat. "It would be a shame for something bad to happen out there in the wilderness and word to spread that being in your company is dangerous."

"I'll know who to hold accountable if it does," Jubil said. "And I'll come for you."

McTavish turned and walked across the lobby and out of the hotel. Jubil's whole body trembled with rage as he watched him leave. He would not cancel the tour and disappoint all the people waiting for him in the dining room. If word got out that he had cancelled—and Black would make sure it did—his hopes of leading adventure tours would be dashed.

His thoughts returned to his clients, who were most likely curious about what was keeping him. He took a few deep breaths to calm himself before walking back into the dining room. All eyes moved to him as he took his place again at the head of the table.

"My apologies, folks," Jubil said. "Some last-minute arrangements for our tour required my attention."

His clients looked to be enjoying their supper and seemed

unconcerned by his absence, but Nelly and Eli were obviously alarmed. He smiled at them reassuringly.

The rest of the evening came off without a hitch. Over dessert, the conversation grew lively, aided by the additional champagne Jubil arranged for. As the guests rose in twos to return to their rooms, Jubil said good night to each of them. When the last one had left the private room, he closed the door and turned to Nelly and Eli.

"It was McTavish," he told them. "Bowler hat and all—he's Lucius Black's security man." He related the essence of their conversation.

"There must be something we can do," Nelly said, fuming with anger.

"Before we leave," Jubil said, "I'll send a telegram to the sheriff in Council Bluffs and in Bismarck telling them who instigated the assaults, but I doubt it's enough evidence for them to arrest him. I'm going to have to give some thought to what else we can do. The main thing is to be very cautious."

"Do you think he'll disturb our tour?" Nelly said.

"He might as well have said so," Jubil said. "I don't think he'll do anything violent, but some sort of harassment is likely. Eli, you and I will work out a system to keep watch around the clock."

Eli nodded.

"Would you spend the night in the livery stable," Jubil said to Eli, "guarding our supplies? I'd do it myself, but I don't want to leave Nelly alone."

Eli frowned and glanced at his sister. "Of course," he said.

CHAPTER 9

Jubil sat in a reading chair in the hotel room, waiting for Nelly to emerge from the dressing room. The night had passed without further incident, and he had managed to get some sleep. Even though he knew what Nelly planned to wear on the tour, he had not yet seen it.

Now, she stepped out from behind the dressing room curtain in her new riding outfit. "What do you think?" she said.

Men's clothes did not hide her beauty—in fact, in his opinion, the outfit accentuated it. She wore a man's tan cotton shirt tucked into the waistband of a pair of straight-legged brown cotton pants that were cinched at the waist with a brown leather belt and rolled to cuffs over her Western boots. Around her neck she wore a bright red bandana, slightly askew—an affect inspired by Custer. Her hair was braided and coiled into a crown that would allow her wide-brimmed Stetson hat to fit securely on her head.

"I am stunned," he said, sincerely.

"In a good way?"

"Yes, definitely. Turn around."

She did a slow pirouette.

"Hmm," he said with a grin. "You're going to attract attention—coming *and* going."

"Jubil!"

He shrugged. She frowned.

"People can think what they will," she said, sniffing. "I intend to be comfortable. And I am."

"That's that, then," Jubil said. "You ready to have some breakfast?"

As they made their way down the corridor and through the lobby to the hotel dining room, Jubil's prediction came true. Every person they passed took note of Nelly, as though she were some exotic creature that had wandered into their midst. He had expected it, but he still found it alarming when most of them turned to continue watching her as she passed. To her credit, and his pride, she carried herself as though she had no idea that people were looking at her.

In the dining room, just as in the lobby, every eye turned to Nelly. Eli frowned as he watched them approach the table. Jubil's clients were scattered throughout the room, and Jubil and Nelly nodded to them politely as they passed and took their seats.

"You make quite a show," Eli said to Nelly, with a hint of scorn in his voice.

"I'm not doing it for show," she snapped back.

Jubil held his hands up. "Don't start, you two." Turning to Eli, he said, "Is everything ready? Did you run into any trouble?"

"Yes, things are ready. No trouble," Eli said. "I've got the wagon outside to transport everybody to the livery, and the mules are packed. We just have to saddle up and go."

"Excellent," Jubil said. "Thanks for doing that on your own. I'll lend a hand from here on."

Eli nodded. Jubil knew he was asking a lot of Eli and was pleased with his attitude.

After the waiter took their order, Jubil sat scanning the dining room.

"I see everybody but Mr. White and his son," he said.

"I haven't seen them," Eli said, "but I got here just before you did."

"I'll ask the others if they've seen them," Jubil said.

"I'll come with you," Nelly said, giving Jubil a knowing look. He thought it was a good idea for her to show confidence—the best defense was often a good offense.

Seated nearest to them were the Smiths. As they approached, Mr. Smith rose from his chair.

"Good morning, folks," Jubil said. "Sorry to interrupt your breakfast."

"No interruption at all," Smith said. "Quite a bold style you have, Mrs. Walker. I approve. Very practical." Jubil had already known he liked Smith, but his reaction to Nelly's clothing clinched it.

"I would never have the nerve," Mrs. Smith said with a wave. "Besides, can you picture me in a pair of trousers like that?" she added with a conspiratorial grin.

Jubil smiled. He had to admit, the effect would not be the same. He was surprised but pleased that the Smiths were so lighthearted. As he looked around the room, he saw plenty of disapproving looks and whispered opinions being shared.

"Thank you, both," Nelly said.

"Have you seen the Whites?" Jubil asked Smith.

Smith looked at his wife. She shook her head. "No, can't say that we have."

"Maybe they came down earlier," Jubil said. "We'll be ready to leave soon."

They approached Mr. Norris, who seemed to take no notice of Nelly's attire. Jubil assumed that was his way of being gentlemanly. His son had been shy around Nelly last night, and he was too embarrassed to even look at her this morning. They had not seen the Whites.

The Laur brothers were over the top with their praise of Nelly's practical fashion sense and her boldness in the face of social norms. Their comments about the beauty she brought to such common attire bordered on lecherous, and they stopped speaking abruptly when Jubil frowned and stepped in front of Nelly. They had not seen the Whites either.

As Jubil and Nelly returned to their table, Mr. White entered the dining room.

"I'd like to have a word with you, Mr. Walker," White said, studying Nelly with an obvious air of disapproval.

"Please join us," Jubil said.

"It won't take long," White said curtly. "My son and I have decided not to travel with you. I was unaware that there would be women in our company. I find that highly inappropriate." He glanced at Nelly. "Your 'adventure' will be more a circus, apparently, and we do not care to play a part in it."

The comment angered Jubil considerably, but he held his temper. He could sense Nelly stewing silently beside him. Jubil was surprised when she did not speak her mind, but he was relieved that she did not.

"I'm sorry to hear that," he said evenly. "I'll have a refund wired to your bank."

"Very well," White said haughtily and left the room.

Jubil and Nelly sat down at the table with Eli, who had overheard the exchange.

"Huh, that's a hell of a note. I'll cancel their horses," Eli said, thinking aloud of the impact. "And we're going to have a surplus of supplies. I suppose that won't hurt anything though."

Jubil nodded, but his mind was on the bigger picture. "This is going to take a bite out of our profits," he said. "Well, there's nothing to be done for it now. Let's move on and make the best of it."

The first day's ride would take the group west out of Denver, high up into the foothills to make camp for the night. Tomorrow they would cross Berthoud Pass, then descend to a lower elevation to make camp again.

Eli had done a good job picking out the livestock for the tour—ten horses, one for each person plus an extra, in case one pulled up lame, and two pack mules. Jubil's mount was a black stallion that he decided to call Diablo, in memory of the black mare he had ridden during his first expedition with Powell. Nelly's horse was a spirited bay with a black mane and black markings. After letting him run to burn off excess energy, for both horse and rider, she named him Mercury. She was thrilled with her decision to ride astride, and claimed it was worth every bit of scrutiny she faced. Eli had chosen a gray stallion that looked similar to Rocky, their carriage horse at home. He named him Buddy, in memory of a horse that had given its life in Eli's service when he rode with Jubil during the 1872 Northern Pacific Railroad survey. Jubil cautioned both Nelly and Eli not to get too attached to their horses. Shipping them home and expanding the stable would be too expensive. He said this to remind himself, as much as to instruct them.

He was relieved to discover that all of their clients were decent riders. On his first expedition with Powell, he had grown weary of chasing down runaway horses that had shed their inexperienced riders.

He chastised himself for having some concern for Mrs. Smith due to her size. She had stepped up into the sidesaddle with ease, and she kept pace with the group without any concession. He thought perhaps her size gave her an advantage with a sidesaddle. She had more padding. Riding sidesaddle did not allow a rider much flexibility in shifting or distributing their weight. When riding astride, you could take a load off by standing in the stirrups. It was a joy to watch Nelly stand in the stirrups and let Mercury run. It reminded him of racing their horses when they were children together in Bloomington.

He had been keeping an eye out for anyone following them,

without being too obvious about it, but the timber was usually too heavy for a clear view. Occasionally they would reach an open expanse, and he would take out his field glasses to scan the area.

Late in the afternoon, he spotted a grassy clearing near a stream. He held up his hand to stop the procession and rode back to address the group.

"The clearing up ahead is a good spot to camp for the night," he said.

Once they reached the clearing, Eli unpacked the mules, and Nelly helped organize the items as they were unpacked—tents, mess kit, and staples. In the meantime, Jubil led the travelers to the nearby stand of timber and fixed a rope between two trees to tether the horses. Then he helped the riders dismount and hitched the horses to the line with lead ropes that allowed them some freedom to graze. Once they were hitched, he helped unsaddle them.

Then Jubil helped the campers set up their tents, while Eli gathered firewood. Nelly built a fire, then she and Eli made preparations for a simple supper of ham, beans, and cornbread. They had brought along two cured hams, but those would only keep for a few days. After that, their staples would be enhanced by whatever game and fish they could procure.

Jubil hoped that as the tour progressed, he would be able to enjoy it more. Most of his time so far had been spent worrying about Black, both in the present and the future, and thinking about keeping his clients safe and fed. By the time dusk fell, he finally felt relaxed. He and Eli arranged some downed logs around the fire to act as crude benches.

"Anything I can do to help with supper?" he asked Nelly.

"No," she said, brushing back a wisp of hair that had escaped its braid. He wondered what her Vassar College and New York friends would think if they could see her now. He thought she was more beautiful than ever. "It's ready. You can gather people up."

The company seemed in good spirits as they passed through the chow line.

"My compliments on the cornbread, my dear," said Mrs. Smith graciously. "It's not that easy to do over an open fire. You're an excellent camp cook."

"Thank you," Nelly said. "I hope you're still of that opinion on the way home. Actually, my brother taught me what I know about camp cooking."

Eli looked at her with surprise, unaccustomed to hearing compliments from her.

"She's a quick study," Eli said lightheartedly. "Vassar girl, you know?"

Nelly smiled at her brother. Jubil was pleased to see them making an effort to get along.

He had just stood up to fetch himself more ham and beans when a piercing scream rang out from the dark beyond the campfire, in the direction of the trees. The horses perked up and began to mill about, nickering and stamping.

"Oh, my Lord!" Mrs. Smith said, wide-eyed. "What on earth was that? Was that a person?"

Everyone was looking into the dark with concern.

"No, ma'am," Jubil said, handing his empty plate to Nelly. "That's a mountain lion. Some people call them California lions, some call them panthers. It's a big cat." He picked up his rifle. "He won't come near the fire." He turned and said to Eli, "I'm going to keep an eye on the horses. Come over when you finish supper."

"I'm finished," Eli said.

Nelly took his plate.

Eli picked up his rifle and followed Jubil to where the horses were tethered. Jubil found Diablo alert but calm, as was Eli's horse, Buddy. Nelly's Mercury was tugging at his lead and prancing—not wild-eyed and out of control yet, but close. This concerned Jubil, because wildlife could take a rider by surprise easily out here. If the horse was inclined to panic, that was not good. He would have to warn Nelly. The other horses were nervous but did not look ready to bolt. He would remind everyone to stay focused in the saddle.

"I'll take the first shift on the watch," Eli said.

"All right," Jubil said. "I'll help Nelly clean up, and then get some sleep. I'll relieve you at two o'clock."

"Do you think Black will try to pull any mischief on us tonight?" Eli said.

"I don't know," Jubil said, "but I'll be surprised if he doesn't do something before we cross the pass. Surely, he won't stalk us all over Colorado."

"Right," Eli said, sounding unconvinced. "What should I do if I see someone? Shoot, or come fetch you?"

"That's good, Eli," Jubil said, "to be thinking ahead like that." He reached out and gave him a pat on the shoulder. "Come fetch me, if you think you have time. Otherwise, do whatever you have to."

Eli nodded. Jubil knew he had to set a tone of caution but still give everyone a sense they would be fine. Not all of them were fully dependent on him for safety. Smith was carrying a rifle and wearing a sidearm. Mr. Norris also had a rifle, but his son was unarmed, as were the Laur brothers.

"Tomorrow we'll rise above the tree line and reach open ground," Jubil said. "As we cross the pass, we'll have a clear view behind us for miles. If we don't see anyone following us, then I think we'll be in the clear."

"That makes sense," Eli said. "I hope you're right."

The lion had not screamed again, and Jubil and Eli's presence and conversation had calmed the animals. Most of them had returned to grazing, though Mercury was still a little nervous.

"I'm going to go back to camp," Jubil said. "Stay awake!"

Eli grinned.

As Jubil approached the campfire, the group quieted and looked to him for a report. He assured them they were safe but reminded them to be prepared for anything.

"If we come across any wildlife or other travelers," Jubil said, "don't confront them. Come to me or Eli and then be prepared to help if called on."

The Laur brothers exchanged a worried look, but the Smith and Norris families took the advice calmly.

"May I ask you something, Mr. Walker?" Mr. Norris's son Darrell said. "That buckskin pouch you're wearing. What's it for? It looks like an Indian token."

"It is," Jubil said with a grin. He sat down among his clients and told the story of how he had come to own White Dog's medicine bag, and described the power that it held.

"You have magic charms to keep you safe?" Darrell said, looking at him in awe. "I hope it rubs off on me."

Jubil recalled how Ike and Eli had been in awe of his adventures when they were Darrell's age. "It's mighty powerful," he said. "But keep in mind we're in the wilderness, where anything can happen," he said, maintaining his light tone.

Darrell nodded excitedly. The others listened soberly.

The cleanup after supper was an easy chore. All hands pitched in to wash up rather than leaving it to Jubil and Nelly, which he appreciated. He and Nelly stayed up until everyone else had retired, then he stoked the fire, and they went to bed.

When the position of the moon told him it was about two o'clock, he went to relieve Eli, and then spent the rest of the night ruminating on what to do about Lucius Black. Dawn came without incident, and Jubil was anxious to move on.

The morning was warm and clear as the group packed up and mounted their horses. As they rode up the mountainside, the vegetation became short and brushy, until they were finally in the open ground above the tree line. They traveled for an hour with a clear view behind them, and Jubil allowed himself to hope that by some stroke of luck they were not being followed.

By noon they reached the top of the pass, where they

stopped for lunch. There, on the ridge of the Continental Divide, his clients got the most expansive view of the world they had ever seen. Jubil could not help but enjoy the exhilaration he usually experienced on his adventures. In these moments, he had a deep appreciation for life and the mystery of what had created the wonder around him, and he took great pride in living his life boldly. And now, as he watched Nelly regard the panorama, awestruck, his own sense of satisfaction doubled.

He was also happy to facilitate such an experience for his clients, but their safety was a burden he was unaccustomed to. On most of his adventures, he had not been responsible for anyone's life but his own. He had served as a guide for Captain Barlow during the 1871 Yellowstone survey and felt some responsibility for keeping him and his men safe, but they were all accustomed to looking out for themselves. Eli had ridden with him on the 1872 Northern Pacific Railroad survey, but Jubil had relinquished most of his oversight at Eli's insistence—which had not turned out well for Eli. On this tour, he felt the burden of protecting everyone—not only from natural dangers but from whatever mischief Lucius Black had in store for them.

After a lunch of ham sandwiches and dried apples, they prepared to move out again. Before Jubil mounted up, he took out his field glasses for one last look behind them. As he scanned the mountainside, three shapes emerged from the trees into the open ground above tree line. They were too far away to make out any details.

Jubil waved Eli over. Nelly joined them.

"It's probably nothing," Jubil said, "but three riders are heading this way."

Eli and Nelly looked at him with the same expression of concern.

"What do you want to do?" Eli said.

"I'm going to stay here for a while," Jubil said. "I'm not sure what good it'll do, but I want to get a closer look at them. You go ahead and set up camp in the spot where we stayed last year on the honeymoon trip. I'll be there before dark."

"What should we tell the others?" Nelly said. "Won't they be worried?"

"I'll tell them I'm going to stay here, and see if I can get us a goat for supper."

"You won't try to take on those men by yourself, will you?" she said.

"No. They won't even see me."

"Good," she said.

Jubil explained his plan to the group, and as they mounted up to cross the pass, Mr. Smith approached him.

"Is everything all right?" Smith asked. "My wife will be fine with your wife and Mr. Boswell, if I can help."

"Everything's fine," Jubil said, "but I appreciate your offer. You can be sure I'll call on you if I need you." Jubil was grateful to have a guest along who might be helpful in a crisis. Smith was obviously at home outdoors.

Eli set off, leading the pack mules, and the travelers fell in behind him. Nelly waved and blew Jubil a kiss, then turned Mercury to join the procession. Jubil led Diablo over to a little stream to drink and graze on whatever he could find nearby, and then he found a spot for a lookout: a flat rock that gave him a clear view of the trail as it came up the pass. He sat on the rock, elbows on his knees, gazing through his field glasses at the approaching riders. It would take them at least two hours to reach him, so he lay down on the rock for a nap. When he awoke, the position of the sun told him that he had slept about an hour. He sat up and scanned the trail again. The riders were now clearly visible. They were an odd lot. Two of them were dressed like mountain men, or wolfers, with fur hats and coats and rawhide leggings. The other wore a vest and a bowler hat.

CHAPTER 10

By the time Jubil caught up with the tour group, it was midafternoon, and Eli and Nelly were off to a good start making camp. The site was similar to the one where they had stopped the previous night—a nearby stream, an open grassy area for tents, a stand of timber for animals and firewood. As Jubil rode into the clearing, Mr. Smith noticed him and picked up his rifle and cradled it in the crook of his arm. Jubil raised his hand in greeting, and Smith recognized him and lowered his gun. Jubil was grateful for Smith's company.

Jubil dismounted and joined Eli and Nelly where they were working. Most of the other travelers were nearby.

"Where are the Laur brothers?" Jubil said.

"They went off on a hike," Eli said. "I told them to stay in sight of the stream so they don't get lost."

"Good," Jubil said. Twice on his adventures, people had wandered off and gotten lost, and it was an unpleasant experience for everyone involved.

Nelly was adding wood to the campfire. She wiped her brow with the back of her glove, then came to join their conversation.

"Did you see anything?" Eli asked Jubil.

"McTavish," he said, "and two wolfers."

"What's a wolfer?" Nelly said.

"Ask your brother," he said.

Eli frowned. "They're hunters who follow cattle drives and protect the herd by killing wolves for their pelts," he said. What he didn't say was that he had been assaulted and robbed by one on the 1872 Northern Pacific Railroad survey. "You think they'll try something?" he asked Jubil.

"I don't think they're here to take in the scenery," Jubil said. "If Black holds true to form, it'll be mischief of some sort. He's trying to ruin my business and scare me off. I think it will be something to frighten or inconvenience us, or both."

"What should we do?" Nelly said.

"Be prepared for anything," Jubil said. "But I don't think there is any need to upset folks by telling them our concerns. Agreed?" He didn't normally like withholding information, but he did not see how that would help matters here.

Nelly and Eli both nodded.

Jubil tethered Diablo with the other stock, then helped finish setting up camp. He visited with each of his clients, who, thankfully, seemed enchanted by their experience so far.

Late in the afternoon, two riders entered the clearing. It was the wolfers. McTavish was not with them.

Jubil asked Smith and Norris to guard the others, then he and Eli walked to the edge of camp with their rifles pointed to the ground. Smith stood with his rifle also pointed to the ground, his wife and Nelly nearby. Norris stood a few yards behind Smith holding his rifle by the barrel, with the stock resting on the ground. Behind Norris stood his son. The Laur brothers had not yet returned to camp. As the wolfers ambled across the clearing, Jubil scanned the perimeter for some sign of McTavish, but he didn't see him. When the wolfers were about fifty feet away, Jubil took a step forward and raised his right hand, with his rifle cradled in the crook of his left arm.

"Just hold up right there, gents," Jubil said, "and state your business. What brings you to our camp?"

The riders stopped and studied Jubil. It was hard to judge

their ages through all the fur and hair, but they weren't notice-ably young or old. They looked seasoned and hard. It was unlikely that Jubil or any of his group could overpower these men hand to hand. If trouble started, he would have no choice but to shoot.

"Just being neighborly, mister," one of the wolfers said. He wore a wolf's head cap with the pelt draped over his shoulders like a cape. He leaned over and spat on the ground. "We was just passing down the trail and seen your camp. Thought we'd say howdy, that's all."

"Well . . . howdy," Jubil said. "I'll ask you to move along now. We're not entertaining guests."

"Well, that ain't very neighborly of you," the wolfer said. He lifted his arm and pointed behind Jubil. "Looks like you got some more visitors coming in. Unless that's more of your own."

Jubil motioned toward Eli with his head, keeping his eye on the riders. Eli turned and looked.

"It's the Laur brothers," Eli said.

"Deal with them," Jubil said. "Then come back."

"We'd be mighty grateful for a decent supper," the wolfer said to Jubil.

"Sorry," Jubil said, "we only have rations for our current number."

"Huh," the wolfer said, turning to his partner. "Don't that beat all. Downright inhospitable." He turned back to Jubil. "We'd be glad to go fetch up a deer or some such to add to the pot."

"No, thanks," Jubil said. "We don't want company. I'm lead-ing this group of folks through Colorado to take in the scenery. I don't want strangers at their table and outside their tents. Now, please—move along." Jubil shifted his right hand to rest over the trigger of his rifle.

Eli returned and stood next to Jubil. The wolfer's eyes ticked back and forth between them.

"Fine," the wolfer said, turning his horse. "We sure wouldn't want to make you gentlefolk uncomfortable."

"Where's McTavish?" Jubil said.

The wolfers exchanged a glance.

"Who's McTavish?" the wolfer said.

"The man with the bowler hat. I watched the three of you ride up the pass," Jubil said, smiling humorlessly. "You should give him back whatever money he paid you to harass us and ride out of here before somebody gets hurt."

"We ain't harassing nobody, mister," the wolfer said. "And I don't know no McTavish."

Jubil shrugged. "Have it your way," he said. "Now, move along."

The wolfer stared coldly at Jubil, then he and his companion rode away.

Jubil watched them until they left the clearing and entered the forest. It wasn't until then that he noticed Nelly was standing beside him.

"Do you think they'll stay away?" Nelly said.

"Seems unlikely, doesn't it?" he said.

"Yes," she said, "unfortunately."

"Do you think they'll come back tonight?" Eli asked, which was what Jubil was thinking.

Jubil nodded.

"For the horses and mules?"

"Yes," Jubil said. "What better way to put an end to our tour?"

"Want me to follow them? Stop them before they can start anything?" Eli said.

"No," Jubil said, patting Eli on the shoulder, "but it's a brave offer. Let's get some supper going and make an early night of it. We'll get up early and move toward Hot Sulphur Springs trading post. Jack Sumner will be there, and I'm hoping he can lend us a hand with security."

"But what'll we do tonight?" Nelly said.

"I'll come up with something," Jubil said confidently, even if he wasn't feeling entirely confident. "Let's get some food in everyone and try to calm their nerves."

Jubil told the rest of the group about the plan to move on early the next morning. He got no objections, but the wolfers' visit had cast a shadow over their lighthearted mood. As he helped Nelly and Eli prepare supper, Darrell Norris approached him.

"Too bad you didn't get a goat," the young man said. "I've never eaten mountain goat."

Jubil looked at him with puzzlement, then remembered his excuse for staying behind earlier at the pass.

"They're elusive," Jubil said with a smile. "Maybe we'll get one later." Jubil wanted to give this young man a taste of adventure, and he felt his ire rise anew at Black for interfering with his clients' enjoyment of the tour.

Eli diced potatoes into a pot for boiling and then made biscuits while Nelly fried up slices of ham. By the time supper was over and the cleanup complete, night had fallen. Jubil assured the travelers as they rose to go to their tents that he and Eli would guard the camp overnight as they had the night before. Smith volunteered to help, but Jubil told him he'd feel better if Smith stayed with his wife and the others. After everyone had retired but Eli and Nelly, Jubil sat with them and stoked the campfire.

"I have an idea," he said, "but I'm going to need help from both of you." He explained his plan. "Do you think you can do it?"

Eli grinned and nodded, but Nelly looked worried.

"I'll do my best," she said, her hands tightly clasped.

First, they reconfigured the tethering system they were using to hitch the horses.

"We don't want the wolfers to be able to just cut the tether line and lead the whole string of stock away," Jubil said. "We'll take down the long line and tether them individually instead. It will take the wolfers longer to free them. We'll take the stakes from the extra tent that was meant for the Whites, drive them into the ground, then tie the lead ropes to the stakes. I don't want to hobble the horses though. One of them might get hurt in the panic we're going to create."

The group went to work and completed the task in short order.

"Now we need to create some shelter to hide behind. We want a good view of the horses, but we don't want to be too close," Jubil said. "That stand of brush over there is a good start. Let's fill in the gaps with more brush, but leave spots to peek through."

Soon Jubil was testing their work.

"I'll walk through the area where the horses are tethered," Jubil said. "You two make sure you can see me clearly from behind the brush, and I'll make sure I can't see you."

Afterward, Eli said, "I could see your silhouette, but I couldn't make out your features."

"Good enough," Jubil said. "Now we wait."

By the position of the moon, Jubil figured it was around midnight when they heard the faint snap of a branch and the rustling sound of footsteps. They exchanged glances in silent anticipation. Jubil had positioned their cover on the far side of the horses, facing toward camp. The fire was still blazing brightly, and a dim glow reached to where the horses were tethered. From this vantage point, they would clearly see the silhouette of anyone tampering with the stock.

Another rustling sound, this time closer—behind them. This was not good. Had the wolfers chosen a path to the horses that was going to take them right to where Jubil and the others were hiding? Jubil put his finger to his lips and then pointed in the direction of the sound. It came again—this time Eli and Nelly both nodded. The steps were coming closer. Jubil lay down flat on the ground and signaled Eli and Nelly to do the same.

Then he saw the wolfers—stalking toward the horses on a trajectory that would take them perilously near their hiding place. Jubil could not risk moving now, so all he could do was lie prone and keep his rifle ready.

The wolfers passed within a few feet of their hiding place without noticing them—focused on the horses and the camp beyond. Once they had reached the horses, the wolfer in front signaled his partner to stop, then he stood looking around the area, probably expecting someone to be guarding the camp, but he did not spot them behind their brush cover. When the wolfer looked away, Jubil sat up and signaled Nelly and Eli.

The wolfer in the lead looked over the tethered stock, then drew a large knife and cut the tether on the first animal he came to—one of the mules. He held the mule's lead in one hand as he whispered orders to his companion, pointing animatedly with his knife.

"Ready?" Jubil whispered to Nelly and Eli.

They nodded.

"Remember," he whispered to Nelly with a grin, "you're a wildcat! Go!"

Nelly took a deep breath and let out a scream that made the hair on Jubil's arms stand on end. Eli looked at his sister with his mouth agape, eyes wide open—as if she had been possessed by the beast itself and sprouted a tail. Nelly let the pitch of her scream fall off and put in a guttural growl that gave her performance an astonishing authenticity. Jubil was amazed.

"Again," he whispered.

She did it again—even better this time. He smiled and shook his head in amazement. She looked pleased with herself.

He turned his attention to the wolfers. They were both crouched down, looking up into the trees and circling to keep from having their backs exposed.

"One more time," he said to Nelly. Once again, she filled the night with the scream of a mountain lion.

"Okay, Eli," he said, "shoot."

Eli raised his rifle and shot a round into the trees over the heads of the trappers. They looked frantically for the lion overhead, and into the darkness from which the shot had come. Eli fired again. The lead wolfer dropped the tether of the mule, and both of the wolfers ran into the woods.

Jubil stood, took careful aim, and fired. One of the wolfers stumbled as Jubil's shot hit a tree near him. "Don't come back!" Jubil shouted. "I won't miss next time!"

Eli stood and extended his hand to help Nelly up.

"That was unbelievable!" he said to her, wide-eyed.

"Thank you," she said and gave him a hug. "I even frightened myself."

The trio walked over to where the animals were tethered and calmed them. The mule the wolfer had freed and a horse the other one had cut loose had both bolted when the gunfire started. It was too dark, and too risky, to search for them now, but Jubil would set out after them at first light. They could make do without the horse but not the mule. They needed him to carry their gear.

He looked toward camp and saw Smith and Norris standing near the fire, rifles at the ready. Mrs. Smith, Darrell Norris, and the Laur brothers all stood in front of their tents.

"We'd better go settle everybody down," Jubil said. "We can't move on until I find that mule, so I hope they can still get some sleep. I'll stay on guard and ride out first thing in the morning. Eli, get some sleep now, if you can. You'll guard the camp while I'm gone in the morning. Nelly, you try to keep everyone's spirits up. Does that sound like a decent plan?"

Nelly and Eli agreed.

Jubil told his clients the wolfers had returned, probably with the intent of causing mischief because Jubil had refused to feed them. He apologized for the scare, but reminded them again that they were in the rowdy West and should be prepared for anything.

It did not take long for Jubil to find the stray mule in the morning. It had wandered downstream and found a grassy spot with a rocky overhang that provided protection from the weather, and the animal had seen no need to go any further. The horse was another matter. He followed a string of hoofprints along the stream, but the horse had waded into the water, and Jubil lost the trail. When he rode back into camp, however, he found the horse had returned on its own.

"I wasted half the morning looking for that nag," Jubil said as he handed the lead rope for the mule to Eli.

"Well, I'm glad you're back," Eli said. "We've got a situation here. The Laur brothers have decided they want to go back to Denver."

"Have they left?" Jubil said.

"Not yet," Eli said. "I told them I wouldn't stop them, but they'd be walking and taking none of our gear. I said if they want another verdict, they'll have to take it up with you."

"Good thinking. At least they didn't set out walking," Jubil said, shaking his head.

As he hitched Diablo, Nelly came to meet him.

"What's your take on the Laurs?" he said.

"They're afraid those men will come back and shoot us in our sleep," she said.

"If they wanted to do that," Jubil said, "they would've done it last night."

"That's what I told them," Nelly said.

"Let's go talk to them," Jubil said. "Come on, Eli. Stand with us."

As the trio approached the camp, the whole group gathered at the campfire.

"I'm sorry about the ruckus last night," Jubil said. "But like I said, I think those men intend only mischief. I was planning to stay here a few days, depending on the weather, but we'll move on today to the trading post at Hot Sulphur Springs. You'll enjoy meeting Jack Sumner, and the facilities at the trading post are perfectly secure."

"We've had enough of your adventure," Nick Laur said. "You should cancel this trip and lead us all back to Denver."

"Does anyone share Mr. Laur's opinion?" Jubil asked, just to be sure. He looked at the others for any sign of agreement but saw none.

"I think we're all a little concerned," Mr. Smith said, "that those ruffians might not be done with us. But Mr. Walker has handled them adeptly so far, and I trust him to continue to do so. I'll do what I can to help him. My wife and I agree—we're out here, so we might as well make the best of it."

"My son and I agree with the Smiths," Mr. Norris said.

"Thank you for your confidence," Jubil said. "I'll do all I can to live up to it."

"We don't share their confidence," Nick Laur said. "My brother and I want to leave."

"That presents some logistical challenges, gentlemen," Jubil said. "I won't make you walk, but I will hold you accountable for returning your horses to the livery in Denver. And I'm not leaving everyone else here for days while I take you back to Denver. The trail is obvious. If you can't stay on it . . . well, good luck."

"You can't just send us off into the wilderness alone and unprotected," Nick Laur said.

"I have no choice," Jubil said.

"We want a refund then," Mark Laur said, finally speaking up.

"I used the money you paid me," Jubil said, "to hire the horses you're riding and to buy the food you've been eating and the gear used to get you this far."

"We'll sue!" Mark said. "See what a lawsuit does for your already sketchy reputation."

The comment exhausted what was left of Jubil's patience. Refunding their money would mean he would be lucky to break even on this tour. Any hopes for profit to help keep the store afloat and to continue to be a viable vendor for the army were fading. In the event that the store failed, the option of falling back on his tour business was beginning to look unlikely. His goals of developing Yellowstone Park and ending the corruption at the Crow Agency now seemed even more difficult and maybe impossible. He felt like Black was winning his campaign to put him out of business. He was about to ask the Laur brothers what they had imagined when booking an adventure tour in the wilderness.

"I'll take them back," Eli said, with evident disgust. "But no refund!"

Jubil studied Eli and considered his offer.

"I'll catch up with you at Hot Sulphur Springs," Eli said confidently. "I'll be there in five days at the most."

"All right," Jubil said. "But if they do anything to slow you down, ditch them and ride back. I need you." He looked at Nelly to gauge her level of concern, but she was nodding and regarding her brother with pride. Jubil was very pleased with Eli for stepping up in this way. He was proving over the course of this trip that he could be trusted in any situation.

"Does this arrangement suit you?" Jubil said to the Laur brothers.

The brothers exchanged a glance. "I suppose it will have to do," Nick said.

"All right," Jubil said. "Let's get on with it."

Jubil helped Eli decide what he would need for the trip.

The tour had an overabundance of supplies now, so Jubil and Eli divided the food and gear. Jubil insisted Eli use the extra horse they had brought as a packhorse—and as insurance in case anything happened to Buddy.

As Eli and the Laur brothers rode off, Jubil and Nelly directed the others in packing up camp. It was about forty miles to Hot Sulphur Springs. Too far to travel in one day, especially with the late start they were getting. Jubil felt that if they could get through the night tonight, they would be fine. Surely McTavish and his crew wouldn't be foolish enough to harass them at the trading post. Jack Sumner would be an ally and a formidable aide in their defense, if it came to a fight.

Eli's bold and generous effort had saved Jubil from the trip being a total financial failure, but he was worried about Eli traveling back to Hot Sulphur Springs alone. And any more trouble could wipe out the trip's now razor-thin profit margin. Whether Jubil's reputation could survive remained to be seen.

CHAPTER 11

Jubil rode at the front of the procession on the way to Hot Sulphur Springs, leading the mules. He had asked Smith to ride at the rear to keep an eye on their flanks, which Smith did enthusiastically. They would make it at least halfway today—if all went well.

As Jubil rode, he pondered what to do about Lucius Black. His greatest concern was that he might be wrong that Black would not resort to violence. Perhaps Black's patience would run out as Jubil stymied his less aggressive efforts. But for the sake of the others, he had to project confidence that there was no danger, while preparing for the worst. He was unaccustomed to thinking one way and acting another, and he didn't much care for it.

They made camp late in the afternoon, a little beyond the halfway point, in an open meadow within the pine forest, with a stream nearby. Jubil set about securing the animals and unpacking while Nelly began work on a campfire. As Jubil helped the guests set up their tents, Nelly used the last of the ham to make a pot of ham and beans. The mood in their small group was surprisingly relaxed and congenial, and, over supper, conversation turned to what they might expect at the hot springs.

Jubil told them about the trading post and entertained them with tales of Jack Sumner. He warned them that Jack had a tendency to know everything, whether he actually did or not. He gave them their first real laugh of the tour with his story of encountering a narrow ridge on the way to Longs Peak and his description of Jack's method of crossing it by scooting across on his rump. Then, to be fair, he told of how Jack had proven his skill as a boatman the following year. Sumner had rescued Jubil and two others from a Colorado River sandbar in the Grand Canyon, after their boat had been crushed on the rocks by the rapids.

After the supper dishes were cleaned, just before sunset, Mr. Smith told Jubil he was going to accompany his wife into the woods, to make their toilet before retiring for the night. As Jubil watched them walk away, he was pleased that he did not need to remind Mr. Smith to carry his rifle.

Jubil and Darrell Norris went to collect more firewood, while Nelly and Mr. Norris stoked up the fire. They had been at their tasks for about ten minutes when a scream rang out from the direction the Smiths had gone, followed by a shot. Jubil dropped his armload of firewood and ran back into camp for his rifle, then ran to the edge of the woods. He stopped and looked for the Smiths but could not see them. Another shot sounded. He didn't want to run into the woods and be mistaken for a target.

"Smith!" he called out. "Smith!"

"Over here, Walker!"

Jubil ran in the direction of Smith's voice and saw him about fifty yards into the woods. He stood holding his rifle at the ready with his wife behind him, huddled against the trunk of a large pine tree. As Jubil neared, he could see Mrs. Smith was crying.

"Are you both all right?" Jubil said when he reached Smith. "What was it?"

"We're all right," Smith said. "Just shaken. It was a man— on foot in the woods. Gala was indisposed, and he stepped out from behind a tree a just a few yards away. She screamed, and I came to her aid. The man dashed off into the woods. I fired at him twice but missed."

"Get her back to camp," Jubil said. "I'll go make sure he's moved on."

"I'm afraid my wife has had an embarrassing accident," Smith said. "She was in an awkward situation when she was badly frightened. She needs some clean clothes."

"I'll get Nelly," Jubil said, embarrassed for poor Mrs. Smith. "She can help her."

"Thank you," Smith said.

Nelly quickly and discreetly found a change of clothes in Mrs. Smith's bag while Jubil explained in general terms to the Norrises what had happened. Then Jubil and Nelly returned to the woods. Nelly helped Mrs. Smith change while Jubil and Mr. Smith stood guard, then they all returned to camp, where Mr. and Mrs. Smith retired to their tent. While Jubil searched the area in the fading light, Nelly took Mrs. Smith's soiled clothing to the stream to wash it.

Jubil found no sign of anyone and did not want to search alone after dark, nor did he want to further upset Mrs. Smith by questioning her about the incident. It was likely that the man had been one of the wolfers. Jubil hid his surprise that the wolfers had not given up their goal of harassing him. Mr. Norris volunteered to help stand guard overnight, which Jubil appreciated, but he declined the offer. He did not expect to be able to sleep anyway.

In the morning, the mood was somber as they broke camp. They reached the trading post midafternoon, and found Jack Sumner at home, doing the same thing he had been doing the day Jubil first met him in 1868—ranting profanely at a group of Ute Indians camped nearby. As Jubil led the tour group toward the trading post, Sumner noticed them. He shouted at the Indians one more time, then walked away and stood watching the group ride in. In his mid-thirties, with a wiry build and a bushy mustache, Sumner was a rough-looking character in his well-worn buckskins and broad brimmed hat.

"Well, well," Sumner said, "if it ain't Jubilee Walker. Last time I talked to Byers, he said you might be coming my way. And there you are."

Jubil had never met Byers's daughter, Sumner's wife, who lived in Denver, but he had always been curious about her. He would have assumed the daughter of a successful newspaper publisher would be a more genteel sort than would take up with Jack Sumner, but who was he to judge? His own wife, a Vassar graduate, was out here in the wilderness with him, dressed in men's clothes, astride a spirited horse.

"Hello, Jack," Jubil said, pulling Diablo up near Sumner. The rest of the group rode up and gathered nearby. "I'm glad to find you at home. Nelly and I missed you last year on our honeymoon trip. Nelly, meet Jack Sumner," Jubil said. Nelly nodded to him.

"Howdy do, Mrs. Walker," Sumner said. "Pleased to make your acquaintance. I like your style, ma'am. You show good sartorial judgment—though I must say your taste in husbands is questionable. I suppose Walker's not a bad sort though, once you get used to him."

Nelly smiled broadly.

Jubil introduced the members of his tour.

"Want us to make camp in any particular spot?" Jubil said.

"Suit yourself," Sumner said. "I was just explaining to those Ute that they can't take up residence here all summer, but they'll be here a few more days. Some of their lot is out hunting, and they'll leave when they get back. They're harm-less—but I'd keep an eye on your possessions. Your animals will be fine though. They won't dare steal them. How long you figure on staying?"

"Under a week," Jubil said. "My partner, Nelly's brother, is riding here from Denver. We'll move on after he arrives. I was planning to take these folks up to Grand Lake for a few days. Maybe hike up and have a look at Longs Peak."

"Sounds like a dandy adventure," Sumner said. "But I had some visitors this morning who may alter your plans."

Jubil's jaw clenched, and his mood darkened. Nelly and the others looked uneasy.

"Three fellers rode up early," Sumner said. "Said they'd like to rest up here a spell, but they were concerned they might run into a feller they'd recently had a scuffle with. Some inhospitable and violent feller named Jubilee Walker had run them off in a hail of gunfire. Said if you'd be showing up here, they'd camp elsewhere."

Jubil steamed at this news.

"That's all true," Jubil said. "Did he mention it was them trying to steal our stock that prompted the gunfire?"

"He did not," Sumner said, "but I figured they were up to no good. I told them I'd known that rogue Jubilee Walker for some time now and would trust him well before I would the likes of them. From their reaction, I'd say they was unaware that we were acquainted. I told them their plan to move on was a sound idea."

"Thank you," Jubil said. It was a relief to be here with Sumner. He could be difficult to tolerate, but he was a good man to have around in a pinch.

"I could round up some of Tall Bull's Dog Soldiers," Sumner said, "and we'll get those boys off your tail for good. You'd need to stash that medicine bag you're wearing though. It'd raise suspicions amongst the Cheyenne as to how you came by it."

"Maybe rightly so," Jubil said. "White Dog gave it to me

after a skirmish with Dog Soldiers—maybe some of the same fellows."

"Hmm," Sumner said. "Well, you wouldn't want to bring that up."

"It would be unavoidable," Jubil said. "I'm not taking it off. I'm proud of it."

"Just tell them you took it off a Pawnee you killed in battle," Sumner said. "That'll make you a hero with them."

"I'm not going to lie about it, Jack," Jubil said. "Anyway, I don't think we'll be needing their help. But thanks for the offer."

He looked at Nelly to see her reaction. She frowned and shook her head. The rest of his group just stared at him, taking in this new information about their guide and the situation they were in.

"You could just rely on the Utes," Sumner said. "Have them scout. At least you wouldn't have to worry about them turning on you."

"That might be best," Jubil said. "If we need them at all."

"Suit yourself," Sumner said. "Make yourselves at home wherever you want. I'll join you for supper later."

Jubil's patience had just about run out with Lucius Black and his lackeys. He did his best to control his anger in front of his clients, but he wasn't going to allow McTavish and the wolfers to terrorize his clients any longer.

"We'll have no trouble while we're here at the trading post," Jubil said to his clients. "Our stock will be safe in the corral. We won't need to set a guard, so I hope you'll do your best to relax. We'll camp near the hot springs. Eli will be back in three or four days. Once he returns, we'll decide whether to go up to Grand Lake, or return to Denver. Mr. Sumner will help us with security."

"So," Smith said, "you are somehow acquainted with these men?"

"I'm acquainted with the man who hired them," Jubil said.

"What does he hope to accomplish by this?" Smith said.

Jubil gave the group a brief summary of his difficulties with Phineas Black. As he spoke, Mr. and Mrs. Smith's expressions grew concerned, while Mr. Norris and Darrell Norris stared at him blankly.

"I see," Smith said. "Well, you're in a tough spot. But you could have told us that."

"I'm sorry," Jubil said. "I was hoping to spare you further concern."

Jubil slept fitfully again that night. In the morning, he told Nelly the conclusion he had come to. "I can't keep looking over my shoulder," he said, "and let them continue to upset the folks we brought out here. I'm going to ride out and look for McTavish and his men."

"You're going alone?" Nelly said.

"Yes. If I go with reinforcements, McTavish will feel more threatened," he said. "I'll be armed, but I want to avoid violence, if possible. I'm just going to ask him to call the job done, and leave us alone. He's made his point and done enough damage."

Nelly silently studied Jubil before she replied. "I don't like the idea," she said, "but I won't presume to tell you what to do."

"I'll be all right," he said, taking Nelly's hands. "I'll ask Jack to stay here and keep an eye on everybody while I'm gone."

Nelly looked worried, but she nodded. Jubil hugged her and then went to find Sumner. He was inside the trading post, talking to two Ute men and looking over some hides laid out on a table.

"Morning, Walker," Sumner said. "These fellows just rode in from their hunt. They were telling me they'd come across some white men camped a few miles north of here on the Grand River. Sounds like it might be your stalkers."

"That's handy to know," Jubil said. "I came to tell you I'm going to ride out to look for them."

"Hang on a bit until I'm finished here," Sumner said, "and I'll ride with you."

"Thanks," Jubil said, "but I'd rather go alone. I'd feel better knowing you're here to keep an eye on everybody while I'm gone."

"All right," Sumner said. "If you're sure you don't want no help."

"I'll be fine," Jubil said. "Thanks. I'm going to try reasoning with them."

Sumner looked skeptical, but he shrugged and returned to his conversation with the hunters.

Jubil rode Diablo north along the Grand River with his rifle in the scabbard. He also wore his Colt revolver. His ability to see up river was blocked by stands of cottonwood and brushy bunches of chokecherry, so he rode slowly to avoid coming up on the campsite unexpectedly.

About a mile north of the trading post, Jubil spotted them on the opposite side of the river, about a hundred yards upriver of his position. As he continued north, they noticed him and went for their rifles. The two wolfers came to stand at the edge of the riverbank with their rifles pointed at Jubil, while McTavish remained seated on a stump near the campfire. Jubil rode up even with them and stopped, looking across the hundred-foot span of the river. He held Diablo's reins loosely and rested his hands on the pommel of his saddle.

"I'm not looking for trouble," Jubil said, speaking up to be heard across the river. "I just came to talk face-to-face."

McTavish got up and walked down to the edge of the river and stood between the two wolfers.

"Then talk," McTavish said.

"I'm tired of looking over my shoulder for you," Jubil said. "Your job is finished. You set out to ruin my tour business— well, you have. Go back and tell Black he's won."

"He'll be happy to hear that," McTavish said. "You'll abide

by his terms then?"

"I didn't say that," Jubil said. "What he's doing at the Crow Agency is illegal and immoral. And I remain opposed to that."

"He won't be happy to hear that," McTavish said.

"I'm tired of toying around here, McTavish," Jubil said, readying himself to draw his pistol if his instincts demanded it. "Here's what's going to happen: You and your boys are going to ride out of here today and be on your way back to Denver. If you're still here in the morning, you're going to face a band of Tall Bull's Dog Soldiers, and that will not end well for you."

McTavish studied Jubil as he considered his response.

"This isn't over, Walker," McTavish said.

"It can be," Jubil said. "All Black has to do is be honest with the Crow people. He can afford to do that—he's a rich man. He's got gold mines. He doesn't need to rob those poor folks. If he stops that, I won't be a thorn in his side any longer."

"Mr. Black does not share your pity for Indians," McTavish said. "And he's not going to bow to you—or anyone, for that matter."

"I can see we're done here," Jubil said. "I'm going turn my horse now and ride back to the trading post. I'd appreciate it if you wouldn't shoot me in the back. If you do, the Dog Soldiers will get even for me."

Jubil turned Diablo and started south. He let the horse walk slowly along the riverbank and forced himself to slouch calmly in the saddle as he awaited a gunshot. After a few minutes, he had rounded a bend in the river and felt safe. He did not look back.

He felt better having taken some action, even if he had made matters worse. He could no longer sit idly by and wait for Black's next move. On his return to Hot Sulphur Springs, he went straight to the trading post and found Sumner.

"I made a demand," Jubil said, "that I'll need your help backing up." He described the ultimatum he'd given McTavish.

"I can make that happen," Sumner said. "I'll send some of the Ute boys up to keep an eye on them and let us know if they move out. If they don't, I'll call in a favor from Tall Bull."

"Thanks, Jack," Jubil said. "I appreciate having you on my side."

Sumner waved him off, not having an ounce of sentimentality in him.

Jubil found Nelly sitting at a comfortable spot on a hillside, writing in her journal. He told her what he had done.

"That was very brave of you," she said, looking worried. "I hope they leave."

Jubil decided not to tell the others anything until he knew what McTavish intended to do. He sat with Nelly while she worked and thought about how to bring this whole situation with Lucius Black to a conclusion. It was almost noon when Sumner came to find him.

"The scouts say your boys have packed up and are heading east," Sumner said. "I told them to tail them back to the pass."

"I hope they don't run into Eli on his way back," Jubil said. Nelly looked at him with concern. "He'll be fine. He can take care of himself." Jubil hoped this was true.

That evening at supper, Jubil told the group that McTavish and his men had moved on. He had hoped for a show of relief and perhaps even enthusiasm for the rest of their time in the mountains. But his quiet supper companions only nodded somberly.

Over the next two days, while they waited for Eli to return and McTavish to get clear of the area, Jubil took the men out hunting and fishing, and they brought in some grouse and trout for supper. Darrell Norris seemed to be relaxing and enjoying the beautiful setting, but Mr. Smith and Mr. Norris, no matter how Jubil tried to draw them out, were quiet and cautious the whole time, especially while they were in the woods hunting. Jubil and Darrell were the only ones who took birds. The other men spent more time looking over their shoulders than they did looking for grouse.

Mrs. Smith seemed to be enjoying herself at the trading post. She bought a pair of fancy moccasins and talked with the Ute woman who had made them. The Ute woman spoke a little English, and she helped Mrs. Smith make a simple pair of moccasins herself. Mrs. Smith also graciously volunteered to help Jubil and Nelly prepare supper, which was much appreciated. Even though Eli said he didn't enjoy cooking all that much, he was better at it than either Jubil or Nelly.

The evening before Eli was expected to arrive, the group was gathered around the campfire for a dinner of grouse, fried potatoes, and biscuits, with fresh blackberries for dessert. Jubil offered some news he hoped would help lift everyone's spirits.

"The Ute scouts returned today," Jubil said. "McTavish and his men have cleared the pass. Eli should arrive tomorrow, and we'll be ready to set out north for Grand Lake for a few days—if you still want to."

Mrs. Smith looked at her husband. So did Mr. Norris and his son. Apparently, Mr. Smith had become the spokesman for the group.

"We know you've been in a tough spot," Smith said, "and we appreciate how you've handled matters. But we've discussed it, and we're ready to go back to Denver. We all signed up for an adventure, and we've certainly had one. But we've had enough. You don't need to refund our money. It's a shame it turned out like it did, but . . ."

"I understand, Mr. Smith," Jubil said, sparing Smith the need to explain further. "As soon as Eli gets here, we'll head back to Denver. I also intend to refund half your money. You've only gotten half the trip I promised, and even that didn't go as intended. We'll do our best to make the trip back safe and pleasant."

"No hard feelings, Mr. Walker," Mr. Norris said. "Darrell and I enjoyed ourselves."

"Thank you," Jubil said. "I understand."

"We'll say good night then," Smith said.

They all retired to their tents.

Jubil and Nelly sat silently staring at the fire. He got up and put on more wood.

"What are we going to do about Lucius Black?" Nelly said. "We can't let him push us around forever."

"No," he said, "we can't. I need to find a way to put an end to this—within the law if at all possible. But I haven't been able to think of a way to do that. We've got to come up with a strategy."

Nelly moved closer to him and hooked her arm with his. "We'll think of something," she said. "I'm surprised to find myself wishing you would put an end to this however you can."

Jubil patted her hand and kissed her cheek. Despite the difficulties they were having, he was glad to have her with him.

"I have another question," Nelly said. "I was expecting to leave a few articles here at the trading post for the mail courier to deliver to Mr. Byers, while we went on to Grand Lake. It appears that won't be necessary now, so I'll just carry them back to Denver. But before we get there, I need your thoughts on which set of articles to deliver."

"Which set?" he said.

"Yes," she said, "I've written two different sets of articles about our trip so far. One set is mainly a travelogue describing the planning and preparation that has gone into the tour, the people who have joined us, and the beauty of the scenery along the way. But the articles make no mention of Black and the difficulties he has caused us. The other set tells the whole story about Black and the harassment you have suffered. But it also details your past and the reasons why he carries a grudge. I'd like your thoughts about which set to make public."

"I appreciate your asking," Jubil said. "As a writer, you'd

probably rather tell the more dramatic story about Black. But I wonder how it would affect our cause. Do you think a public shaming will motivate him to stop his harassment campaign or escalate it? So far, his strategy has been to try to drive me out of business, which he's done a decent job of doing, but he hasn't resorted to real violence. What if the publicity provokes him to go further?"

"All right," she said. "I'll ask Mr. Byers to print the more innocuous articles, and hold onto the others in case you change your mind. They're very well written," she added with a grin.

"I'm sure they are," he said, and he kissed her.

Jubil was in the corral grooming Diablo the next day when he saw Eli riding toward the trading post. He gave him a wave, and Eli returned it casually. He seemed more subdued than usual. A younger Eli would have ridden into camp at a gallop, waving his hat. Nelly saw him from her spot on the hillside, and she picked up her papers and started toward the corral, arriving at the same time as her brother.

"Welcome back," Jubil said. "You made good time. Everything go all right?"

"On the way to Denver, yes," Eli said, "but on the way back, I had a little scare. I saw McTavish and his men riding east."

"Did they see you?" Jubil said.

"By luck they didn't," Eli said. "I'd stepped off the trail into the woods to do my business and taken Buddy with me. I spotted them coming down the trail, and we hid behind some rocks as they rode past. What happened?"

Jubil updated him on what had happened and how everyone was ready to return to Denver.

"Can't say I'm anxious to ride back over the same ground again already," Eli said, "but I don't disagree with the plan."

In the morning, they said their goodbyes to Jack Sumner and set off for Denver. Four days later, they were back at the hotel. As Jubil, Nelly, and Eli said their goodbyes to their guests, both Smith and Norris assured them that they hoped to travel with them again one day. Jubil couldn't help but feel that day would never come.

Nelly stayed at the hotel while Jubil and Eli led the stock back to the livery. The tour had lasted one day short of two weeks, and Jubil had lost money on it. Hardly an auspicious start to his adventure tour business.

That evening, after they had taken naps and gotten themselves cleaned up, Jubil had the hotel deliver a message to Mr. Byers, asking him to join them for breakfast in the morning so Nelly could deliver her articles. Then he, Nelly, and Eli had a late supper in the hotel dining room.

"Have you forgotten what day it is?" Nelly said.

Jubil puzzled over the question.

"Oh," he said, remembering that it was July 13.

"Happy twenty-fifth birthday," Nelly said.

"Hey—happy birthday, Jubil," Eli said.

"That's very kind. Thank you," he said. "I wish I felt more like celebrating. We've got a lot to sort out before we leave here."

"What are you thinking?" Nelly said, reaching across the table and covering Jubil's hands with her own.

"Black wants me to stay out of Bozeman, Yellowstone, and the Crow Agency," Jubil said, looking into Nelly's eyes. "Am I really going to give those things up and allow him to dictate what I can and cannot do?"

"While I am tempted to say yes, just for the sake of peace," Nelly said, patting his hands, "I cannot imagine you being able to do that."

"Thank you," he said, lifting her hand to his lips and kissing it lightly. "That was a lot easier to establish than I thought it might be."

"Ugh," Eli said, anxious to clear the air of romance. "So, what are we going to do?"

"I'm thinking there's hardly any point in my returning to Council Bluffs to reopen the store," Jubil said. "Not until I've found a way to free myself from Lucius Black. If he doesn't get some sign from me that he's won, he'll just keep up his campaign against me."

"How can you free yourself of him," Nelly asked, "without resorting to violence?"

"I'll admit, it may not be possible," Jubil said, "but what if I can find hard evidence that Black is engaged in illegal dealings with the Crow Agency?"

"You don't think Black will take offense," Nelly said, "at your snooping around?"

"I hope to avoid his notice," Jubil said.

Both Nelly and Eli looked at him skeptically.

"What else can I do? I'm open to suggestions," Jubil said, waiting for one or both of them to suggest abandoning the idea of correcting the situation. When they didn't, he continued. "I think it's time to make another trip to visit Flynn at the agency. Maybe I can convince him to help me find the evidence I need to prove Black is operating the agency illegally. It's only a matter of time before he gets swallowed up by the law too."

"I'm going to guess he'll be more afraid of Black than the law," Eli said.

"You may be right, but at least I can try," Jubil said. "It'll also give me a chance to talk to the commander at Fort Ellis, and maybe White Dog."

"And Eli and I are supposed to do what?" Nelly said, with an air of suspicion.

"Go back to Council Bluffs?" Jubil said. "Or maybe Bloomington, to see your folks?"

"That's not going to happen," Eli said.

"No," Nelly said, "it's not."

"You can't go out there with me," Jubil said. "It's too dangerous. Especially for you," he said to Nelly.

"Careful, Jubil," she said, "what did you just say about allowing someone else to dictate what you can and cannot do?"

"But Nelly," Jubil said, "surely you see—"

"That you're free to risk your life for what you believe in," Nelly said, "but I'm not?"

He held his tongue while he fought with the double standard that he knew existed in his heart. Their relationship was built on Jubil's acceptance of Nelly's desire to control her own destiny. She didn't want him to put himself in harm's way, but she wasn't trying to stop him. How could he do any less for her? His plan was to maintain a low profile on his visit to Montana. Now he would have to keep Nelly's and Eli's presence hidden as well.

"It's a long hard trip," Jubil said. "A week's ride there and back."

"Am I not handling that sort of travel to your liking?" she said.

"No," he said, "you're doing fine. Very well, in fact."

She gave him a look that said, *I rest my case.*

"All right," he said. "You win. I'll let the Garcias, your parents, and Abe and Lily know that our return has been delayed. I'll just say that we're going to Bozeman for a while. We'll leave after breakfast tomorrow."

At breakfast, William Byers was disturbed by the story of Jubil's difficulties, and he argued for publishing Nelly's full narrative of the events—reminding Jubil of the power of the press—but Jubil thought it would be taking matters too far.

Byers studied Nelly's face. "We won't begin publishing your journals until two weeks from today," he said, "so just contact me if you change your mind."

"Thank you," Nelly said.

Jubil shook hands with Byers. "We'll be in touch," he said.

CHAPTER 12

McTavish had not shown himself since their return to Denver, but Jubil had a suspicion that he was still there, watching to make sure they returned to Council Bluffs. He was proven right when they arrived at the Denver train depot. At the platform where they would board their train to Cheyenne, he spotted McTavish waiting several cars up to board the same train.

"We've got company," he said to Nelly and Eli, nodding in McTavish's direction. He was ignoring them but making no effort to hide his presence.

"Oh . . . wonderful," Nelly said with annoyance.

"Want me to go tell him to take another train?" Eli said boldly.

"No," Jubil said, "ignore him. Just stick to our plan, and we'll try to lose him when we reach Cheyenne."

Over breakfast, they had made a plan to board the train bound for Council Bluffs, wait until the last possible moment before it pulled out of the depot, and step off. If they lost McTavish, they would buy tickets for Corinne. If he foiled their plan, they would regroup.

In Cheyenne, when they stepped back off the train bound for Council Bluffs, McTavish was nowhere in sight. Even so, Jubil kept a close watch on the crowd until their train to Corinne left the station. Once aboard, he walked the length of the train twice to make sure McTavish hadn't followed them. By suppertime that evening, he had finally accepted the fact they were in the clear—for now. McTavish would figure out pretty quickly that they had not taken the train east, and he would notify Black that Jubil had lost him. McTavish might even head back to Bozeman, guessing that's where Jubil had gone or to seek new marching orders from Black.

They had brought along some of the gear from their tour—cooking supplies and two tents—and had shipped the rest back to Council Bluffs. In Corinne they had to supplement their supplies, starting with horses, and Jubil got a very good price on them, thanks to the good relationship he had established with the liveryman there. Jubil had purchased Apollo at the same stable—twice—first for the 1870 Yellowstone expedition and then again for the 1871 expedition, after which he had taken Apollo home with him. The horses they bought were strong and healthy, but Jubil was not feeling sentimental this trip, so he simply thought of the horse he was riding as the mare. The money he saved at the livery came in handy at the mercantile, where they were charging steep prices for the staples they needed. He still had some reserves in his money belt, but funds were tight and only getting tighter.

During the ride to Montana, Jubil pointed out to Nelly the spot where he and Eli had been ambushed by O'Brien and the spot he was considering for an inn that would serve as his western entry point to Yellowstone. He longed to show Nelly and Eli the wonders of the park, but there was no time for that now.

When they reached Bozeman, Jubil steered them well south of town and headed east for Fort Ellis. In another hour, the scattered white buildings of the fort came into view, and he headed for the quarters of his friend First Lieutenant Cheyney Doane. He and Doane had grown close on Jubil's first expedition to Yellowstone in 1870, then traveled together again on his second expedition in 1871, and yet again on the first Northern

Pacific Railroad survey in 1872. Jubil led Eli and Nelly up to the small house where Doane and his wife lived. They tied up their horses.

"Let me make sure this is still their quarters," Jubil said and went to knock. The door opened, and there stood a six-foot-three-inch man with broad shoulders and long black hair.

"Well, I'll be," Doane said, smiling through his walrus mustache. "Jubilee Walker. There must be adventure afoot!"

Jubil laughed. "You've got me pegged, Lieutenant."

Doane looked over Jubil's shoulder. "And your partner on the survey—sorry I don't recall his name. And . . . someone else."

Jubil motioned Nelly and Eli forward.

"You remember Eli Boswell. This is his sister, Nelly," Jubil said, "my wife."

"Ah, well," Doane said, nodding approvingly. "How do you do? I've spent an evening or two listening to Mr. Walker pine over you," Doane said. "I can see why he was anxious to get back home. It's a pleasure to meet you." Doane towered over Nelly as he shook her hand. He made no comment about her attire.

"Welcome back to Montana, Mr. Boswell," Doane said.

"Thank you, Lieutenant," Eli said. "It's good to see you again."

Doane shook Eli's hand, then turned back to Jubil.

"Come in—come in," he said, stepping out of the doorway.

Jubil and the others stepped into the parlor of Doane's quarters and were greeted by Doane's wife.

"Walker, you remember Amelia?" Doane said. Doane introduced Eli and Nelly.

Doane's wife was the picture of gentility in a full skirt and a white blouse with puffed sleeves, her long hair elegantly rolled up. She acknowledged Jubil and Eli with a nod and regarded Nelly with a polite smile and an air of bemusement.

Jubil said, "You might be interested to know, Mrs. Doane, that Nelly introduced the Lieutenant's Yellowstone journal to her literature class at Vassar College. She's a journalist herself now."

"Thank you!" Doane said. "I appreciated that very much."

"Oh, he certainly did appreciate it," Mrs. Doane said, her face lighting up. "He bragged of it for days. I hope we have time to become better acquainted, my dear."

"Sit down," Doane said. "Tell me what brings you out here."

Jubil began his story with the incidents in Bismarck and Council Bluffs, then McTavish's appearance in Denver, followed by the events during the tour, and finally why they had come to the fort.

"I know of Lucius Black," Doane said. "Another bad apple—just like his brother. Not sure why he finds this place worth his time."

"My first order of business," Jubil said, "is to stop his mistreatment of the Crow. I'm going to ride out to visit Flynn at the reservation, to see if I can gather any support for stopping Black in a court of law."

"If Black gets wind you're here," Doane said, "that'll turn ugly."

"Yes," Jubil said. "I was hoping the new commander wouldn't mind if we stayed at the fort a few days. I don't think Black can get to us here."

"I'm sure he wouldn't mind," Doane said.

"I was also hoping to meet him," Jubil said. "I'd like to talk with him about supplying the fort if we open a store in Bozeman. Perhaps you could vouch for me?"

"My pleasure," Doane said. "He might not mind dealing with someone other than Black."

"Good. Thank you," Jubil said. "I'll go to see Flynn tomorrow. Maybe we could see the commander the day after?"

"I'll see what I can do. You can stay with us." Doane looked to his wife for confirmation.

"It would our pleasure," Amelia Doane said.

Jubil and Nelly collected their things, and Mrs. Doane settled them into their room. Eli preferred to stay in the barracks, so Doane went with him to assign him a bunk with his men and to tell the commander there were guests on the post.

Jubil was a little surprised that Nelly preferred to stay at the fort while he and Eli rode to the reservation to see Flynn and, they hoped, White Dog, but the prospect of a proper bath, wearing a dress for a while, and not being on horseback had won her over. Mrs. Doane had also insisted on showing her off to the other officers' wives at the fort and was planning a tea to introduce her new friend—the Vassar graduate, former resident of New York City, freelance journalist, and woman suffrage advocate, who had ridden there in men's britches with her adventurer husband. Jubil had taken great pleasure in seeing Nelly befriended by Libbie Custer, and now again she was winning over everyone she met. Granted, these army wives were starved for an opportunity to break the monotony of post life, but Nelly was an impressive person to meet under any circumstances. Having her along had added a new dimension to Jubil's travel and to his understanding of his wife, and he could see how happy and comfortable she was with this new life.

The only negative aspect to Mrs. Doane's plan was the attention it might draw to his presence in the area. People were often coming and going between the fort and Bozeman. Word might spread about the guests at the post.

After breakfast, Jubil and Eli set out on the thirty-mile ride to the Crow Agency. The weather had cooperated since they'd left Corinne, and the dry spell continued that morning. They would ride back to the fort this evening, unless White Dog was there, in which case, they would spend the night.

They reached the Bozeman Pass about an hour after leaving the fort and stopped for a few minutes to enjoy the magnificent view.

"I wish we were going that way," Eli said, pointing south.

"My thoughts exactly," Jubil said. He was proud of Eli for swallowing his disappointment and not complaining.

They followed Trail Creek down the mountainside until they reached the Yellowstone River. To Jubil's surprise, the river was lower here than he had ever seen it. He selected a point to ford on a gravel bar, and they easily walked their horses across, saving them a couple of hours they would have spent traveling around the riverbend to the ferry crossing. The last time he had been here, the river was a churning flood. He had risked his life to cross it, in order to keep Jay Cooke's railroad survey from failing before it even started.

Jubil had never approached the reservation and the agency from this direction. Along the way, they passed farm fields tended by Indians. The Crow weren't traditionally farmers, but they had done a respectable job of raising some produce— mainly out of necessity. The small herd of pathetic undernourished cattle revealed the ongoing food scarcity caused by Black's corrupt practice of sending the tribe livestock that no one else would accept, along with inedible fodder. If not for hunting, fishing, and farming, the tribe would starve—which would suit Secretary Delano just fine.

It was early afternoon when Jubil and Eli rode through the open gates of the agency compound, approached the central building, and hitched their horses to the rail. Flynn was not sitting on the porch this time, so Jubil and Eli went inside, stepping into the large room that looked like a ramshackle general store. Standing at a table covered with furs, Flynn was talking to an old man in a mix of Crow and sign language, with an occasional burst of English and cursing when he lost his patience. Flynn looked over to see who had entered the store. When he recognized Jubil, he stopped talking and walked away from the old man, who looked after him with a confused expression.

"Hello, Flynn," Jubil said.

"Jayzus, Mary, and Joseph—it's you again!" Flynn said with mock dismay as he came to shake Jubil's hand. "And who might this fine lad be?"

"This is my partner, Eli Boswell," Jubil said.

"How do you do, Mr. Boswell?" Flynn said. "You must be a bold fellow to ride with Walker."

"I try to keep up," Eli said with a grin.

"And what are you doing here this time?" Flynn said to Jubil. "If I dare ask."

The old man that Flynn had abandoned at the table approached them, but Flynn said something in Crow and waved him off. The Indian looked offended and walked out muttering to himself.

"I need to bring you up to date on some matters," Jubil said. He told Flynn about his encounter with Lucius Black on his previous trip, and about his meeting with Secretary Delano.

"My name is on a ledger on his desk?" Flynn said.

"Mr. Shawn Flynn—agent of record," Jubil said. Flynn frowned at the use of his Christian name. "You're accountable for any corruption."

"Sure, and we all know that's not true now, don't we?" Flynn said. "And yet there you were, in the nation's capital, calling attention to me and my dire situation."

"It was Lucius Black I intended to call out," Jubil said, "but Delano didn't give me the chance. As soon as I mentioned there was corruption out here, he shut me down. But somehow, word of my meeting with the secretary very quickly traveled back here to Black."

"I don't suppose you're here to apologize for putting me in a bad light with the powers that be?" Flynn said.

"I'm here to warn you about what's going to happen," Jubil said, "and to give you a chance to get on the right side of it." He told Flynn about the harassment campaign that Black had been waging and Black's ultimatum to Jubil. As he told his story, he could see the surprise on Flynn's face and the calculation behind his darting eyes as he tried to sort out what all this had to do with him.

"This isn't going to end until I give in to Black or get the better of him," Jubil said. "I'm going to try to work within the law, but I'm determined to do it one way or another."

"I don't see why we need to worry about staying within the law," Eli said. "Black sure hasn't."

"I haven't heard a word around here about Black's campaign against you," Flynn said.

"I'll give you the benefit of the doubt on that," Jubil said.

"I'm not sure I will," Eli said. "This'd be a good time to come clean if you know anything."

Flynn looked at Eli with scornful disregard.

"What is it that you want from me then?" Flynn said to Jubil. "I've got a bad feeling you are going to tell me exactly how I'm supposed to 'get on the right side of it,' as you say."

"I need your help," Jubil said. "If we're going to build a legal case against Black, we'll need hard evidence that we can present in court to prove what he's been up to—ledgers, invoices, letters, whatever we can get our hands on. The lawyers will probably want you to testify, too, especially if we're presenting you as having been coerced into following Black's orders. That'll be the only way to clear your name."

Flynn stared at Jubil for a long moment. Finally, he said, "Are you daft, man? I'll be dead the day Black learns I've turned on him. And it won't just be me. You're dreaming if you think you'll see him inside a court of law. He'll hunt you down and put paid to your complaint with a bullet—and you can count on it. No sir, Mr. Walker, your plan of going to the law will not happen."

Jubil wasn't surprised by Flynn's response, but he wasn't ready to concede his point. "Why is he going to all this effort to put me out of business?" Jubil said. "The Crow Agency business can't amount to that much money to him. I hear he was rich before he moved out here. It just doesn't add up."

"Maybe the Crow Agency and the mercantile don't add up to much," Flynn said. "But his mining operation is another story. Last I heard, he was operating a gold mine, down near Cooke City."

"That's no secret," Jubil said.

"The presence of the operation is common knowledge," Flynn said. "But not the yield."

"It was richer than they let on?" Jubil said.

"Aye, by far," Flynn said. "But they are keeping that a secret to avoid starting a rush."

Jubil and Eli exchanged a glance. Eli looked impressed by Flynn's story.

"How much richer?" Jubil said.

"From what I heard," Flynn said, "Phineas and his men hit a lode. Then when Lucius came to town, he started bringing his own gold into the mine, to store it there rather than trust the banks. They're hiding a fortune in there. They just use these other businesses as a cover for their activity and wealth."

Jubil remained skeptical. "How do you know all this, and why didn't you tell me when I was here before?"

"The mines had nothing to do with what you came to discuss before, now did they?" Flynn said.

"I knew he was hiding something," Eli said.

"I wasn't hiding anything, lad," Flynn said to Eli dismissively. He looked to Jubil.

"It was McTavish," Flynn said. "He talks too much. Neither Murphy nor O'Brien ever so much as whispered a word to me about how much the mine produced, but when Lucius Black entered the picture and brought McTavish in, he talked as though I'd been in on it all along. I never disabused him of the notion."

"I suppose not," Jubil said.

"Your promotion of Yellowstone Park is likely to bring a passel of folks to the area," Flynn said. "Black has to move his plunder in and out by passing through a section of the park—the mountains down there dictate the route. As the park gets more popular, his mine activity will be too public for his liking. If he can keep you far away from here and prevent you from stirring up a fuss, it eliminates the problem—or at least delays it."

"The park border is somewhere in that vicinity," Jubil said. "Do you know exactly where the mine is? If it's inside the park boundary, then he's mining illegally, and all that gold belongs to the US government. That would be a good reason for him to be so secretive."

If Jubil remembered the wording correctly from the Congressional bill, the northern boundary of the park extended from the confluence of the Gardiner and Yellowstone Rivers, ten miles to the east of the most easterly part of Yellowstone Lake. But he couldn't remember the rest of the description. He didn't think the boundaries had ever been surveyed. He thought Hayden might have just drawn a big square on a map, and then described it for the bill. Jubil had never seen that map.

"If that were so and the mine were on government property," Flynn said, "then why haven't they already come down on him?"

"The government hasn't followed through on its promises to protect the park," Jubil said. "They haven't appropriated funding to enforce any of the law's provisions. Jack Baronett still operates his toll bridge over the Yellowstone, and McCartney operates his bathhouse at Soda Mountain. By the letter of the law, they should be put under government control too. But Langford can't do it all by himself. Secretary Delano told me he has a big appropriations bill that he thinks has a good chance of passing. If that happens, then the boom is on. Maybe Black has gotten word and is hustling to mine that spot out and move his gold out before anyone starts paying too much attention and enforcing the law."

"Interesting theory," Flynn said. "Or maybe it's not within the park's boundaries, and he's secretive about it because he's a greedy bastard."

Jubil and Eli laughed.

"Yes," Jubil said. "But that's probably true in either case."

The situation was clear to Jubil now. All this bother wasn't about the Crow Agency or Jubil building a store in Bozeman—it was about gold. What Black wanted was secrecy. If Jubil had a means to deny him that, it would be a powerful negotiating tool or, if it came to that, a powerful weapon. Maybe making public Black's actions and linking them to his ownership of the mine was the only way to beat him. Jubil was certain Nelly would agree to write a new article, a final installment in her series, to that effect.

Maybe it was time for Jubil to deliver an ultimatum to Black directly. Tell him that if he met Jubil's terms, Jubil would respect Black's secret about the mine and even help him find a way to avoid tourist traffic. But if Black insisted on persecuting him, he would publish everything he knew about the mine.

He would have to be prepared for the backlash. His instincts told him that Black was unlikely to negotiate. He would come for him. If so, Jubil might have to resort to following the advice of his friend General Sherman and shoot it out. Either way, he was not going to allow Black to control his life.

"I've got an idea," Jubil said, "one that Black's not going to like one bit."

"No great surprise, that," Flynn said. "Let's hear it."

"I'm pretty sure you're not going to like it either," Jubil said.

CHAPTER 13

"You want me to deliver your ultimatum to Lucius Black?" Flynn said incredulously. "He'll kill me just for talking to you."

"We're going to paint you as a victim," Jubil said, "not an accomplice. You tell him that I turned up on your doorstep and threatened to kill you if you didn't deliver my message— and you give him a sealed envelope containing a letter. You're just supposed to hand it to him and then deliver his reply to me at Fort Ellis."

"And if I refuse," Flynn said, "what'll you do? Shoot me?"

"No," Jubil said. "But when I ride away from here, you become part of the problem. No more friendly visits. You're going to have to take sides in this, Flynn. Your days of staying out of the fray are nearing an end. I want you on my side. What kind of a future have you got out here anyway? Is this what you came to America for?"

"Well, the fact is, I was dragged to America more than came voluntarily, you might say," Flynn said. "Murphy and O'Brien dragged me into trouble in County Cork, and then they dragged me here to get away from it. Now here you are, trying to drag me into your own trouble."

"I'm offering you a way to take charge of your own life," Jubil said.

Flynn looked away and stewed over Jubil's comment. As Jubil studied him, another idea came to mind.

"I intend to open a store out here," Jubil said, "and I hope to supply the Crow Agency. If I do that, you can stay on here at the agency if you like, but you could also come work in my store. In fact, I already have a store in Council Bluffs that I could use help with. Eli and I need someone to run it when we're out leading tours. You could join our business and be your own man. Maybe even earn enough money to go back to Ireland, if that's what you want to do."

"Now wait a minute," Eli said. "Don't I get a say in this? You would trust him to run the store?"

Jubil looked at Flynn, who met his gaze.

"I would," Jubil said.

Flynn looked at Jubil with surprise, and Jubil imagined that he might have never heard anyone say that before.

"How do you see us getting out of this without getting killed?" Flynn said.

"I hope Black will make a smart decision," Jubil said, "and see that being at war with me is more trouble than it's worth. I hope he'll give up the sham of running the mercantile and supplying the agency, and focus on his gold mine. My letter to him will propose that I open a store to supply the reservation, the fort, and the community, and I'll lead tours in the park. But I'll keep quiet about his mine and even use my influence to keep the tourist trails away from the northeast corner. He and I can coexist peacefully. That's what I'm going to propose."

"It's a rosy picture," Flynn said, "I'll give you that. But what if he doesn't go for it?"

"I'll defend myself if I have to," Jubil said. "And everyone around me."

Flynn gave him a searching look. "I do believe you will try, Mr. Walker," he said.

"Black has resisted violence so far," Jubil said. "I'm hoping he will continue to do so."

Flynn and Eli shared a skeptical look, which they then turned on Jubil.

"Which brings up another subject," Jubil said. "Is White Dog here?"

"I don't believe he is," Flynn said. "He and Standing Horse went out hunting, but they'll be back soon."

"Good," Jubil said. "I want to see him. In the meantime, I'll need a pen, paper, and an envelope."

Flynn went to his desk in the corner by the fireplace and set the items out for Jubil, who sat down and composed his letter, handed it to Eli to read, and then gave it to Flynn.

"Any suggestions?" Jubil said.

"Forget all this and go back to Council Bluffs?" Flynn said.

Jubil ignored the comment. "Take it to Black," he said. "Once you deliver it, come find me at the fort. I'm staying at Lieutenant Doane's quarters."

"I'll ride back with you," Flynn said. "I'll leave you at the fort and go on into town and check in at the Metropolitan Hotel. I'll talk to Black tonight, then come see you at the fort tomorrow morning. On our way, we'll go by Standing Horse's lodge. You can tell his woman you're looking for White Dog."

"Rains in Winter," Eli said to Flynn. "Her name is Rains in Winter."

Flynn shrugged.

Jubil was proud of Eli for remembering her name and honoring her. She and Standing Horse had fed and entertained them one evening as they made their way back with White Dog from the failed 1872 Northern Pacific Railroad survey. That had been the highlight of the trip for Eli, and he beamed with joy later that day when she greeted him by name. She said she expected the hunters back tomorrow or the next day. Jubil's spirits rose now that he was almost certain he would see his friend. His confidence also rose considerably regarding his ability to defend himself, Nelly, and Eli.

It was a quiet ride to the fort. Jubil could see that Flynn was unnerved about having to pick a side in the conflict between Jubil and Black, but he wouldn't have minded hearing some of the tales of leprechauns Flynn had spun to pass the time back in the summer of 1867 as their Warner and Company freight wagon rattled its way across the dusty plains.

When they neared the fort, Jubil and Eli wished Flynn luck, and he gave a lackluster wave and continued west to Bozeman.

"I honestly do not understand," Eli said, as they watched Flynn ride away, "why you trust him."

"He's a sly one, I'll grant you that," Jubil said, "but he's got a good heart—I just feel it."

Eli looked at him doubtfully.

"Well, if you recall, you and your brother burned down my farmhouse and barn," Jubil said with a grin. "And I still trust you."

Eli rolled his eyes and turned his horse toward the fort.

At Doane's quarters, Jubil found the lieutenant sitting in his chair by the fire reading, while Mrs. Doane sat on the nearby sofa doing needlework. It was a domestic scene that was hard for Jubil to reconcile with the marauding warrior he knew Doane to be.

"Could I speak to you for a minute?" Jubil asked Doane. "Maybe we could step outside?"

"All right," Doane said, studying Jubil. "We'll only be a moment, dear," he said to Amelia, and they stepped outside.

"Some new information has come to light about Black's situation," Jubil said. "I'm going to have to use a different strategy than bringing the matter of the Crow Agency to a court of law." He explained his terms and the letter he'd asked Flynn to deliver.

"I'll be surprised if he agrees to that," Doane said, "but I suppose it's worth a try. It might possibly have the opposite effect, however, and rile him up even more."

"I've got to do something," Jubil said. "I can't let him run my life."

Doane nodded thoughtfully. "I'll keep this under my hat," he said. "And it's best not to talk of it with Amelia."

"Understood," Jubil said.

Back inside, Jubil wished the Doanes a good night and went to find Nelly, who had retired to the bedroom to write. He tapped lightly on the door and peeked in.

"Are you decent?" he said.

"Yes," she said.

"What a shame."

She was sitting at the desk, which was covered with papers. She put down her pen and turned to face him. He went to her and kissed her, then sat down at the foot of the bed. She was wearing a dress again, which was strange to see after having gotten used to her in pants.

"How was your day with the ladies?" he asked.

"Very nice," Nelly said, but without enthusiasm. "I felt like Amelia's prize pig, but she meant well. It was fine, really. I'm just unaccustomed to talking about myself so much—or talking so much in general."

"I'm sure you are the high point of the season here," he said with a grin.

She waved him off. "Did you find Flynn?"

"We did," he said. He told her what Flynn had shared with them about the gold mine.

As Nelly listened, her jaw dropped. "Oh my," she said, "that does change the picture."

"I wish I had been able to discuss it with you beforehand," Jubil said, "but I made a threat to expose him that I'll need your help to make good on." He explained how Flynn had scoffed at the idea of using the law bringing Black to heel, and he described the letter he had written to Black and the terms it spelled out.

"You told him you'd help keep his mine a secret if he agreed to your other terms?" Nelly said. "Are you sure you can live with that?"

"I know it sounds a bit shady. But if that's the only way to both help the Crow and keep the peace"—he shrugged—"I'll do it."

"Do you think there's any chance he'll accept your terms?" Nelly asked.

"There's always a chance," he said.

"Of course, you would say that," Nelly said, becoming lost in thought.

"I'll write another article," she said, "about Black's secret gold mine, and if Black refuses your terms, we'll tell Mr. Byers to run it, along with the others about Black that we left with him."

"Good. That will do it," Jubil said. "Thank you."

Nelly studied him for a moment, then offered a sad grin. "I know you're trying to do what's right—and I love you for it," Nelly said. "We'll face the consequences together."

The next morning, Eli joined them for breakfast at the Doanes' quarters. Amelia Doane kept up a lively conversation, and the rest of them followed her lead, temporarily distracted from the suspense of waiting for word from Flynn. They were just finishing the meal when there was a knock at the door. Doane rose to answer it.

"Good morning, Lieutenant," Flynn said. "I'm here to see Mr. Walker."

"Come in, Mr. Flynn," Doane said.

"Good morning," Jubil said, rising to greet him. "You don't

look any worse for wear. How did it go?"

"Morning, Walker. Morning, ladies," Flynn said, with a nod in their direction.

"Let's retire to my office," Doane said.

Once Jubil, Flynn, Doane, and Eli were behind closed doors, Flynn said, "Well, I was relieved Mr. Black didn't shoot the messenger, but my ears are still burning from the tirade he unleashed after reading your letter. I was impressed he could be so colorfully profane."

Despite the seriousness of the situation, Jubil grinned. "Did he have anything to say," Jubil asked, "that you can repeat?"

"He did," Flynn said. "Once he got calmed down, he got all pensive-like. And then he says to me that he's going to propose some amendments to your terms. He'll have a letter delivered this afternoon, he says. Then he took McTavish aside—"

"McTavish is in Bozeman?" Jubil said.

"Yes," Flynn said.

He must have caught on to their game, searched the passenger cars for them, and gotten off at the next stop. McTavish's presence coupled with Black's delay made Jubil wonder what scheme they were dreaming up. Why would Black need so much time to compose a counteroffer? "I don't trust his reasoning," he said.

"What are your orders after you leave here?" Doane said to Flynn.

"I'm to go back to the reservation," Flynn said with a shrug, "and carry on with business as usual."

"My offer still stands," Jubil said.

"I have not entirely dismissed your offer," Flynn said. "I'm thinking I'll lie about here at the fort until Black's message arrives. Then we'll see which way the wind blows."

"Fair enough," Jubil said, then turned his attention to Doane. "While we wait, would this be a good time to meet your new commander?"

"He's expecting us sometime today," Doane said. "Might be good to catch him early, before other business draws him away."

Jubil looked out the window toward the headquarters building and saw a rider approaching.

"It's White Dog," Jubil said excitedly. "I'm going out to meet him." Jubil said, leaving the office and stepping outside. Nelly, Eli, and Flynn followed him out, while Doane and Amelia stood in the doorway behind them.

Jubil raised his hand in greeting, and White Dog did the same. His friend looked no different than the last time Jubil had seen him—buckskin britches and moccasins, a well-worn army shirt, his long hair worn straight, with one black feather hanging from a braid on the right side.

Jubil looked at Nelly, who was taking in the scene with an awestruck smile. He could see the joy and wonder in her eyes. He was looking forward to the day he could read her description of this first meeting with White Dog.

When White Dog reached them, he dismounted and hitched his horse. He and Jubil greeted one another with a grasp of the right forearm and a grip on the shoulder.

"It's good to see you, my friend," Jubil said. "Thank you for coming." Jubil turned to Nelly and Eli. "You know, Eli."

Eli stepped up to shake White Dog's hand.

"And this is my wife, Nelly."

Nelly smiled and gave a shy wave, and White Dog responded with a perceptible nod.

"I've got a lot to tell you," Jubil said. "Can you stay for a while? The lieutenant, Eli, and I were just on our way to talk with the fort commander. You can come along if you like. Eli and I have a business proposition that might see us putting a new store in Bozeman."

"You have trouble?" White Dog said. "Rains in Winter says you are with Flynn, and here at fort, not in town. I wonder why."

"I'm in a tight spot with Lucius Black and his men. Can I explain it to you after we see the commander?"

"Yes," White Dog said. "You talk. I go to corral and sleep." Jubil realized that for him to have arrived so early, he must have left the reservation in the middle of the night.

"Your friend is onto a good plan," Flynn said. "I didn't sleep much last night myself. But I'll take the barracks rather than the hayloft."

"All right," Jubil said. "Eli and I will get our business done, and we'll all reconvene later." He turned to Nelly. "Will you stay here with Mrs. Doane?"

"Oh, yes," she said. "I have some writing to do."

"Yes," Jubil said with a smile, "I imagine you do."

The new fort commander, Major N. B. Sweitzer, was available to talk, and Jubil, Eli, and Doane were ushered into his office in the headquarters building. Major Sweitzer was a West Point graduate who had served under General McClellan during the war. He had also been the commander of the regiment that had tracked down and killed John Wilkes Booth. The major was a congenial host and very interested in Jubil's expeditions and acquaintances—Major Powell and the Grand Canyon expedition; his friendship with General Sherman and his service as a guide in Yellowstone for Major Barlow's survey; riding with General Custer on the successful railroad survey in 1873. He particularly enjoyed the story of Jubil and Custer helping the survey leader, Thomas Rosser, smash up the whiskey kegs to prevent General Stanley from following Baker's drunken example and ruining the survey.

As the conversation turned to business, Major Sweitzer was also interested in hearing about Abe Warner's original Warner and Company supply service to other Division of the

Missouri forts under General Sherman and General Sheridan, as well as Jubil's recent supply agreement with Custer at Fort Lincoln. When Jubil finally got around to making his supply proposal for Fort Ellis, he found the major encouraging and open to doing business with Warner and Walker.

Their visit took most of the morning, and as Jubil took his leave, he promised to stay in touch. He had made no mention of the Crow Agency, Lucius Black, or his previous encounters with Phineas Black and his men, and neither had Major Sweitzer. Either the major didn't know about these incidents—which was unlikely—or he hadn't allowed it to affect his view of Jubil or his reputation. It occurred to Jubil for the first time that maybe Lucius Black's attempts to ruin his reputation would have ultimately proven unsuccessful, even if Jubil had done nothing to counter them. But there was the matter of the Crow Agency, and there was no turning back now. He had set out on a trajectory that would have to play out.

As he, Eli, and Doane walked back to Doane's quarters, he felt his luck might be taking a turn for the better. With Major Sweitzer's support, he would be guaranteed enough business to give his new store a fighting chance. He was confident he could also pick up a respectable amount of business from the community, though there would be little market for the stylish line of clothing that he and Luke had started. People would probably be more interested in basic goods at a low price, and that was fine with Jubil. That's what Warner and Company had originally offered, and Abe had done quite well with it. The new store would go back to basics.

When they reached the house, Doane opened the door and then stopped abruptly on the threshold, putting his arm out to keep Jubil and Eli from entering. He turned his head side-to-side as if searching for something, then he rushed into the room. With his bulk no longer blocking Jubil's view, he saw what had stopped Doane in his tracks. Amelia Doane sat in one of the dining room chairs—bound, gagged, with tears coursing down her face.

Jubil stood in the doorway in shock, watching the lieutenant free her. Doane removed her gag, and her mouth trembled as she looked up at her husband with terror in her eyes.

"They took Nelly!" she said, and then she began to sob uncontrollably.

Jubil rushed through the house looking for his wife.

She was gone.

CHAPTER 14

"What happened?" Jubil said, kneeling beside Amelia as Doane freed her hands.

"Give her a minute, Walker," Doane said sternly.

"Of course," Jubil said apologetically. He got to his feet and stepped back. His mind and his pulse raced. Black had taken Nelly—but how? He was finding it hard to breathe. *All right, keep your wits about you*, he told himself, but it seemed almost impossible to do. If anything happened to Nelly—

Eli remained in the open doorway, a stunned look on his face. When Jubil met his eyes, Eli came to stand next to him and clasped his shoulder briefly with a trembling hand.

Doane, kneeling in front of his wife, handed his handkerchief to her. Her crying had calmed from hysteria to a steady weeping that shook her frame. Jubil paced back and forth across the room and waited for her to regain enough composure to speak. She was wasting valuable time.

"Can you tell us what happened, dear?" Doane said gently, cupping Amelia's shoulders tenderly in his large hands. She wiped her eyes and nose, and took a shuddering breath.

"They came shortly after you left for headquarters," she said shakily. "I had begun to clean up after breakfast, and Nelly offered to help. I insisted I didn't need it and sent her off to write. A knock came at the door—it was two soldiers carrying a large rolled-up rug. They had come in a covered wagon driven by a man in civilian clothes. One of the soldiers told me that Major Sweitzer had ordered a new rug for our dining room. I told them I'd heard nothing about such a replacement, but he said that was not his concern. He had orders to bring it in and remove the other one. I was confused, and I probably should have sent them away . . . or sent for you . . . but I let them in. They—they—oh, Nelly! I should never have let them come in!"

She broke down crying again.

Jubil tried to compose himself as he watched Doane massage his wife's rope-burned wrists.

"Did you recognize the soldiers?" Doane said gently.

Amelia shook her head. She dabbed at her eyes with the handkerchief.

"How about the man driving the wagon?" Jubil said. "Was he wearing a bowler hat?"

She thought a moment, then nodded.

"McTavish—Black's henchman," Jubil told Doane.

He stepped out of the house, slamming the door behind him without thinking. As he paced in the yard, he swore under his breath, desperately trying to form a useful thought—all that came to mind was images of Nelly struggling as the men kidnapped her. He felt as though he was about to explode with rage. He threw his hat to the ground and kicked it.

Eli stepped out of the house and watched Jubil for a moment, then he walked over and picked up Jubil's hat, knocked the dust off of it, and handed it back to him.

"We'll get them, Jubil," Eli said, his voice low and quavering. "Whatever it takes—we'll get her back."

Jubil took his hat and met Eli's gaze. Eli's eyes were brimming with tears. Jubil struggled to take a few deep breaths to calm himself enough to think straight.

"Do you think Flynn was in on it?" Eli said, wiping his eyes and collecting himself.

"I doubt it," Jubil said. "Why would he stay here if he had something to do with it? Anyway, we'll find out soon enough. Go over to the barracks and bring him here. You better strap on your pistol first, just in case."

Eli nodded and bolted for the barracks.

Composed enough now to face Amelia without upsetting her further, Jubil went back into the house. Amelia had stopped crying.

"Is she up to telling us more?" Jubil asked Doane. "Did they hurt Nelly?"

"Can you tell us what happened, dear," Doane said, "after the men came into the house?"

"They came in with their rug and put it down in the parlor," she said. "Then they went to stand at either end of the dining table. One of them asked me to remove the tablecloth so they could move the table to switch the rug. As I did that, Nelly came out of her room to see who had come in. The man closest to her reached out and grabbed her. He wrapped an arm around her while he covered her face with a handkerchief. She tried to fight him off, but he was too strong. I was frozen with shock. Suddenly, the other man grabbed me. He pushed me into a chair and told me if I wasn't quiet, they would hurt Nelly. He tied me up and gagged me. By this time Nelly was unconscious—maybe from ether?"

As Amelia talked, Jubil stared at her in disbelief, the image of Nelly being manhandled and sedated burning into his mind.

"They unrolled the rug and laid her down on it. Then they wrapped her up in it. The man who tied me up took a letter out of his pocket and put it on the mantel. He said to tell Mr. Walker it was Mr. Black's response to his offer. Then they carried Nelly out the door."

Jubil spun around and saw the envelope on the mantel. He tore it open.

Walker,

This would not have happened had you heeded the terms you were given in Denver to stay out of Bozeman, Yellowstone, and the Crow Agency. Your offer to coexist out here is of no interest to me. I don't trust you, and I never will. You killed my brother and two of his men. I was willing to forgo a bloody revenge if you stayed out of my affairs, but you are determined to have your own way at my expense, which I will not allow.

I would prefer that no one lose their life because of our differences, but it seems I must prove to you that the unthinkable is possible. If you cooperate, your wife will be safe and reasonably comfortable, hidden where you have no hope of finding her. Here are my terms:

You leave immediately and ride to Corinne, where you board the eastbound train to Council Bluffs. I have a man in Corinne who will tell me when that has happened. Mrs. Walker will then be escorted to Corinne and sent home. Once you reunite, you will live out your lives without any mention of my business, and you will never set foot in Montana again. If you ever break these terms, I will find you.

If you ignore my warning and come after your wife, I will shoot you on sight. Unfortunately, after your demise, she will have to be eliminated, too, to avoid her publishing anything about my private affairs. If you come for her, you will be the death of her.

Jubil walked to the window to hide his fury as he considered Black's terms. Eli and Flynn were just stepping out of the barracks, Eli with his gun drawn. He gave Flynn a shove, and Flynn stumbled forward. Jubil hadn't meant for Eli to be so aggressive.

"What does the letter say, Walker?" Doane said.

Amelia had largely regained her composure but still looked as though she might burst into tears again at any moment.

Jubil handed the letter to Doane, who rose from his knees

and sat in a chair beside Amelia so that they could read the let-ter together. Jubil supposed that Amelia had earned the right to know the details of the situation. Doane then handed the letter back to Jubil.

"What's your plan?" he said.

"I'm going after her," Jubil said.

Doane nodded. Jubil knew that he would do the same if it were Amelia who had been taken.

The door opened, and Flynn stepped in the house, followed by Eli, who still had his revolver trained on Flynn.

"You can holster your weapon, Eli," Jubil said.

"Thank you," Flynn said, giving Eli the evil eye. "As God is my witness, Walker, I had nothing to do with Black's mischief. I had no idea he planned to do this."

"I'm inclined to believe you," Jubil said.

Jubil handed the letter to Eli, who read it and handed it back to him, his mouth a grim line.

"Maybe Black sent him to spy on us," Eli said, "or shoot us in the back."

"I'm not armed now, am I, lad?" Flynn said, showing his empty hands. "And how will I send my messages? Smoke signals?"

Eli stared at him scornfully.

Jubil could tell that Eli was desperate to do something to save his sister and that he was not thinking any more clearly than Jubil was. They both needed to get ahold of their wits if they were to do Nelly any good.

Jubil handed the letter to Flynn, who read it and shook his head.

"I'm very sorry, Walker," Flynn said, sounding sincere. "I did tell you the man has a vile temper."

"Since you know him so well," Doane said, "where do you think he might have taken Mrs. Walker?"

"Well," Flynn said, giving the question some thought, "he

might have just stashed her in the Metropolitan Hotel. But with all the people in town and the law handy, that seems unlikely. I'm guessing he actually will head someplace where he has more control and no witnesses."

"Let's say he's not in Bozeman," Doane said. "Where do you think he'd go? Is there any place near the Crow Agency that he might take her?"

Flynn shook his head. "I think he'd take her somewhere hard to get to and easy to defend," Flynn said. "In all my years working for the Black brothers, I never heard about any secret hideaway. But"—his eyes lit up as he thought of it—"there is the gold mine."

"All the way down in Cooke City?" Doane said. "That's a three-day ride."

"And you'll not get close to that mine without him and his men having you covered," Flynn said with raised eyebrows.

"We can't trust what Flynn says," Eli said impatiently. "Let's ride to Bozeman and sack the Metropolitan Hotel and the mercantile—and anywhere else in town he might have hidden her."

Jubil looked to Doane.

"As Mr. Flynn points out, their top priority will be secrecy," Doane said. "But Mr. Boswell's plan would be quick to execute. Maybe it's worth a search, before heading off into the countryside for days."

If Black's men weren't in town but were headed to the mine, they would probably already be over the Bozeman Pass by now. But Black was a conniving man. It was possible he had directed his men to sneak Nelly into the hotel in Bozeman wrapped in the rug. A quick search in town made the most sense.

"We'll ride into town first," Jubil said.

"I regret to say I don't think I'll ride with you," Doane said. "I need to stay here with my wife."

"No!" Amelia said, gripping Doane's arm. "You have to find Nelly! I won't rest until she is safe! I'll stay with Mrs. Slocum until you return."

Doane stood and kissed his wife's hands. "Get your things, dear," he said, "and I'll deliver you to your friend." He turned to Jubil. "Then I'll tell the commander what's happened and meet you in the stable. Do you want me to scare up some volunteers?"

"No," Jubil said. "Stealth may be more important than fire-power for this operation."

Doane nodded.

Jubil went to his and Nelly's room and collected his jacket, slicker, and rifle. It broke his heart to see the pages of Nelly's writing strewn across the desk. He had to believe he could get her back alive, that she would be all right.

He put two boxes of fifty cartridges, one for his rifle, one for his revolver, into his saddle bags. There was no time to pack provisions for what might be a week on the move. They would have to live off the land, which was easier said than done. They might have a few hungry days ahead, but that was of no concern to him right now.

He rejoined his friends in the parlor. "Let's saddle up," he said, opening the front door. He did not want to waste another moment. He looked over at Flynn as they walked toward the stable. "Can you lead us to the mine?"

"I rode down there a time or two with Mr. O'Brien," Flynn said, "so I have a fair notion of where it is. But I'm not sure I could lead you right to it."

"Cut him loose, Jubil," Eli said. "We'll manage. We can't trust him."

"Maybe all the more reason to keep him close," Jubil said.

"I knew that the Black brothers were not model citizens," Flynn said, "and still I went along with their shenanigans. But kidnapping a woman, I cannot abide. I'm going to throw in with you, Walker. And if you don't survive, I'll make a run for it. I have a knack for that."

Jubil nodded curtly. "You'll need your rifle."

"I'll fetch it from the barracks," Flynn said. He broke off and jogged toward the barracks.

Eli shook his head.

When they went into the stable, White Dog was coming down the ladder from the hayloft. As Jubil explained what had happened, he struggled to manage his rage and sorrow.

"We will find her, my friend," White Dog said, putting his hand on Jubil's shoulder.

White Dog's own wife had been killed during a battle with another tribe. He listened carefully as Jubil described their budding plan. White Dog offered to gather men from the reservation to help. Jubil knew they would be stealthier than soldiers, but he decided to keep the team small.

Jubil approached Doane as he saddled his horse. "Should we stop in to see Sheriff Mendenhall—tell him what's going on?" he said.

"He's a good man," Doane said. "But he goes by the law. He's liable to round up his own posse to do the job. Is that what you want?"

"No," Jubil said. "And now that I think about it, why would Black incriminate himself by writing this letter?"

"He's arrogant enough to think the law won't get involved," Doane said. "And he's connected enough that, even if it does, he probably thinks he could keep any judge or jury from holding him accountable."

Jubil had heard similar theories about why no one had ever tried to put an end to Phineas Black's illegal dealings. You couldn't raise a jury or find a judge that would convict him for fear of their lives.

Doane mounted up, and they were ready to go. Jubil and his small army set off for Bozeman at a gallop.

They rode straight for the Metropolitan Hotel. As they pulled up outside, Jubil said, "Eli and I will go in first. If we're not back in five minutes, come in after us."

Doane, White Dog, and Flynn maneuvered their horses away from the front door as passersby stole glances at the collection of riders.

In the lobby, Jubil and Eli looked around, their hands on their pistols. A few people milled about, and the dining room was crowded, but there was no sign of Black or McTavish. The desk clerk took notice of them standing there.

"Can I help you, gentlemen?" he said.

Jubil and Eli approached the counter. Jubil drew his pistol and laid it on the countertop with the barrel pointing at the clerk.

"I'm in a hurry here," he said evenly, "so I don't have time for evasive answers."

"Yes, sir," the clerk said, looking nervously from Jubil to the pistol to Eli and back to Jubil.

"Is Lucius Black here?"

"No sir."

"Do you know where he's gone?"

"No sir."

"When did he leave?"

"Very early this morning. He woke the cook well before dawn to fix breakfast for him and the men before they left."

"How many men?"

"Mr. Black, Mr. McTavish, and two other men."

Jubil and Eli exchanged a glance.

"We're looking for a young lady who may be held here against her will," Jubil said. "Would you have seen anything to make you suspect such a situation?"

"Oh no, sir," the clerk said emphatically. "All of our guests are quite happy to be here."

"Any empty rooms?"

"None," the clerk said, gesturing to the empty key slots behind him.

"What if we want to have a look in these rooms for ourselves?" Eli said.

"Well," the clerk said nervously, "I can't stop you, but I urge you not to create a disturbance. This is a reputable place, and we want to keep it that way. I assure you that no one is being held here against their will."

"All right," Jubil said, holstering his weapon. "If you see anything, you tell the sheriff."

"Yes sir," the clerk said.

Outside, Jubil and Eli mounted their horses, and the others joined them.

"We're wasting time," Jubil said. "Let's head for the mine."

CHAPTER 15

It was midafternoon before Jubil and his posse cleared the Bozeman Pass. From there, it was about a hundred twenty miles to Cooke City, a three-day ride on horseback at a steady pace. They might cut a day off that with a brisk pace and a night ride, but they couldn't push the horses too hard, or one of them might founder. If Jubil had been riding Apollo, he could have done it, but he wasn't sure about the mare.

As they rode south through Paradise Valley, along the west bank of the Yellowstone River, Jubil took no notice of the magnificent scenery and felt no joy at being there again. He had never felt the sense of urgency he was now experiencing. Images invaded his mind of Nelly being overpowered by McTavish's henchman, sedated, bound, and trapped in a rug. Surely, they had freed her by now and allowed her to revive. Had they harmed her in any way, beyond binding her and tossing her around like baggage? Amelia Doane's wrists had been rubbed raw after just a few hours. Surely, they had unbound her by now. Would they give her any privacy to answer nature's call? Would they manhandle or violate her? He could feel his face flush as murderous thoughts arose in his mind. *We're coming, Nelly*, he thought grimly. *Hold on.*

His companions moved around him and may have even spoken to him, but Jubil hardly noticed them. It was as though he were encased in a shroud that nothing could penetrate. Nothing would be right again until he got to Nelly and made sure she was safe.

The sun had dropped behind the Madison Range to the west as they approached Bottler's Ranch, about thirty miles from the pass. Though it was called a ranch, it was more a rest and supply center for miners and hunters. It was a collection of rough-built structures—a house, bunkhouse, stable, sheds—owned by a German hunter, Fredrick Bottler, and his fellow-bachelor brothers, Philip and Henry.

As Doane started to cross the river toward the ranch, Jubil stopped. "I think we should keep moving," he said.

Doane looked at him and frowned, and the others appeared to share his concern.

"That's not a good idea, Walker," Doane said calmly. "We can't get through Yankee Jim Canyon in the dark. The trail is too narrow. You know that."

Yankee Jim Canyon was twenty miles beyond Bottler's Ranch. McTavish and his crew would have passed through the canyon in the daylight, and they would be well on their way tomorrow before Jubil and company cleared it, unless they rode on tonight. Their horses had the stamina to continue.

"We need to catch up with them," Jubil said firmly. "There's no time to spare. I'm going on."

Doane pursed his lips as he stared at Jubil. Flynn and Eli exchanged a glance but neither spoke. White Dog rode up beside Jubil.

"No moon tonight, and rain may come," White Dog said. "The canyon will be very dangerous. Your heart is heavy, but you must stay alive to free her."

His friend's words penetrated Jubil's irrational resolve. He thought of White Dog's wife and how it must have felt to lose her.

Doane said, "The horses need to rest."

Eli nodded in agreement, and Flynn looked concerned but kept his thoughts to himself. Jubil relented and turned the mare to cross the river. As they approached the ranch, Fredrick Bottler stood watching.

"Evening, gents," Bottler said. He did not look askance at White Dog, which Jubil appreciated. "Will you be wanting to stable your horses?"

"Yes," Jubil said. "We could use a meal too."

"You've come to the right place," Bottler said, "if you'll eat venison stew."

"Did you happen to see some men traveling with a woman today?" Jubil asked.

"I did," Bottler said, sizing Jubil up with a look of curiosity—or suspicion.

"Were they traveling in a wagon or on horseback?" Jubil said.

"Three men and a woman pulled up in a wagon," Bottler said, "along with a bunch of other riders."

"A bunch?" Jubil said. "How many?"

"Not sure," Bottler said. "Seven? Eight, maybe?"

Jubil turned to his companions. "He must have picked up some guards along the way," he said. He asked Bottler, "Did the woman look all right?"

"More or less, I suppose," Bottler said. "Kind of nervous maybe. She didn't say anything. I thought it was an odd arrangement, but it wasn't my business."

"Did they stay around, or leave right away?" Jubil said, hoping they might have loitered there to allow him to gain ground on them.

"They bargained their wagon for two more horses," Bottler said, "and moved on. Something wrong?"

"We're trying to catch up with them," Jubil said, offering no more information.

"Hmm . . . well, ride on over to the corral, then come into

the house for supper," Bottler said, including White Dog in his invitation.

That night, Jubil lay awake for a long time, his mind racing, and then he finally fell into a fitful sleep. They had breakfast at dawn and made ready to leave. Jubil purchased a sack of jerky and one of hardtack, in case game or fish proved unavailable, and they were on their way south along the river. The weather since leaving Corinne had been dry, but it looked like their luck was about to run out. Gunmetal gray clouds roiled in the sky above them, and a fresh breeze whipped against Jubil's slicker.

Late that morning, they reached the point where the mountains closed in to form Yankee Jim Canyon—a narrow gap named after a prospector who had struck gold there in the 1850s. The trail rose steeply up the western side of the canyon wall until it reached a ledge that traversed the wall before winding back down to the river as the canyon opened up again. As they entered the canyon, a steady drizzle began. This would make the trail ahead even more hazardous, but waiting for better weather was out of the question. Even in good weather, the quarter-mile trail was challenging to cross. The surface was covered by an uneven layer of stones embedded in, or sitting loosely on, a bed of sandy dirt. The rain soon turned the dirt into puddles of slippery mud filling the gaps between the slick stones, making footing for the horses treacherous.

They rode single-file as they climbed up the canyon wall, Jubil in the lead, then Doane, White Dog, Eli, and Flynn. The trail leveled out and narrowed to a ledge wide enough for a wagon. There was plenty of room for a rider on horseback, but the long drop to the river made it feel precarious. If a horse faltered or if anything startled the animal, the consequences could be fatal.

Everyone but Eli was familiar with this stretch, and even though Jubil had traversed it several times, the horse he was riding probably had not. So far, the mare had proven calm and reliable. Jubil turned in the saddle to see how Eli was faring and saw no outward sign of panic.

The wind picked up and pushed Jubil's hat tighter to his head as he rode with his face down, helping his horse navigate the sloppy trail. He estimated they had covered almost half the distance of the ledge when the clouds opened up, and the drizzle turned into a downpour, reducing visibility to a few yards. Had it been raining this hard before they entered the canyon, he would have waited out the weather, but it was too late to turn back now.

Jubil's horse slipped on a rock, causing him to catch his balance in the saddle. At the same time, he flinched instinctively as he heard the sound of a rifle shot on his left and a ping to his right. A second later another shot, but this time no ricochet. He looked to his left across the canyon, but the rain was too heavy to tell where the shots had come from. The distance to the bottom of the canyon was several hundred feet, too far for the shots to have come from there.

Jubil stopped and called to Doane, behind him.

"Did you hear that?" Jubil said.

"I did," Doane said, his rifle at the ready. "Came from straight across from us."

Someone had climbed up the opposite wall, intending to ambush them by firing straight across the canyon.

The rest of his fellow riders were strung out in a line a few feet apart, all of them looking toward the opposite side of the canyon.

"Ambush!" Jubil shouted to his group. All of them already had their rifles in hand.

"Should we turn back?" Eli shouted.

"I wouldn't advise that," Doane said. "It's as far back as it is forward. Besides, at this distance, with this wind and rain, it'd take a lucky shot to hit us."

But bad luck for whoever they did hit, Jubil thought.

"Think we should fire back?" Jubil said to Doane. Again, he wished for Apollo. This was a poor place to learn whether his horse was gun shy. He should have thought of that earlier and tested her out.

"Wouldn't hurt," Doane said. "Probably a waste of ammo though."

Jubil raised his Henry rifle, levered a round into the chamber, and fired straight across the canyon, at nothing in particular. The mare remained calm, so he fired again. He waited a few seconds for a reply and looked for any sign of the shooters. He was surprised they did not return fire.

"I suppose we should move on then." Jubil said.

"Slow and steady," Doane said.

Jubil stood in his stirrups and shouted to the group.

"Five more minutes, and we'll be across," Jubil said. "Fire if you see anything, but otherwise don't waste the ammo."

White Dog slid off his horse, took its reins in hand, and walked forward, using the horse as a shield.

"Do what White Dog's doing," Jubil shouted to the others.

As soon as Jubil took a step forward, another shot rang out, then a ping and the buzz of the ricocheting bullet. That was close. The mare flinched a bit, but Jubil had the reins wrapped tightly in his left hand, and she walked forward with him. The puddles were getting deeper, hiding slick rocks and making the footing more precarious. He stumbled and nearly dropped his rifle into a muddy pool—he could not let that happen. He heard another shot but no ricochet. Behind him, someone returned fire.

Jubil's focus narrowed to nothing but the next few feet forward. One careful step at a time, and soon he would be at the end of this hazardous stretch. He had experienced a similar hypnotic focus once before, crossing the narrow ledge on the way to Longs Peak.

Another shot came his way, and Jubil impulsively felt the need to return fire. He stepped out in front of the mare and fired straight across the canyon. His horse had not flinched when he'd fired from her back, but the shot right in front of her face startled her. She stumbled backward and tried to rear but lost her footing and sat down in the mud. Jubil nearly lost his grip on the rifle as he tried to hold it and the reins at the same time. He tried to calm the mare by talking to her as she struggled to stand. Once she had regained her feet, he glanced behind him to see if the others were all still there. They were, and they were waiting for him to move.

He started forward again. He estimated another minute, maybe two, before they reached safety. The gunfire continued at random intervals, not a steady hail of bullets but a constant reminder of danger. As he plodded forward, a memory came of Sitting Bull during a battle with the soldiers who accompanied the 1873 Northern Pacific Railroad survey. At one point, as his men were fighting the soldiers, Sitting Bull had walked down the embankment on which his men were positioned and sat down. With gunfire from the soldiers spraying all around him, he sat calmly and lit his pipe. When he finished his smoke, he stood up and walked back up the embankment without being hit. *He must carry strong medicine,* Jubil remembered thinking. He patted the medicine bag that he was wearing and hoped its power held out, not only for him but for its original owner, White Dog, and the rest of the group.

He was now only a few yards from where the trail went behind a ridgeline and began its descent to the river.

Jubil was the first to reach safety, followed by Doane, White Dog, and Eli. The gunfire had never ceased, but none of the bullets had found its mark—until now. As Jubil watched Flynn make his way along the final yards of the trail, he heard the scream of a horse and saw the neck of Flynn's mount erupt in a spray of blood. The horse reared and stumbled, pulling Flynn off balance with the reins still wrapped tightly in his fist. The horse floundered, then gained its footing and panicked, still towing Flynn alongside it. It tried to run but slipped and slid over the edge of the trail. At the last second, Flynn freed his hand from the reins, but he could not stop the momentum from carrying him over the edge. Jubil watched in horror as the horse hit a flat-topped boulder about ten feet below the ledge, then rolled off and plummeted to the canyon floor. Flynn landed on his feet on the same boulder but fell no further. On three sides of him was a sheer drop.

Jubil and the others ran back along the ledge to help Flynn, leaving their horses tethered as best they could. Flynn was sitting on the boulder, huddled against the canyon wall with his knees up and his arms wrapped around them. Another shot rang out, and Jubil felt a rage rise in him that he could not control. He raised his rifle and fired round after round across the canyon, until his magazine was empty. Breathing rapidly, he reached in his pocket with a shaky hand to retrieve more ammunition and felt a hand on his shoulder.

"Take it easy, Jubil," Eli said with concern. "We need to conserve our ammunition."

Of course—Jubil had just reminded everyone else of that only moments ago. He took a deep breath and nodded to Eli, then stood his empty rifle against the canyon wall.

He had to do better if he was going to be of any use to Nelly. He turned his attention to Flynn.

"Stand up," Jubil called to him. "I'll try to reach you."

"It's my ankle," Flynn said. "It may be broken. I don't know if I can stand on it."

"Come on, Flynn," Jubil said. "You can do it. You have to."

Slowly, Flynn turned to face the wall, put his weight on his good ankle and stood, then tested his weight on his bad ankle. He flinched but found he could stand well enough to keep his balance.

"All right," Jubil said, "let's see if I can reach you."

Jubil lay down and extended his arms over the ledge toward Flynn, but a gap of about three feet still separated them. He considered jumping down and boosting Flynn up the side of the canyon, but there was barely enough space on the boulder for Flynn alone, and it was too wet and muddy to trust a stable landing. It was a miracle Flynn had landed there.

"Hold steady," Jubil said. "I have another idea."

During the Grand Canyon trip in 1869, Major Powell had found himself stranded on a rock wall, a short distance from the top. His and Jubil's climbing companion had removed his pants and dangled them over the edge for Powell to grasp. Then Jubil helped pull Powell up to safety. Jubil considered removing his pants but reconsidered and removed his slicker. It was longer and made of sturdier material.

"I'm going to lower my slicker down for Flynn to grab onto," Jubil said to Doane. "Once he has a grip, you and White Dog hold onto me and help pull him up."

White Dog nodded, and Jubil got in position. He lay flat on his stomach and dangled the slicker over the edge. White Dog and Doane sat on either side of him, braced and holding him by his legs.

"All right, Flynn," Jubil said. "Wrap the arms of the slicker in your fists and hold on tight. We're going to pull you up."

Flynn did as he was told.

"All right, he's got it," Jubil said to his companions. "Pull!"

White Dog and Doane struggled to find rocks in the trail to push against with their feet. Slowly, they pulled Jubil backward and pulled Flynn up. Jubil winced as the sharp rocks beneath him scraped his chest and belly. Flynn's hands cleared the edge, then his head. When his waist cleared the edge, Doane reached down and grabbed him by the belt and boosted him over the edge. Flynn collapsed on the ledge, panting. As Jubil stood up, another shot rang out, as if their attackers had been too busy watching Flynn's rescue to bother firing.

Jubil started to reload his rifle, but Eli covered the magazine chamber with his hand.

"We need to get out of here," Eli said, patiently. Jubil nodded. Eli was thinking more clearly than he was, and he was grateful for that.

With Jubil and Eli's help, Flynn was able to limp off the ledge. They had finally reached safety.

Doane took a look at Flynn's ankle, which had begun to swell. He moved it around a bit, which made Flynn wince.

"Just a bad sprain, I think," Doane said. "It's not broken."

"What do you think," Jubil said. "Can you manage with it?"

"I can," Flynn said.

Jubil saw determination in Flynn's face.

"All right, you're going to have to ride double with Eli," Jubil said. "Can you do that?"

"I can ride, but I'll need help mounting," Flynn said. "I lost my rifle too."

"Take this," Jubil said. He unbuckled and removed his revolver holster and handed it to Flynn. "I'll give you more ammunition later."

The rain finally stopped as they made their way down to the floor of the canyon. When they reached the river, White Dog rode up beside Jubil.

"I will find the shooters," White Dog said. "Make sure they do not follow us. Flynn needs a horse."

Jubil turned and looked at Doane for his opinion.

"Not a bad idea," Doane said.

"I'll go with you," Jubil said.

"No," White Dog said. "You go to your wife."

Images of Nelly being abducted flashed in his mind again, and he knew his friend was right—he could not stop moving forward toward freeing Nelly. He imagined White Dog must wish he could have done more to save his own wife.

Doane said, "I'll go with him."

"No," White Dog said. "I go alone. Meet you tonight."

"Be careful," Jubil said, knowing there was no point in quibbling with his friend. "We're going to push on to Baronett's Bridge. I hope to make it there by nightfall."

White Dog handed his reins to Jubil and crossed the river on foot. He headed north into the canyon as Jubil and the others continued south. The toll bridge was near Tower Falls, another thirty miles distant. Jubil hoped the horses would hold up.

The hours dragged by, and the rhythm of the falling rain and the syncopated clop of the horses' hooves became mesmerizing. As Jubil rocked in the saddle, he regretted that he had never mastered the art of sleeping while riding. He wished desperately for his mind to cease plowing the same ground over and over again.

Did he believe, as Abe had said, that he was invincible, or was he just selfish and stubborn? Why could he not let something go when it was so obviously out of his control? Now he was leading his friends into battle with the most ruthless man he had ever encountered, and any of them might be hurt or even killed. For the first time, he regretted ever going West, ever following what now seemed like a childish impulse to seek out adventure in the wilderness.

But as he explored his regrets, he recalled something Lucius Black had said about his brother—*whatever differences he had with you, that was no way to go about resolving them.* Obviously, he had said that only for the Bozeman sheriff's benefit, but the sentiment was still right. There was no reason he and Black couldn't coexist here peacefully, and kidnapping Nelly was uncalled for under any circumstances. This was all Black's doing, not Jubil's. He would do whatever was necessary to get her back, and if Black hurt or killed her, Jubil would dedicate his every breath to avenging her.

Late in the afternoon, it finally stopped raining, and Jubil and the others stopped to rest at a shady bend in the river near the confluence of the Yellowstone and Gardiner Rivers. Jubil had just passed the sacks of jerky and hardtack around when he saw White Dog coming their way riding a saddled horse and leading two others. He came to a stop beside Jubil.

"Shooters won't need them now," White Dog said.

Jubil felt no remorse for what had happened to their attackers.

Flynn chose the mount he preferred, and they set off again. The second horse was for Nelly, and the third they would leave with Jack Baronett.

They followed the Yellowstone as it veered off to the southeast and rose onto the high plateau of the Yellowstone Basin. A few miles ahead, they would cross the Yellowstone at the toll bridge and head northeast to the mine, where Jubil would recover Nelly or die trying.

CHAPTER 16

Throughout the afternoon, Jubil and the others were alert for another ambush, but none came. As they passed the point where Blacktail Deer Creek met the Yellowstone River, Jubil recalled camping there in 1871, when he was the guide for Captain Barlow, now Major Barlow, on his survey of the basin for the army. He and Barlow had not hit it off, and a lack of communication had resulted in their parties getting separated. Barlow had set off for the day expecting Jubil to catch up with him, but Jubil had not asked where Barlow planned to camp. They found each other again at Blacktail Deer Creek, where they both admitted their part in what could have been a deadly mistake. At the time, Jubil's focus was clouded by grief over the recent death of his business partner and friend, Luke Warner, and he had behaved recklessly. He couldn't let his worry over Nelly cause similar lapses of judgment now.

As sunset came, the party reached the bridge, just past the confluence of the Lamar River and the Yellowstone. It was constructed of heavy timbers, set in two spans, each about fifty feet long. Near the bridge was a small cabin and, beside it, a shed.

Standing outside the cabin stood a burly bald-headed fellow holding his rifle in the crook of his arm, cautiously watching as Jubil and his companions approached. Jubil stopped and turned to the group.

"Hold up here for a minute," Jubil said. "The lieutenant and I will ride up and talk to him."

As they approached, Jubil noticed Baronett's posture and expression relaxing a bit. Perhaps Doane's uniform was reassuring to him. They stopped but remained mounted.

"How do you do, Mr. Baronett?" Jubil said. "My name is Jubilee Walker, and this is First Lieutenant Doane, from Fort Ellis. You might recall, we passed through here a few years back, in 1871, with a survey crew."

"I knowed you looked familiar," Baronett said, "but I couldn't place you. Now I recall—you're that fellow that shot Phineas Black."

"Yes sir," Jubil said, not proud to be remembered as such.

"Well then, you're a friend of mine," Baronett said. "If I recall right, you knew that Everts fellow too."

"I did," Jubil said. "He's still alive and well, thanks to you."

A reward was offered after Truman Everts got lost during the 1870 Washburn Expedition, and Jack Baronett and a couple of his friends had located him, nearly starved to death after almost a month alone in the basin.

"Good for him," Baronett said. "What brings you here today?"

"I've got a serious problem." Jubil briefly explained their mission to rescue Nelly and why he had cause to believe it was Lucius Black who had abducted her.

"Damn! I'm surprised he would stoop that low," Baronett said, shaking his head. "He's even meaner than his brother. Phineas was a hothead, which you well know. But Lucius . . . he's cold."

"Did you see any riders come past today," Jubil said, "who had a woman with them?"

"I just might have," Baronett said. "Some riders passed by around noon—maybe a half-dozen in the group. The one that paid the toll, I recognized him as a miner. I couldn't see the rest of them real good cause it was raining like blazes, and they all had their heads down and covered. But one of them looked up and eyed me kind of strange-like. And that one had a mighty pretty face for a miner."

"Thank you. This information helps a lot," Jubil said. It was a relief just to hear that Nelly was alive and alert. As badly as he wanted to move on, he knew he needed sleep if he was to be alert himself when he caught up with Black, and the horses could go no further today.

"My companions and I need a spot to camp for the night," Jubil said. "We'll lay up here, if you don't mind. Maybe you can tell us something about the mine and where they might be holding her."

"Sure," Baronett said. "Pick a spot, and make yourselves to home. I just took down an elk yesterday, so I'll rustle us up some supper."

"Much obliged," Jubil said. He turned and signaled his companions to approach, then introduced them to Baronett.

They tended their horses and gathered wood for a camp-fire, and Baronett brought out a small cauldron of venison, potatoes, and carrots and hung it over the fire to boil.

As they ate supper, Jubil questioned Baronett.

"What can you tell us about the mine?" Jubil said.

"Funny thing about that since Lucius Black took over," Baronett said. "He's out for every penny he can squeeze. He's raised the ante for my protection money while increasing his use of my bridge considerably—back and forth to his mine." Jubil knew that Baronett had been paying Phineas Black to keep him from burning his bridge. He was not surprised to hear Lucius had continued that policy.

"Why do suppose that is?" Jubil said. "Is he taking more yield out of the mine?"

"Oddly," Baronett said, "he seems to be hauling more loads in than what he's hauling out. What he's carrying beats me."

Jubil and Flynn exchanged a look.

"Do you know where the mine is?" Jubil asked Baronett,

"I went up with O'Brien once," Baronett said. "Phineas Black was anxious to see my bridge built, and we rode up to get some men to help set the pilings." He described how to get there and the mine buildings and shafts. Flynn chimed in with additional details.

"All right, good," Jubil said. "Where do you think he's most likely to hold Nelly?"

"Well, the most comfortable quarters—if he's concerned with such," Baronett said, "would be the foreman's house. That's got a room in the back of the office where the foreman sleeps. Other than that, there's the bunkhouse and the barn. Surely Black is not evil enough to put her in the men's bunk-house or in the barn."

Jubil's stomach churned at the mental image of Nelly being held under such conditions. He felt his ears burn as his anger threatened to overflow.

"We need a plan," Doane said. "We can't just ride in there and shoot the place up. He'll kill her for sure if we do. We have to catch them by surprise." Doane turned to Baronett. "This meadow where the mine is situated. Is there another way into it, other than the main trail?"

"Yes, but you'd have to go in on foot," Baronett said. "The slope up through the trees is too steep for the horses."

"You're thinking we sneak in and rescue her?" Eli said.

"I am," Doane said. "We'll creep in the back way and make our way to the barn. Then we'll create some kind of distrac-tion, and in the confusion, some of us will free Mrs. Walker and take her to safety, while the others hold off the guards and try to capture Black and McTavish."

"I have a thought," Jubil said, looking at Flynn, "but it will require some boldness from you, Flynn. We need someone to find out exactly where Nelly is being held, how many guards there are and where they're posted, and where Black and McTavish are. Once you find out, you can meet us in the barn."

Flynn looked at Jubil incredulously. "You expect me to just ride in there and have a look around."

"Why not?" Jubil said. "You still work for him, don't you? He still trusts you, doesn't he?"

"Aye, but what earthly reason would I have for showing up at all?" Flynn said.

Jubil thought about it.

"Tell him I came back to the agency and threatened to kill you if you didn't tell me where he had taken Nelly. You tried to throw me off the trail by telling me that he had taken her to his mine camp near Idaho Falls. Then you high-tailed it to the Cooke City mine to tell him that I had rejected his terms."

"And how was I to know where to find him?" Flynn said.

"You made an educated guess—you've come to the mine before with O'Brien," Jubil said. "You injured your ankle on the way here."

Flynn frowned as he puzzled over Jubil's proposal.

"I don't think this is a good idea," Eli said. "I don't think we can trust him. What if he tells Black that we're coming for him?"

"He won't do that," Jubil said, looking at Flynn. "Will you, Shawn?"

Flynn met Jubil's gaze. "No."

White Dog said, "I go with him. For security."

"Does that make you feel better about the plan, Eli?" Jubil said.

"Yes," Eli said.

"White Dog," Jubil said, "while Flynn is with Black and McTavish, find out where they're holding Nelly and how many guards they have. Then wait for us in the barn."

White Dog nodded.

"Aye, it might work," Flynn said with a shrug. "I may as

well try to be useful. With this gimpy ankle, I won't be any use in a sneak attack. Black's a suspicious sort though."

"That's my main concern," Jubil said. "I'm not sure how he'll react when the attack starts—whether he'll turn on you. You need to separate yourself from them before we set the plan in motion. Tell them you have to relieve yourself, and then come meet us in the barn."

Flynn considered this for a moment. "Sure, and if he does suspect me," he said, "I'll try to lie my way out of it somehow, and failing that, I'll defend myself with your Colt revolver."

Jubil wished he had his revolver for the attack, but he would not leave Flynn unarmed.

"You believe that?" Eli said, shaking his head.

Jubil looked at White Dog for any sign of concern but saw none.

"I think it's a clever enough plan," Doane said. "Black might buy it and let his guard down. If he doesn't, it will at least confuse and worry him. Still some details to work out. Any suggestions about what kind of distraction to create?"

No one had any ideas.

"Hmm," Doane said. "We'll give that some thought. And after the distraction occurs, what is each of our assignment?"

"I want to help free Nelly," Eli said.

Jubil hesitated. He worried that Eli might panic, as he had on the Northern Pacific Railroad survey. But he couldn't deny him the chance to help rescue his sister.

Jubil nodded. "You and I will go after Nelly," he said. "White Dog, Doane, and Flynn hold down the guards and target Black and McTavish."

"Are we agreed then?" Doane said, and went over the whole plan again.

The group exchanged glances and nodded in agreement.

"I reckon I could join up with you fellows," Baronett said. "Lead you into the mine. Be another gun for you."

Jubil considered the idea. "I appreciate your offer, Mr. Baronett, I do," Jubil said. "But this isn't your fight. It's personal for us. You've been help enough."

Baronett nodded. "One more thing to consider," he said. "I think you'll find the trail on the other side of the river guarded. You might want to scout that before you set off."

Exhaustion finally brought Jubil a few hours of deep sleep, but he awoke while it was still full dark. He lay awake on his bedroll, staring at the stars and waiting for dawn. But dawn wouldn't come for another hour or so, and the others were still sleeping soundly. The campfire had burned down to a pile of glowing embers, and he decided to get up and stoke it.

He added some wood to the fire and then sat on a log, staring into it and poking it with a long stick. Jubil had been struggling mightily to keep his darkest thoughts from dragging him into the pit of despair, but there were times when he was unable to resist them. What if Black killed Nelly as soon as Jubil attacked? What if he had already killed her? How could Jubil ever avenge her death? How could he live with the guilt of having brought her into this world of lawlessness and murder? How could he live at all? What joy would there ever be in life again? It would be nothing but a series of activities with no purpose.

He had to get his wits about him, or he'd be no use to Nelly when he finally reached her.

Just then, White Dog arose and came to sit silently with him and watch the fire. A few minutes later, Doane stirred and got up to join them.

Jubil poked at the fire and looked at his companions. He was grateful to have them by his side. There was no one he would trust his life with more than them. An urge to get on with it drove the dark thoughts back into their lair. He was ready to move on.

"Maybe we should go see if Baronett was right about those guards," Jubil said.

"White Dog and I took care of that while you were sleeping," Doane said. "We can expect to find seven men at the mine camp: Black, McTavish, and five guards."

Jubil did not question how Doane had gained this information or what had become of the guards. The lieutenant had his own grudge to settle with these men for their treatment of his wife. How he did that was of no concern to Jubil.

Soon enough, Eli and Flynn joined them at the fire. They finished off Baronett's elk stew, then made ready to leave. Flynn's ankle was more swollen and painful than it had been yesterday, but he insisted he could do his part. Jubil wondered vaguely if he could really trust Flynn, who had always gone whichever way benefitted him most. But what choice did he have at this point? Doane gave Flynn the holster and revolver of one of the guards, and Flynn returned Jubil's Colt revolver. They were ready to go.

CHAPTER 17

The trail to the mine meandered along the path of the Lamar River as it flowed toward the Yellowstone. They went straight east for a while, then angled southeast into the Lamar Valley. The weather was warm and dry, and it would have been a pleasant day for a ride, if not for their mission. Jubil felt oddly calm. He knew the importance of keeping calm in order to survive, and nothing was more important than what he was about to do. Nelly was depending on him.

It was around noon when they reached the confluence of the Lamar River and Soda Butte Creek, about halfway to the mine. Doane rode up beside Jubil.

"You want to take a short break?" Doane said.

Jubil agreed, and everyone dismounted. They ate a meager lunch of jerky and hardtack and then rode on. Jubil took the time to appreciate his horse.

"I can't get too attached, old girl," he said patting the mare on the neck, "but thank you. You've been a good partner. Keep up the good work."

The horse turned her head and gave Jubil the side-eye. Growing up, he had always talked to Star as if she were a friend, and he had just continued the habit with other horses. He had a moment of yearning to be back in Council Bluffs, tending to Star, Apollo, Comet, and Rocky. He imagined Nelly sitting in the gazebo reading a book, the ends of her beautiful black hair lifted by the breeze. The thought that he might never witness a scene like this again was almost too much to bear.

"How much longer before we get there?" Eli said, waking him from his daydream. He had ridden up beside Jubil without him noticing.

"We're about halfway," Jubil said. "How are you holding up?"

"I'm ready," Eli said. "You can count on me, Jubil. I won't choke. We're going to get her out of there and teach those men a lesson."

"Yes, we are," Jubil said. He was glad to hear Eli's boastful bravado. This was the Eli he had known growing up. Always making bold declarations. But then the first time he had faced real danger, on the 1872 Northern Pacific Railroad survey, he had panicked. It had taken him some time after that to regain his confidence, but you wouldn't know it hearing him today. Jubil hoped Eli's bravado would hold up when they needed it most.

Midafternoon, they reached a bend in Soda Bluff Creek where its course turned east. A few hundred feet beyond the bend, Jubil spotted the narrow trail Jack Baronett had described, rutted by wagon tracks and pack animals, that led away from the main trail and headed north toward the mountains.

"Is this our turnoff?" Jubil stopped and turned in his saddle to call out to Flynn. The group rode up to where Jubil had stopped.

"Yes, I think so," Flynn said, looking around to get his bearings.

They followed the wagon tracks north until they came to a creek running along the base of the mountains. They followed the creek for another thirty minutes before Jubil noticed something that made him stop.

"There's where the creek comes down the mountainside,"

Jubil said once the others had joined him. He pointed several hundred feet further down the trail. "Just to the right of the creek, you can see the trail winding up the slope to a flat spot. I think that's the meadow we're looking for."

"Good eye," Doane said. He reached inside his jacket and drew out a small collapsible telescope. He scanned the area that Jubil had indicated and then handed the telescope to Jubil.

Through the glass, Jubil could see the whole layout clearly. Part of the mountainside had sheared off, leaving a solid rock wall as a backdrop for the large meadow spread out in front of it. According to what Baronett had told them, the entrance to the mine was in that rock wall, and the mine buildings sat in the meadow.

"That's it all right," Jubil said.

"Good," Doane said. "They'll have guards on that trail coming up to the meadow, but if we go up the mountainside right here until we're even with the meadow and then make our way over to it, we can bypass the trail and come into the meadow right at that rock wall."

Jubil handed the telescope to White Dog, who looked through it and then passed it to Flynn, who passed it to Eli.

"We need to split up here," Jubil said.

He turned to White Dog and Flynn. "You two go on up to the mine. When you come to the guards, what will you tell them, Flynn?"

"That I work for Black at the Crow Agency. That I have important news for Black. Assuming they don't just shoot us," he concluded, his old sarcasm reinvigorated.

"Defend yourselves if you have to," Jubil said. "We'll go on with the raid as best we can."

Jubil turned to White Dog. "You'd better go by another name. Black won't recognize your face, but he might recognize your name as associated with me."

"Call me Standing Horse," White Dog said to Flynn.

They reviewed the plan once more.

"I'll not be able to make much of a run for it on this bum ankle," Flynn said, with raised eyebrows.

"Just do what you can to help keep the guards at bay," Jubil said to Flynn, "while Eli and I get Nelly."

He turned to Eli. "Then you'll take her to where we leave our horses, and wait there for me."

Eli nodded.

"Thanks for your help," Jubil said to Flynn, offering a handshake. He rode over to White Dog. "Thank you," he said, and they clasped forearms. "Be careful."

White Dog nodded.

Flynn turned his horse and rode up the trail toward the mine, with White Dog following. Jubil's stomach began to flutter as he thought about how close he was to Nelly. She was just ahead in one of those buildings, hoping with all her might that he would come for her soon. He struggled to get ahold of his wits.

"Let's ride up the slope into the woods," Doane said, "and find a place to leave the horses."

They left the trail and crossed the shallow creek, then rode up the slope of the mountain through the trees until the terrain became too difficult. They hitched their horses near a little brook with a grassy bank, hidden from the trail below by a pile of boulders, then they continued up the slope on foot.

The climb was not difficult, but it was littered with rocky outcroppings, boulders, and deadfall. If they delayed too long in freeing Nelly, and Eli had to escape this way in the dark, the footing would be difficult, and it would be impossible to cover at a run. Finding the horses would also be a problem. Jubil looked up at the mountain for a landmark to guide them back to the horses, and pointed out a notched spire of rock to Eli.

After they had been climbing awhile, they came even with the meadow and started across the mountainside, through the trees. The forest was thinner there, as the tree line was only a few hundred yards further upslope. This made travel easier but left them more exposed as they approached the mine. Doane suggested they spread out and, one at a time, dash from one point of cover to the next. Soon, Doane stopped and signaled Jubil and Eli to come to him.

Doane handed Jubil the telescope. "This is a good spot to scope out the mine," he said.

Jubil saw through the scope that the meadow was covered in knee-high grass. The creek flowed down from the mountain and into a pond in the meadow. The mine buildings were all in a row facing them on the far side of the mine entrance—the barn closest to the rock wall, the corral attached to the barn. The bunkhouse and the foreman's house were situated closer to the front of the meadow, where the trail came up from the valley. There was a guard patrolling the foreman's house. Jubil could not see the back of the house, but he imagined a guard would be posted there as well. As Doane had predicted, two guards were posted at the front of the meadow, where the trail came up from the valley below. Their most immediate threat was the guard posted where they would come into the meadow near the rock wall, probably placed there to prevent anyone coming in from the very direction from which they approached. This guard was sitting on a rock beside the pond with his back to them, about fifty yards out from the rock wall. Jubil handed the telescope to Eli.

"Do you think we need to take that guard by the pond out in order to get to the barn?" Jubil asked Doane.

"I'm concerned about drawing the attention of the other guards," Doane said. "It would be better to sneak past him."

"I don't see any sign of Flynn or White Dog," Eli said. "Is that good or bad? Shouldn't they be there by now?"

"We could keep watch for a while," Doane said.

"I think we should get on with it," Jubil said.

Doane nodded. Eli handed the telescope back to Doane, who pocketed it.

"Maybe we could creep along the rock wall through the meadow grass?" Eli said.

"That might work," Jubil said. "Good thinking."

"Let's move to that outcropping right at the edge of the rock wall," Doane said. "We'll be exposed as we cross the creek, so we'll have to hustle."

Doane led out, dodging between trees, then ducking low and wading across the creek. From there he stayed low and sprinted for the cover of the outcropping. Eli followed, then Jubil.

From this angle they could see the guard rolling a cigarette. As he busied himself, Jubil peered around the corner to study the length of the rock wall.

This close, he could see that the meadow grass did not extend all the way to the wall. The ground was barren for about thirty feet in front of it, so Eli's idea to conceal themselves would not work. It was about five hundred feet from their position to the barn. The entrance to the mine was about halfway to the barn. Between their position and the mine entrance, three wooden ore carts were parked in a row. Between the mine entrance and the barn sat a pile of lumber and timbers stacked about four feet high, parallel to the wall. Jubil ducked back as the guard looked up and licked his rolled-up smoke to seal it.

Jubil described the way forward to Doane and Eli.

"We're just going to have to watch the guards closely," Doane said, "and when we have a chance, sprint from one cover to the next."

"What if we're spotted?" Eli asked.

"We'll have to shoot it out," Doane said. "Go for the closest guard first."

"If we're seen," Jubil said, "We should make a dash for the foreman's house."

Doane nodded. "I'll lead out, then Eli, then you," he said.

"Move smartly."

The guard lit his smoke, then stood up and stretched. He turned his back to them and looked across the pond, his rifle propped against the rock he had been sitting on. The guard in front of the house was also looking in another direction. Doane made his move. He rounded the corner of the rock wall and crouched low as he moved quickly toward the row of ore carts. Reaching them safely, he turned and signaled to Eli, who followed Doane's example and also made it safely to cover.

The guard at the pond reached down, picked up a stone, and skipped it across the water. Then he strolled along the bank as he smoked, looking for another suitably flat one. As he reached down, Jubil made his move. As he reached cover, Doane and then Eli moved on to the next point, successfully ducking into the entrance to the mine.

Jubil peeked between two of the ore carts. When the pond guard finished his smoke, he tossed the butt into the water and picked up his rifle. As he turned to have a look around, Jubil pulled back out of sight. He crouched and listened for the sound of the guard's footsteps approaching but heard nothing. He made sure his feet were out of sight behind the cart's wheels. He was about to peek out from around the cart again when he heard the guard whistle. He felt a surge of alarm and risked a look to see if the guard was summoning someone to come to his aid. But he was signaling to the guard in front of the foreman's house by pointing into the woods. Was he drawing the other guard's attention to something? No, when the house guard nodded, the pond guard tucked his rifle casually into the crook of his arm and walked into the woods—probably for a toilet break.

Doane signaled to Jubil to move again. As Jubil dashed for the mine entrance, Doane and then Eli ran behind the pile of lumber stacked parallel to the rock wall. They were now close to the barn.

Jubil ducked into the entrance of the mine and ducked

behind an ore cart parked just inside the entrance. The guard returned from the woods and began a conversation with the guard in front of the foreman's house. While the two of them were occupied, Jubil moved from the mine entrance to the lumber pile. From there he was out of sight of the foreman's house. He removed his hat and peeked around the end of the lumber pile at the guard by the pond. When his moment came, Jubil slipped out from behind the lumber pile, ran behind the barn, and slipped inside, where Doane, Eli, and White Dog were sitting on bales of hay.

"Any trouble?" Jubil asked White Dog.

White Dog shook his head. "Trail guard knows Flynn. Rode right in. No problem."

"Good," Jubil said. "And Black?"

White Dog shrugged. "Flynn sends me to stable horses. He goes with Black."

"Where to?" Jubil said.

"Bunkhouse."

"Was McTavish there?"

White Dog nodded.

"But you've heard nothing from him since?"

White Dog shook his head.

"All right," Jubil said. "We can wait for him a little while longer. Is Nelly in the foreman's house?"

"Yes," White Dog said. "I ask guard for smoke. He tell me front part of house is office, back part bedroom. She is in bedroom. I count five guards—two at house, two at trail, one at pond."

Jubil nodded. "That confirms what we saw as well. Thank you."

"While we wait for Flynn," Doane said, "we should discuss your idea for a distraction. I think we need something big."

"Maybe we should burn down the barn," Eli said.

"That's good," Doane said.

"Whatever you think," Jubil said, anxious to get on with it.

CHAPTER 18

It was all Jubil could do to keep himself from heading straight for the foreman's house and gunning down anyone who tried to stop him. He sat calming himself, gathering his wits. He had to stick to the plan.

He looked around the barn. Tools for logging, carpentry, and mining lined the walls. In the center of the main room was a new ore cart under construction. Stacked along one wall were dozens of small empty wooden boxes, probably used to haul ore out—or Black's gold in. Against another wall were two large wooden crates. Jubil walked over to examine them. One was a crate of dynamite with five sticks remaining. The other held rolls of fuse cord. The thought came to him unbidden: *Black took from me what matters most, and I'll do the same to him.*

"I have another idea," Jubil said to his companions, brandishing a roll of fuse cord. "I'm going to blow up Black's gold mine."

Eli's jaw dropped. Doane grinned. White Dog nodded.

Jubil and Doane examined the crates of dynamite and fuses.

"Do you think this is enough?" Jubil said. The only experience he had with explosives was black powder. When Jubil was very young, his father had used it to blow stumps out of the ground. But he had only watched that process. He had never set a charge himself.

"Four sticks will make a hell of a blast," Doane said. "Place two at each top corner of a set of support timbers, and you'll bring down at least enough rock to block the entrance—but maybe a lot more. We'll hold one stick in reserve."

Doane unrolled one of the coils of fuse cord. "These are about four feet long," he said. "Once you light the fuse, you'll have about two minutes to get clear."

Jubil picked out four sticks of dynamite and four rolls of fuse cord.

"I thought we were going to wait for Flynn," Doane said.

"What time do you think it is?" Jubil said.

"I'd say we have about two hours of daylight left," Doane said.

"I hope he's all right," Jubil said. "But we have to get on with it."

"Maybe he's perfectly fine," Eli said. "After Black accepted him without question, maybe he's switched sides again. Or maybe he never was on our side."

Since Black hadn't come for them yet, he either didn't know they were there, or he was waiting for them to make their move.

"We don't have time to wait around to find out," Jubil said. "I'm going to set the charges, light the fuses and get back here. As soon as it blows, we'll rush the foreman's house. Eli and I will break in and free Nelly. Doane and White Dog, you hold off anyone who tries to stop us. Eli will take Nelly back to where we left the horses." He looked at White Dog and Doane. "Then we will finish the job of bringing Black and his men to justice. I hope we'll find Flynn in the process."

Jubil looked to each man for confirmation.

"All right then," he said. "Here I go."

He crept out of the barn. The pond guard wandered up and back along the shore. These guards took their duties very casually. Maybe Flynn had told Black that Jubil was on his way to

Idaho Falls, and maybe Black believed him. Jubil ducked behind the lumber pile, then waited and watched for another opportunity to move. When it arose, he ran for the mine entrance.

He ducked inside and looked down the horizontal tunnel ahead of him. Only a few feet in, the sunlight faded to shadow and then to inky darkness. A musty, earthy smell hung in the air. He felt drawn to see what was at the end of this tunnel. Was Flynn's secondhand story about a cache of gold true? There had to be something big behind this campaign that Lucius Black, and his brother Phineas before him, had waged against Jubil. Was the answer at the end of this tunnel? He would never have another opportunity to find out.

On the wall beside him was a crude wooden shelf holding three lanterns and a matchbox. He lit one of the lanterns and started down the tunnel. Log support timbers placed every few feet shored up the walls, and the floor was covered by planks used as a track for the ore carts.

He had gone no more than a hundred feet in when the full realization of what was overhead captured his imagination. He was an ant, crawling along a little tunnel inside a massive conglomeration of earth and rock. He had experienced this feeling of smallness once before, the first time he rode the ferry across the sound to Nantucket Island and saw the expanse of the ocean. Now, he was unsettled by the complete silence of the tunnel, broken only by the dull thud of his boots on the plank railway. His lantern flickered, casting shadows that danced on the walls. He hoped his lantern did not run out of oil—he hadn't checked it.

As he walked further into the mine, he passed side tunnels, but most of those played out only a few yards in. The ones he could not see the end of, he did not venture down. He could not get lost. Ahead, another tunnel branched off, and he decided to look into it but go no further. When he reached the mouth of the tunnel, he could see immediately that there was something different about it. Where the main tunnel support timbers were spaced out every few feet, this tunnel was lined with them. The tunnel was only about twenty feet long, and what he saw at the end of it gave him chills—a set of iron bars with a door chained and padlocked like a prison cell.

As he walked toward the barred chamber, the timbered walls closed in tight around him, and the eerie sense of his own insignificance returned. But this time, that odd sensation was combined with a feeling of dread, bordering on fear. The place was sinister. Jubil fought back thoughts of being buried alive in there.

When he reached the wall of iron bars, he turned up the wick on his lantern and slipped it between two bars, extending his arm slowly while searching for any sign of a trap that he might be about to trigger. But nothing happened, and he extended his arm as far as he could reach. What he saw at the back of the chamber almost made him lose his grip on the lantern handle.

The cell was about ten feet deep, and on the floor, near the back wall, sat stacks of gold bars arranged in a roughly four-foot cube. Even in the gloomy atmosphere, the lantern light sparkled off the surface of the gold ingots. There were hundreds of bars there—millions of dollars' worth.

Here was the origin of all the trouble Jubil had endured at the hands of the Black brothers and their henchmen. Some mined and smelted by Phineas, and some brought in for safe keeping by Lucius from his California strike. And Lucius Black wanted as few people as possible to know that it was there.

Jubil made his way quickly back down the main tunnel, seething again with anger. Blowing up the mine would serve two purposes, he decided: he would have his revenge on Lucius Black, and he would keep the gold from anyone else who knew it was there. If he and his crew were successful in freeing Nelly and bringing Black and his men to justice, it wouldn't make sense to leave the mine sitting wide open, for anyone to plunder. If he blew up it up, anyone could mine it out again, but it would take weeks or months. Burying it might give the authorities time to sort out who legally owned the mine, if Black was out of the picture.

Near the mine entrance, Jubil extinguished the lantern. He located a set of four support timbers with gaps large enough for him to slip the charges into the upper corners. He unrolled the fuses, placed them in the charges, and lit them. He ran for the tunnel exit, stopping briefly to look for the pond guard and then running for the stack of lumber.

He looked through a gap between the boards. The pond guard was facing his way with his rifle at the ready. Had he heard Jubil running or caught a fleeting glimpse of him? If Jubil ran for the barn now, the guard would see him, but he couldn't stay there for long—he didn't want to be this close when the charges blew. He moved to the end of the lumber stack and looked at the barn, a hundred feet away.

When he looked around the end of the lumber pile, he saw that the guard had taken a few wary steps in his direction. Jubil crouched low and ran. A shot rang out, and a spray of dirt flew up a few feet in front of him. Jubil heard the guard running toward him, and then the dynamite exploded.

Jubil fell to the ground and covered his ears and head as the deafening blast shot a cloud of dust and debris out of the tunnel entrance like a massive cannon. He looked back over his shoulder and watched as the guard landed twenty feet back from the mine entrance and lay there, unmoving. Jubil jumped up and ran to the barn, where his friends were waiting.

When Doane saw that Jubil was all right, he grinned. "That should get their attention," he said.

Eli handed Jubil's rifle to him.

"Let's move," Jubil said. His hearing was muffled, and his ears were ringing.

He led out from behind the barn and moved swiftly past the corral. The horses milled about, agitated by the blast. The two trail guards and the two guards at the foreman's house had abandoned their posts and were running toward the mine and their fallen companion. Black and McTavish burst out of the bunkhouse and, like the others, ran toward the mine. Thirty seconds later, Flynn emerged and limped toward the meadow.

Jubil and his friends took advantage of the confusion to make their way to the bunkhouse, situated between the barn and the foreman's house. As they ran for cover, the guards gathered around their fallen companion. One of the guards knelt to check for signs of life, while the others stood watch with rifles at the ready. Black started toward the mine entrance, but McTavish held him back.

Jubil said to Eli. "We've got to make a break for it. Ready?"

Eli nodded.

"We'll cover you," Doane said. "Go!"

Jubil and Eli ran toward the foreman's house. Doane and White Dog dove out from behind the bunkhouse and lay prone to fire at the men gathered in the meadow. When the firing started, Black and McTavish dropped to the ground in the tall grass. One of the guards was hit and fell dead. The other three ran for the cover of the lumber pile. When Jubil and Eli reached the back of the foreman's house, Jubil peeked around the corner to make a quick assessment of the situation.

"We've got to hurry!" he said to Eli.

Doane and White Dog moved to the corral, where they were crouched behind the water trough for cover. From there they could keep the guards at bay behind the lumber pile. Flynn was now limping toward the foreman's house, having changed course when Black and McTavish rose from the grass and ran in that direction, fast.

The foreman's house was a small crudely built wood-frame

building with a door in the center of the back wall and one small boarded-up window. Jubil tried the door.

"We'll have to break it down." They threw themselves at the door in tandem, and there was a loud crack, but nothing gave way. The wasted seconds seemed like minutes.

"Again—harder!" Jubil said. This time they made a short run at the door, and when they hit it, the bar inside broke in half, and the door flew open. They stumbled through the doorway to find Black and McTavish already in the back room.

Lucius Black stood to Jubil's right, holding Nelly tightly in front of him like a shield, with his pistol pointed at Jubil and Eli. Jubil nearly cried out at Nelly's bedraggled appearance. Tears streaked her unwashed face. She was barefoot, wearing the same dress as when he had last seen her, but it was now soiled and ripped at the hem. Her hair was bunched up in a rough untidy braid with strands hanging loosely around her face. She clutched her hands to her chest. Her left forearm had been rubbed raw by the too-tight manacle on a chain that tethered her to the iron bedstead. Jubil's heart broke with a desperate love for her, and his head swam with rage.

Standing next to the open office door was McTavish, his pistol also trained on Jubil and Eli.

"Set your rifles down very gingerly," Lucius Black said. "And keep your hands well away from those sidearms. You make a move, I'll shoot her."

Jubil and Eli complied. Outside, occasional gunfire still rang out.

Black turned to McTavish. "Where's Flynn?"

"He was right behind us coming in," McTavish said, glancing back through the doorway.

"I'm right here," Flynn said, stepping into the room and coming to stand beside Black, putting his weight on his good leg. "This gimpy ankle is slowing me down." He held his revolver in his hand. "Followed me here, did you, Walker? Sure, and you've been a thorn in my side for the last time. You're making me look bad amongst my associates."

"I told you we couldn't trust him," Eli said to Jubil with a high note of disgust in his voice.

Jubil stared at Flynn, who stared back, expressionless. How could he have been so wrong about him?

"Where are Walker's other friends?" Black said to Flynn.

"Still shooting it out with your men," Flynn said. "They're at a standoff—your boys are pinned down in front of the mine. Walker's men are behind the corral water trough."

"Check to see that they're not coming this way," Black said to MacTavish, keeping his gun pointed at Jubil.

McTavish walked a few steps toward the front door of the foreman's house before returning to hold Jubil and Eli at gunpoint. "They're still in the corral," McTavish said.

"It's too bad, Walker," Black said, turning his full attention to Jubil. "I thought we might be able to find a way past our differences, but it looks like there's only one way I'm going to be rid of you for certain." Black cocked his pistol, then smiled and turned to Flynn.

"Perhaps you'd like to do the honors, Mr. Flynn?" Black said.

"Don't mind if I do," Flynn said. He raised his pistol, and Jubil had the familiar sensation of time slowing to a crawl. Knowing that he had nothing to lose, he moved to draw his gun. As his hand swung toward his holster, he saw Flynn turn toward Black and fire. Black's head exploded in a spray of blood and gray matter, splattering Nelly.

McTavish recoiled with shock and fired his own gun by accident, sending a bullet sailing toward Jubil. He felt a slap in the palm of his left hand and realized the bullet had passed straight through it—the wound didn't even hurt. He drew his pistol and fired from the hip at McTavish. The round hit him in the chest and threw him backward against the wall. As he fell to the floor, Flynn aimed at McTavish and fired again. The room rang with the echoes of the shots and then went silent.

Jubil instinctively pointed his pistol at Flynn but did not fire. Flynn met Jubil's gaze, and they stared at one another for a long moment. Then Flynn dropped his pistol and put his hands up.

Jubil holstered his gun and ran to Nelly, who collapsed in his arms.

"I knew you would come," she said, weeping uncontrollably.

He pressed her face to his chest to shelter her from the scene and wiped the gore from her hair with his sleeve as best he could.

Eli stepped up to take a look at Jubil's hand. "We've got to get that bound up," Eli said. "The bleeding's steady but not gushing. I don't think it hit any major blood vessels."

He tore a strip from the sheet on the bed and began to wrap a makeshift bandage around Jubil's hand.

"Where have you been?" Jubil said to Flynn as Eli tended to his wound. "Why didn't you join us like we planned?"

"I couldn't join your escape on this game leg," Flynn said. "I should have admitted it before I even rode in here, but I was determined to follow your plan. Once I got here, I realized I would just slow you down. I decided to bide my time and wait for my chance to help out. When the explosion happened, I hobbled after Black and McTavish as fast as I could," Flynn said. He looked down at Black and McTavish. "I was almost too late. You set off that explosion?"

"I blew up the mine," Jubil said.

"Jayzus," Flynn said, shaking his head.

Jubil winced as Eli tied the bandage tightly around his hand. As the shock of the injury wore off, the pain increased.

Eli tore another strip of bedsheet and tenderly wrapped his sister's wounded forearm. "We've got to get Nelly out of here," he said. "I don't hear any gunfire. I'll go check on Lieutenant Doane and White Dog." He went out the back door.

Flynn went to McTavish's body and started going through his pockets. Was he ransacking the dead man for valuables?

"What are you doing?" Jubil said angrily.

Flynn retrieved something from McTavish's vest pocket and held it up—a key. He went to Nelly, removed her shackle, and dropped it to the floor.

Her weeping now more under control, Nelly rubbed her bandaged wrist. "Thank you," she said.

Jubil kept Nelly positioned so that she did not have to look at the bodies of the dead men. He was concerned about how she would cope with the bloody scene she had just witnessed. The first time he had seen someone shot in the head, he had vomited and then had nightmares for days. Eli had had the same reaction. Nelly had not vomited, but that did not mean she wasn't deeply disturbed.

Eli stuck his head back inside the door.

"Doane says we're going to have to mount an attack on the guards to root them out from behind the lumber pile," Eli said.

"Tell him to hold up a minute," Jubil said. He turned to Nelly. "Will you be all right staying here in this house for a few minutes more, while we go finish this off?"

Nelly nodded.

"I'll stay with her," Eli said, approaching Nelly carefully.

"Good," Jubil said. "I'll be back soon."

He turned to Flynn. "Will you stay here too?"

Flynn nodded.

Jubil reached for his rifle with his right hand and winced as he laid the stock across his bandaged left palm. He was not going to be able to use it very well. He adjusted it to rest on the back of his left forearm and stepped out the door.

He could see Doane and White Dog crouched behind the water trough in the corral, watching the lumber pile. Jubil crouched low and ran to join them.

"You're hit," Doane said as Jubil settled beside him.

"Could have been worse," Jubil said.

"I think they're conserving ammo and waiting for dark, to make a run for it—or come for us," Doane said.

"I want to try something," Jubil said.

He peeked over the top of the water trough. No one fired.

"You men!" Jubil shouted. "Listen up! Black and McTavish are dead, and the mine has been destroyed. Come out with your hands up, and we'll take you to face the law. Fight it out, and you'll die here."

"We're not coming out!" a voice called out a few seconds later. "You'll shoot us down anyway. We've got more right to that gold than you do!"

"They think this is about the gold mine?" Doane said to Jubil.

"Isn't it?" He told Doane and White Dog what he had found in the mine.

Doane raised his eyebrows. White Dog looked unimpressed.

"I'm not going to be much use in a gunfight," Jubil said, holding up his damaged hand. "I'd sure hate to lose either one of you to that scum behind the woodpile. How can we flush them out without having to charge them?"

Doane stroked his walrus mustache. "There's one more stick of dynamite left," he said. "You go on back to the foreman's house. I'll fetch the charge from the barn and then sneak out and lob it behind the pile of lumber. That should do it. Cover me, White Dog."

White Dog nodded.

Jubil returned to the foreman's house and found Nelly and Eli sitting on the bed. Eli had his arm around her, and her head was resting on his shoulder. He had never witnessed this sort of tenderness between them. Seeing them made closer by this trauma was a bit of a silver lining to an otherwise grim affair.

"Prepare yourselves for another explosion," Jubil said as he entered the room. As if on cue, the blast went off.

"What was that for?" Flynn said.

"Lieutenant Doane was clearing out the rest of the vermin Black brought here with him," Jubil said.

Eli got up when Jubil went to the bed and knelt in front of Nelly, taking her cold shaking hands in his gingerly, being careful of his wound. Her crying was under control now, but her eyes and nose were red.

"Does it hurt badly?" she asked, looking at his bloody bandage.

"Not so much. It'll be fine," he said softly, feeling his eyes begin to burn. "How about you? Did they hurt you?"

"No," she said weakly, "not as badly as I feared. My ears are ringing from the gunfire."

She started to cry again, and he pulled her into his arms, holding her as best he could, and let himself cry with her. Another wave of rage came over him, even though Black and McTavish lay dead on the floor.

He leaned back to wipe his eyes. "Let's get you out of this room."

He stood, took the blanket off the bed, and wrapped it around her shoulders.

"I don't like the idea of spending the night here," he said to Nelly, "but it's too late in the day to set out now. We'll leave first thing in the morning. Let's go get you settled."

Jubil put his arm around Nelly and led her out the back door. Eli and Flynn followed them out. Doane and White Dog were coming their way.

The groups met midway to the bunkhouse and assessed their situation.

"Looks like we got them all," Doane said.

"What are we going to do with those two?" Jubil said to Doane, pointing at the bodies of the guards in the meadow.

"I'll put them in the house with the other two," Doane said. "That's good enough. There's not enough left of the other three to bother with."

Jubil would have preferred that Nelly had not heard that, but she was already in shock, and she showed no reaction. Jubil nodded and looked around at the area. He was relieved not to see any body parts strewn about in the meadow.

"All right," Jubil said. "What about the horses?"

"I'll go fetch them," Doane said.

Jubil nodded and continued with Nelly to the bunkhouse while Eli and White Dog dragged the guards' bodies into the foreman's house.

"Let's get you more comfortable," Jubil said to Nelly. "Would you like to wash up a little?"

Nelly nodded.

Jubil helped Nelly unwrap the bandage from her wrist. She soaked her forearm in the cold creek, which soothed it a bit, and washed her hands and face. Jubil washed his damaged hand and was encouraged that it didn't look as bad as he feared, but it was hurting badly.

In the bunkhouse, Eli tore more strips from the sheet and rewrapped their wounds, then he went through the pantry in the kitchen and Flynn helped him make a pot of beans and rice for supper. After Doane and White Dog returned, they all sat around the table together, and Jubil told them about the gold stash he had found in the mine.

"What do you think will become of it?" Eli said.

"I don't know," Jubil said. "Black may have relatives or a partner he left it to. I'm not sure what happens if he doesn't. It may not matter though. If the mine is inside the park's boundaries, the gold belongs to the government. I think Black suspected it is, and that's why he was so secretive about it."

Eli and Flynn exchanged a look, and Jubil thought they

might yet end up friends. Doane and White Dog had no comment about the gold.

As Jubil told the story of exploring the mine, Nelly showed no signs of her usual inquisitiveness and in fact hardly seemed to register the details about Black's secret motive. Jubil was concerned about the state of her mind, but he hoped she was just overwhelmed by all that had happened to her and that she would soon be feeling more like herself.

Jubil studied Flynn. He was not surprised that Flynn had decided to side with him rather than Black, but he had never imagined Flynn would go so far to defend Jubil and his friends as to shoot Black and McTavish.

"Thank you, Flynn," Jubil said. "You saved our lives."

"Aye, well," Flynn said, "I surprised myself, too, didn't I? Suppose it's a fair trade for the effort you're making to turn me away from a life of crime."

Jubil allowed himself a weak smile. After all they had been through today, Flynn's spirit was unscathed. Jubil not only trusted him, he truly liked him.

After supper, Jubil suggested Nelly could take a bath. Eli and White Dog toted water from the pond to warm on the stove for her, and Eli washed her clothes, but Jubil's hand would not allow him to be much help. After bathing, she wrapped up in a blanket for the night. Jubil and Nelly slept in the bunkhouse. The rest of the men, in an attempt to give Nelly some privacy, slept in the barn. Tomorrow they would set out for Baronett's place and begin to put this ordeal behind them.

CHAPTER 19

Jubil was grateful when the sun finally rose. It had not been a restful night. Nelly had been startled awake several times by nightmares, sitting up in the bed, shivering and crying. When she had dozed off again, the pain in Jubil's hand and the events of the day kept him awake. In the morning, he went to sit beside her when she awoke.

"How are you doing?" he said, brushing her hair away from her face.

"I'm all right," she said weakly, which was not remotely true.

"I'll get your clothes," he said, and retrieved them from where they hung next the woodstove. "They're still a little damp."

She sat up in bed, still wrapped in the blanket, and took them from him. "They're fine," she said, without feeling.

Jubil felt terrible guilt at her suffering. "You go ahead and get dressed," he said. "I'll go check on the others, and we'll get out of here."

In the barn, they were all awake and getting ready to ride.

"How's Nelly?" Eli said.

Jubil appreciated the compassion Eli was showing his sister. "She slept some—but fitfully. Her clothes are still damp, but she says she doesn't mind."

"They'll dry soon enough in the sun," Doane said. "Looks like a decent day."

Jubil looked to Flynn. "How's that ankle?"

"I'm thinking it's a wee bit better," Flynn said.

"Good," Jubil nodded. "Where's—"

Just then White Dog came into the barn, carrying a string of trout.

"Good work," Eli said to him. "I'll take those over to the bunkhouse and fry them up. Do you think it'll bother Nelly to have me busying about?" Eli asked Jubil.

"I think she'll be fine with you," Jubil said. "She's getting dressed—so knock."

Eli nodded and took the fish from White Dog.

Jubil moved to grab his saddle and winced at the pain in his hand.

"Don't," White Dog said. "We can do it."

His injury prevented him from helping much with the horses, and he couldn't hold his rifle properly. The bleeding from his wound had slowed, but it hurt even worse than it had the day before. He was going to be a burden rather than an asset during the trip back—a feeling he disliked intensely. But if Major Powell could look out for himself without the use of half his right arm, Jubil was determined to find ways to manage with a bad hand. He busied himself calming the animals, putting the blankets on their backs, and fetching the tack with his good hand. They would take the horses that no longer had riders back with them to sell.

Once the horses were ready to ride, Jubil turned to Doane. "There's something I want to do before we leave."

The idea had come to him this morning in bed. He began to look around the barn. After a few minutes, he found what he was looking for—a five gallon can of kerosene. He lifted it with his good hand and set it near the barn door.

"What do you plan to do with that?" Doane asked.

"I want to burn the foreman's house," Jubil said. "I'd rather burn the bodies than leave them to scavengers."

"Suits me," Doane said.

After breakfast, which to Jubil's concern Nelly refused, he went with Doane to supervise the dousing of the foreman's house with kerosene, while everyone else mounted up in the meadow. Jubil set the house ablaze, and he and Doane joined their crew.

Doane led out, followed by White Dog. Jubil and Nelly came along behind them, with Eli and Flynn in the rear, leading the string of horses. As they rode away, Jubil stopped to take one last look, to make sure the building was thoroughly afire. Nelly stopped beside him to watch the conflagration. Her eyes brimmed with tears as she watched the house holding her tormentors go up in flames. Jubil leaned over and covered her hands with his good hand as she gripped the pommel of her saddle.

"You're strong," Jubil said, and Nelly nodded. "You'll get past this. You'll be fine again when we get home." He sincerely hoped this was true.

Their procession followed the trail down into the valley and south along the creek. They were about thirty minutes down the trail when Jubil paused again to look back. He watched the billowing black smoke rise from the plateau where the mine had once been. He felt no remorse or satisfaction—only relief that Nelly was alive.

They rode back to the main trail and then silently followed Soda Butte Creek into the Lamar Valley. The day was warm, and Nelly's clothes did indeed dry quickly—at least the outer layer—but she did not complain. In fact, she hardly spoke at all. About noon, they made a rest stop at the confluence of Soda Butte Creek and the Lamar River.

White Dog found a patch of yarrow and made a poultice for Jubil's hand and Nelly's wrist. Eli had stuffed the bedsheet into his saddlebag, and now he tore strips of cloth from it to rewrap their wounds. Jubil's hand hurt badly, and he had begun to imagine what might happen if the wound became infected. During the 1870 Washburn Expedition, Doane had had an infection in his thumb that worsened to the point that Nathaniel Langford had to lance it with his knife to prevent it killing him.

Flynn's ankle was improving—he was able to get on and off his horse unassisted and hobble around.

The war-torn group made it to Baronett's Bridge in the afternoon. Baronett stood outside his cabin, watching them cross. When Jubil and Nelly reached him, he squinted up at Jubil and said, "I reckon you prevailed. This is your wife, safe and sound?"

Jubil made introductions.

"I'm sorry for what those devils put you through ma'am," Baronett said. "High time they got what was coming to them."

Nelly stared blankly at Baronett without replying, and then she looked away. Baronett caught Jubil's eye, a concerned expression on his face. When Jubil shrugged, Baronett nodded knowingly.

"Looks like you all survived," Baronett said. "How about Black and his men?"

Jubil shook his head.

"No great loss there," Baronett said. "I'm anxious to hear the story over supper, if you're up to it."

"All right," Jubil said.

White Dog and Eli went off to catch some fish for supper. Baronett gave Jubil another bedsheet to use for bandages and, most generously, brought out a bottle of whiskey and poured a liberal amount onto the palm and back of Jubil's hand. This hurt like the dickens, but Jubil was reassured at last that the wound would not fester any longer. Jubil swore he would repay Baronett for his kindness. White Dog had also picked enough yarrow to make a fresh poultice, and once he had applied it,

Jubil felt more hopeful that his hand would heal.

They set up camp near Baronett's cabin and enjoyed a boiled supper of fish, potatoes, and onions. Nelly showed no appetite and silently picked at her food. Jubil told Baronett what had happened at the mine but made no mention of the gold he had found stashed away in the tunnel. After supper, everyone retired for the night, but Nelly wanted to sit near the fire for a while. After everyone was abed, she sat wrapped in a blanket, staring into the flames. Jubil sat silently beside her with his arm around her until she was ready to try to sleep.

He lay awake watching her as she tossed and turned, mumbling as she dreamed. When she cried out or woke with a start, Jubil held her until she drifted off again.

In the morning, Nelly still wasn't hungry, but at Jubil's urging, she nibbled at one of the biscuits Baronett had made. Jubil thanked him for his hospitality and left him the string of Black's horses rather than take them back to sell, which Baronett appreciated.

When they reached Bottler's Ranch that afternoon, Eli and White Dog went out hunting and brought back a bounty of grouse for supper. Fredrick Bottler took pity on Nelly for the shabby state of her dress and offered her a choice of items left behind by a prostitute who would no longer be needing them. In a good-natured attempt at humor, he told the wild story of her demise, and the thievery that had led to it. Tears welled in Nelly's eyes as she looked at the dresses, then she burst into tears and ran from the room.

Jubil caught up with her outside, where she stood weeping into her hands.

"I can't wear that poor dead girl's clothes," Nelly sobbed.

He took her in his arms.

"It's all right, your dress is fine," Jubil said. "He meant well."

"I know," Nelly said, gaining a little control over herself. "I'm sorry I made a scene."

He raised her chin and looked into her eyes.

"You have nothing to be sorry for."

She hugged him tightly.

White Dog rode up holding a fistful of yarrow. "More to help your hand, your arm," he said. "Is there trouble?"

"No," Nelly said, making an effort to smile at him. "I'm all right."

White Dog made another poultice, and Bottler had plenty of cheap whiskey, so Jubil was able to tend to his hand again. The pain was now a steady ache. He could not move his middle three fingers, but he could move his thumb and his little finger, though when he did, the pain was severe. As long as he didn't try to use the hand, the pain was tolerable.

They had grouse stew for supper, along with the best freshly baked bread Jubil had tasted in a long time. To his relief, Nelly ate a little.

After supper, Jubil led Nelly down to the bank of the Yellowstone River and found a boulder with a flat top for them to sit on. He put his jacket around her shoulders.

"How are you feeling?" he asked.

"I'm exhausted," Nelly said, resting her head on his shoulder. "But I'll make it."

He was relieved that she was finally speaking and acting a bit more like herself.

"I'm sorry I got us into all this," he said, his voice trembling.

"I don't blame you for anything," Nelly said. "Black and the others brought this on themselves. I insisted on coming with you, not fully realizing the dangers. And I agreed with your plan to expose Black. So . . ."

He kissed her forehead. "It's a relief to hear you say that, although I still bear some of the blame. I know you want to be independent, but I still feel responsible for your safety in dangerous circumstances. I have some explaining to do to your parents, and Abe and Lily."

"Yes," Nelly said, "we do. I dread that."

Jubil knew the Warners would be disappointed in him over this whole episode. But he needed their support, in many ways. He loved them like the parents he had lost, and he hoped they could understand that he couldn't live his life reacting to Lily's fears or Abe's aversion to risk.

"I'm not sure where we go from here," Jubil said. He did not look forward to solving the tangle of business problems Black had created for him, nasty gifts that lingered on after his death.

"Right now," Nelly said, "all I want to do is get clean, eat some decent meals, and sleep in a bed—and you need to get that hand tended to by a doctor. Could we do that in Bozeman?"

"Yes," Jubil said. "The law and the doctor will probably tell us how long we need to stay." For now, he would try to focus on taking one step at a time, which meant getting to Bozeman and taking care of Nelly.

They were on their way up through Paradise Valley the next day, riding toward Bozeman Pass, when Flynn rode up beside Jubil. Everyone had been very quiet on the ride, each one seemingly sifting through what they had been through.

"If you have no objections," Flynn said, "I'm going to split off here and go back to the agency. If the sheriff wants me, I won't be hard to find."

"All right," Jubil said. "My offer still stands about working for Warner and Walker Outfitting."

"I appreciate that," Flynn said. "I'll sit tight until you get things sorted out with Delano about supplying the agency. In the meantime, maybe I can help keep any new scoundrels from getting a foothold."

"I'm going to do my best to prevent that too," Jubil said.

"Let's keep in touch. Get whatever papers you can that prove Black's dirty dealings with the agency. And if you hear that Black has any heirs or other relatives, can I count on you?"

"You can," Flynn said. "I'm not especially proud of what I've done, but Black earned it."

"It was him or us, and you saved our lives," Jubil said. "That means a lot to me."

As they shook hands, White Dog rode up to join them.

"I go with Flynn," White Dog said.

Jubil was not ready yet to part company with White Dog, but he never was. He had a moment of yearning for him to be nearby all the time.

"Once again, I'm deeply indebted to you," Jubil said. "Saving Nelly's life was more important to me than saving my own."

White Dog nodded. "Some things cannot be replaced."

Jubil felt a pang of sympathy for his friend. He had wondered before if White Dog would marry again, but he imagined now that if he had lost Nelly during the violent confrontation with Black, he would never want another wife.

"I'm going to keep trying to get that supply contract with the agency," he said. "And Flynn is joining the effort as well."

White Dog studied Flynn for a moment and then turned back to meet Jubil's eyes. Was there a spark of humor there?

"I'm expecting to be around here a lot more in the future," Jubil said. "I have a real need for your help as a scout for my adventure tours. Will you take the job?"

White Dog studied Jubil. "I will scout for you."

"And my offer of my farm still stands."

"I do not want to live like a white man," White Dog said.

"I'm not trying to make a farmer out of you," Jubil said with a smile. "I think you'll be surprised by my farm." He remembered the story of White Dog being taken to the mission school as a child, after his parents died of the pox. He had escaped the first night. "When I have the next tour planned,

I'll come and ride the train with you—both ways."

White Dog nodded noncommittally.

"Would you do one more thing for me?" Jubil said. "Would you send some men to the mine a couple of times before winter sets in? I'd like to make sure no one tries to open it again."

"Yes," White Dog said.

Jubil waved Nelly and Eli forward to join them. They were both very pleased to hear the news about White Dog scouting for them.

White Dog and Flynn said their goodbyes and then turned and crossed the Yellowstone River, heading toward the reservation.

The rest of the group rode over Bozeman Pass and past Fort Ellis without stopping. They were anxious to get to Bozeman and clarify their standing with the sheriff. As they rode up the main street, side-by-side, road-weary and somber, past Black's Metropolitan Hotel and his mercantile, the townspeople stared at them.

Jubil told Sheriff Mendenhall and his deputy Arthur Barnes the long story of what had happened, beginning with the attack in Bismarck and ending with Nelly's rescue. He did not mention the treasure stashed in the mine, and the lawmen did not ask about it. The sheriff questioned the other members of the party and then accepted Jubil's story as fact. The same sheriff had dealt with the aftermath of Jubil's gunfight with Phineas Black, and he clearly had no more affinity for the elder Black brother than he had had for the younger one.

The sheriff declared that they were all free to go, and with this burden off their shoulders, the group split up. Doane rode back to the fort, Jubil and Nelly went to find the doctor. Eli sent a telegram to Mr. Byers on Nelly's behalf, telling him to run the full account of their Colorado tour, then he went to the Guy House to book two rooms. They would not patronize the Metropolitan Hotel, even though doing so would no longer benefit Lucius Black.

At the offices of Doc Jones, they were greeted by a young woman who remembered Jubil. He was embarrassed to admit he did not remember her, until she reminded him that she was Molly, Doc Jones's daughter, the pigtailed teenager who had helped tend his shoulder wound after the gunfight with Phineas Black. She had grown considerably in three years.

The doctor cleaned and sterilized Jubil's hand, then sutured the open wounds on either side. He said Jubil could thank the whiskey and White Dog's poultices for saving his hand. He applied a splint, then bandaged the hand in a fashion that prevented any movement and padded it against contact. He told Jubil he was not at risk of losing the hand, but he would not guarantee how much use of it he would regain after it healed. Jubil again reminded himself of Major Powell's missing right hand and forearm and counted himself lucky.

Jubil resigned himself to being in Bozeman long enough to get a clean bill of health from Doc Jones—at least two weeks, until the middle of August. There had been plenty of time on the ride back from the mine to think about what he needed to do next.

He had put an end to Lucius Black's part in the corruption at the Crow Agency, but as Flynn said, unless Jubil could get the contract to supply it, someone else would step in—just as Black had done when his brother had died. But it seemed that Secretary Delano would prevent Jubil taking over and also quash his broader hopes of helping to develop Yellowstone Park. Jubil sent Walter Trumbull a telegram urging him to try again to set up a meeting with President Grant. He could not fully explain what had happened in a telegram, so he just said he had an urgent need to talk about the situation at the Crow Agency. Walter replied that he would do his best.

Before he met with Grant, he had to know if the mine was within the park boundaries. That meant hiring a surveyor with some of the cash he had left in his money belt from the adventure tour.

"I'm going to meet with a surveyor today," Jubil said to Nelly at breakfast. "I thought you might like to come along."

Nelly looked surprised. "Am I needed?"

"Not really," he said, "I just thought you might to like to get out of the hotel."

"I suppose I could," she said. After their meal, they set off.

The surveyor was willing to do the job after he finished his current project. But he would need someone to lead him to the mine.

The next morning, Jubil announced his plans for the day to Nelly again, at breakfast.

"Today, I'm going to talk to a lawyer," Jubil said, "about how Black's property will be disposed of. I was hoping you'd come with me."

"I can't imagine I'm needed for that," Nelly said, looking suspiciously at him. "I appreciate your concern, Jubil, but you don't need to keep an eye on me every moment. I'm fine at the hotel. I'd like to use my time to write."

"Oh, certainly," Jubil said. "Much better idea." He was embarrassed by his hovering. He wasn't aware that he had been.

The attorney explained that, unless a will or other legal documentation of ownership turned up, Black's property would be subject to probate. The circuit judge, who would be in town sometime that month, would rule on the disposition of the property. If there were no heirs, the government would auction off the property.

After talking to Sheriff Mendenhall and the clerks at the Metropolitan Hotel and Black's mercantile, Jubil concluded that the Black brothers had done a decent job of keeping the secret of their gold stash, but Jubil knew that total secrecy wasn't possible. The guards at the mine knew, and someone had helped Black transport tons of gold into the mine. Baronett said he recognized one of Black's men as one of the miners. Were Black's men that they had killed the only ones who knew about the mine? That seemed unlikely.

Jubil allowed himself to fantasize about winning the mine in an auction. As appealing as the idea was—an easy solution to all his financial problems—it was also such a remote possibility that it seemed foolish to hope for.

His discussion with the clerks at Black's mercantile uncovered a new disappointment. The store's bookkeeper had absconded with the books the same day Nelly was kidnapped. The only hard evidence of corruption Jubil would be able to produce was testimony from Flynn, which Jubil believed he would provide if necessary. But he would not ask unless it was. Flynn had done enough.

Jubil's unexpected stay in Bozeman and the business of paying a surveyor would deplete his remaining cash reserves. He made arrangements through the First National Bank of Bozeman to write a draft on the McLean County Bank, where the remaining balance of the inheritance from his parents was on deposit. At the rate he was drawing on this money, it would be depleted within a year—and sooner if he didn't start watching his expenses.

While Jubil was occupied with business, Nelly was enjoying the cozy comforts of the Guy House. She was still having disturbing dreams but not as frequently. She was interacting with people normally again, and she was writing each morning. It did not hurt that the proprietor of the Guy House, Mr. Dodson, treated her like royalty. He was a subscriber to Mr. Byers's *Rocky Mountain News*, which he received by mail, and was familiar with Nelly's writing, which pleased her.

Byers had so far run two of her travelogue articles from the Colorado tour.

Their room at the hotel was equipped with a small desk next to a window with a view of the mountains, where Nelly was working on a full accounting of her kidnapping. She did not want Jubil to read it until it was finished.

"I'm not sure what I'll do with it," she told him. "Publish it or burn it. But I know I'll feel better for having done it."

For all of her writing, she had been unable to bring herself to write to her parents—there was too much to tell. She did ask Jubil to let them know they were all right. He sent telegrams to the Boswells and the Warners saying that they were fine and that their departure from Bozeman had been delayed. He felt guilty about saying they were "fine," but it would have to do for now.

Eli was enjoying his time in Bozeman. Jubil had not seen him in such high spirits for quite a while. His gregarious nature had resurfaced, and he spent his days either accompanying Jubil on his business enquiries or wandering about getting to know seemingly everyone in town, including Molly Jones, the doctor's daughter.

Lieutenant Doane and his wife came to town to return Nelly's belongings and to gauge their recovery. Amelia Doane continued to be troubled by her decision to allow the men into the house, but Nelly assured her that she felt no ill will toward her. Jubil was glad to see that Amelia was comforted by Nelly's assurances and her acceptance of what had happened.

Doane also brought news that Mr. Langford had been in the park while Jubil and Doane were embroiled in Nelly's rescue. Langford had shown some of the fearless vigilantism that he once had been known for by confronting a man illegally running a spa in the Lower Geyser Basin. Jubil was disappointed that he had not been able to see his old friend, as Langford had come and gone through the park's west entrance.

It was also while they were in Bozeman that newspaper headlines blared out the news that Custer's expedition had found gold, but the quantities varied depending on the report you read. Nelly pointed out that the further east the newspaper, the more skeptical the tone of the reporter regarding the claims. But facts had little to do with the fire that had been lit. Jubil knew that the secret he carried about Black's mine would transform that spark into an inferno.

When Doc Jones removed the stiches from Jubil's hand two weeks after their arrival in Bozeman, he declared that the wound was sufficiently healed and that infection was no longer a concern. Jubil's hand was still very sore, and the bones had not yet knitted together, so it had to remain splinted and immobilized. But Jubil was relieved that it was not worse.

He asked Eli to join him and Nelly that evening for supper to discuss their next steps.

"Doc says I'm well enough to travel," Jubil told Eli. "I also heard from Walter Trumbull today. He's arranged a meeting with President Grant on September first. I'll tell him about my meeting with Delano and what has happened, and I'll ask him to support my efforts. That meeting will tell us whether we're in business out here or not."

"That's impressive," Eli said.

"I'd like for you to stay here and attend to some things for us," Jubil said. "If you don't mind?"

"I don't mind," Eli said, straightening with pride.

"Good," Jubil said. "When the circuit judge arrives, you'll represent us. If the judge wants testimony, you can provide that and explain where I've gone and why. Your main task is to find out what the judge orders done with Black's property. If he has a will, we need to know who his heirs are. If they know about the gold, they might come after us. If he doesn't have a will, we would like to move forward on acquiring the mercantile, which would allow us to start our own business faster and at less expense.

If Black doesn't have a will and the mine is outside the park's boundaries, we need to know who has rights to the property. Of course, you'll not say a word to anyone about the gold, right?"

Eli nodded.

"We also need to know if the mine is inside the park. I've arranged for a surveyor to map the boundaries up there," Jubil said, "but someone needs to lead him to the mine. I was thinking about Flynn."

"All right," Eli said, with no sign of ill will. Jubil was relieved that he had finally put his suspicion of Flynn behind him.

"He said if we needed help, he'd be willing," Jubil said. "I'd like you to ask him to lead the surveyor to the mine."

Eli nodded. "I can do that."

"Good," Jubil said.

"Assuming Grant supports you," Eli said, "and we open a store out here, who will run it?"

"I was hoping you would," Jubil said.

"I was hoping you'd ask," Eli said. "What will we do with the store in Council Bluffs?"

"I'm going to try to keep that going myself," Jubil said. "I have an idea that I'd like your opinion on—both of you. At first, I was against the idea of trying to convince Ike to stay on and not take the job in Chicago. I didn't think it was fair to him. But he's had a little time to sample his new life, and I'm thinking I might go talk to him—see how he's doing, and ask if he might be interested in coming back to Council Bluffs. What do you think?"

Nelly and Eli exchanged a glance.

"You're closest to him," Nelly said to Eli.

"Do it," Eli said. "A little pressure won't kill him. Tell him he's letting us all down."

"We don't have to go that far," Nelly said.

Jubil laughed. "I'll talk to him once we get the matter of the Bozeman store settled."

"You've got repair expenses in Council Bluffs," Eli said, "plus new inventory to order and salaries to pay. A new store to start up in Bozeman. How are you going to afford all this?"

"I've got some ideas," Jubil said, "but I'm not ready to get into that yet. We need to see how things go with Grant. Then I'm going to talk to Abe before I make any final decisions."

They enjoyed the rest of their supper, and when Jubil and Nelly returned to their room, he asked, "Have you decided where you want to go from here?"

"If you don't mind, I'd like to go with you to Washington," Nelly said. "Just as a tourist. I've never been, and I'd enjoy the sights and the hotel service. I would also like to see Abe and Lily."

"That would be wonderful," Jubil said. He hadn't mentioned it to her, but he had been feeling uneasy at the thought of being away from her for any length of time so soon after their ordeal with Black. "Walter will be pleased to see you. I meant my question in a broader way though. I know you want to write, but I was wondering if you were reconsidering your decision to travel with me quite so much. I thought you might be wanting some peace and quiet, where you could get some work done."

Nelly patted Jubil's hand. "Thank you for asking. I have been thinking that," she said. "You and Eli have been so good about letting me travel with you, and I'd like to do it again sometime, but I've had all the adventure I need for a while. I've gathered enough experiences to write a stack of articles, or maybe a stack of novels, and I'd like to do that. I'll write from Council Bluffs, or Pete's cabin on your farm, or my parent's house, if necessary."

She seemed like herself again, and he was very grateful for that. She would never be completely free of what she had experienced, but her plans were promising. She smiled and leaned into him as Jubil drew her into his arms.

CHAPTER 20

The four-day stagecoach ride from Bozeman to Corinne was just as bumpy and dusty as Jubil remembered, and the inns and suppers just as crude. But compared to another week on horseback and sleeping rough, it would do. In comparison, his and Nelly's accommodations in a Pullman Palace car on the way to Washington felt like the height of luxury. Given their current financial situation, it was an extravagance, but Nelly's comfort was worth any price to him.

They checked in to the National Hotel with a full day to spare before Jubil's meeting with President Grant. After breakfast, they set out on a walking tour to see a few highlights of the nation's capital. Along the way, they stopped at a telegraph office to let the Boswells and Warners know that they were now in Washington on business and would be in touch again soon. They knew these cryptic messages might be as troubling as they were reassuring, but it was the best they could do for now.

When they arrived back at the hotel, a telegram was waiting for Jubil at the front desk. He and Nelly returned to their room, where he opened it and read aloud, *Mine location approximately one mile south of park boundary. Judge arriving in Bozeman late this week. Eli.*

Ever since the park bill had passed, Black had been mining illegally, and the gold would now belong to the government.

"Is that good?" Nelly asked.

"Well," Jubil said, "now we can give President Grant some good news. But I won't breathe easy until I know that Black has no heirs who might want revenge."

That evening they met Walter Trumbull in the hotel dining room for supper.

Walter rose as they approached.

"What a pleasant surprise!" he said, going straight to greet Nelly. "I haven't seen you since your wedding—which was lovely, by the way. Did you enjoy your honeymoon trip?"

"It's very good to see you, Walter," Nelly said, clasping both his hands warmly. "Yes, thank you. We had a marvelous time."

"Hello, Walter," Jubil said, shaking hands with his friend.

Jubil's telegram had not mentioned the events that had led to his most recent request. So after the waiter took their order, Jubil described everything that had transpired since he and Walter last met. When Jubil finished his story, Walter leaned back in his chair.

"How terrible! I'm so glad you're all right," he said to Nelly.

Nelly nodded. She was still having bad dreams occasionally, but she was handling it bravely.

"There's another matter too," Jubil said. "The mine where they held Nelly was a gold mine." He told Walter about the Black brothers' secret operation and the recent news from Eli about the mine's location.

"My goodness," Walter said. "You do find yourself in some situations, don't you?" He sat pondering something, then turned to Nelly. "Would you consider coming along to the meeting with President Grant?"

"Pfft," Nelly said, waving him away.

"When Grant hears what Black did to you," Walter said, "it will make a strong impression about what kind of people Delano supports."

"That's not a bad idea," Jubil said, sitting up straighter in his chair.

"I can't go to a meeting with the President of the United States," Nelly said dismissively. "What would I have to say to him—I'd be humiliated."

"You have plenty to talk about," Walter said. "Your education, your career, your political activism, your many interesting acquaintances. I'm sure he'd be happy to meet you. You're beautiful too—that won't hurt."

"Oh, Walter," Nelly said. "Really."

"I was born a politician, Nelly," Walter said. "I know how they think."

"I don't always agree with Walter," Jubil said, "but this time I do. Come with us?"

Nelly looked as if she were about to be kidnapped again.

"You'll enjoy it," Walter said. "You can write about it."

That got her attention, and her expression changed from fearful to thoughtful. "If you're sure it's all right," she said.

Jubil had grown fairly accustomed to meeting distinguished people, but the president was another level of distinguished. He hoped the flutter in his stomach didn't disturb his breakfast to an embarrassing effect. Nelly wisely had only had tea and dry toast. Walter, a veteran of the political sphere, was unaffected, and he chattered away during their short ride in the hired carriage up Pennsylvania Avenue.

When they arrived at the White House, Walter led Jubil and Nelly to the front door and opened it without knocking, as though entering a hotel or shop. As they stepped inside, they were greeted by a gentleman seated at a small desk in the center of the foyer. Jubil was surprised to see no armed guards present, but perhaps they were kept out of sight.

"Good morning, gentlemen, madam," the man said. "I'm Mr. Babcock, President Grant's personal secretary. May I help you?"

"Good morning," Walter said. "I'm Walter Trumbull, and this is Mr. and Mrs. Jubilee Walker. We have an appointment this morning with President Grant."

The man looked in a register on his desk. "Yes," he said, rising from his chair. "If you'll follow me, I'll see if he is ready for you."

They followed the man up a staircase to the second floor, then down a hallway to a room in the front right corner of the building. Jubil noticed Nelly trying to take in the grandeur of the place without looking like a country bumpkin—which is how he felt. He had felt the same way when visiting an even more opulent mansion—Jay Cooke's Ogantz in Philadelphia. He and Nelly exchanged a brief glance and grinned at one another with contained excitement. Mr. Babcock asked them to wait as he knocked lightly on the door, opened it slightly, and looked in. Then he opened the door wide and waved them forward.

"Mr. President," he said, "Mr. Walter Trumbull and Mr. and Mrs. Jubilee Walker to see you."

Ulysses S. Grant rose from a surprisingly modest desk in the center of a large ornate office and came to greet them with a friendly smile.

"Good morning, Mr. Trumbull," Grant said, shaking Walter's hand first. "I hope you are well. Give my regards to your father. I regret his retirement. I miss having the benefit of his opinion—most of the time."

Walter had shared with Jubil that his father, recently retired senator Lyman Trumbull, was of a similar opinion to General Sherman as to Grant's effectiveness as a president. In some ways they loved him, but in others he frustrated them to no end.

"Thank you, sir," Walter said. "I'll give him your best. I'd like you to meet Jubilee Walker, and his wife, Nelly—spelled with a *y*, unlike your lovely daughter's name."

Grant gave Nelly a little bow as he gently shook her hand. "What a delightful surprise," Grant said, congenially. "I was not expecting such a lovely guest. Welcome to the White House."

"Thank you, Mr. President," Nelly said, with an elegant little nod of her head.

"Mrs. Walker is from Bloomington, Illinois, sir, and a graduate of Vassar College," Walter said. "She's a journalist, and well acquainted with the leaders of the woman suffrage movement. I thought you'd enjoy meeting her."

"I do indeed," Grant said. "You've made an impressive start for a young person from the heartland." Grant turned to Jubil. "And so have you, Mr. Walker," Grant said, shaking Jubil's hand with a firm grip that Jubil couldn't help but characterize as presidential. "I've been looking forward to making your acquaintance."

"Thank you for taking the time to see us, Mr. President," Jubil said.

Grant's warm demeanor calmed Jubil's nervousness.

As they sat down in three chairs set in front of the president's desk, Jubil marveled at Grant's appearance, familiar to every adult in America, and much of the world. He wore a black suit that looked slightly large for him, or perhaps was just comfortably loose. His hair and beard were well-trimmed but not fussily tended. Unlike some other famous men Jubil had met, Grant emanated no aura of the powerful figure he was. If not for his fame, he could have been mistaken for any man on the street. In fact, he was so common in his appearance and demeanor, it almost gave the impression that there had been some mistake. This could not be the fierce general who had saved the Union. But it was. Jubil recalled the impression Grant had made on him at their past brief meeting—the aroma of whiskey and cigars. Neither of those was in evidence this morning. Grant studied his guests and then settled his attention on Nelly.

"I take it, Mrs. Walker," Grant said, "that you are acquainted with Miss Susan B. Anthony and her partner, Mrs. Elizabeth Cady Stanton?"

"Yes, sir," Nelly said. "I have made Miss Anthony's acquaintance and been in her company on occasion. I'm closer to Mrs. Stanton. She is a close friend of Professor Maria Mitchell, who was my governess and benefactor at Vassar College."

"I suppose you share Miss Anthony and Mrs. Stanton's opinion," Grant said, "and disapprove of my support of the Fifteenth Amendment as it was written?" He said this in a conversational tone, with no hint of challenge or threat.

"Yes, sir, that is correct," Nelly said without hesitation. "I believe you had the perfect opportunity to add language to end all voter discrimination, based not only on race but sex as well."

"But there is where we disagree," Grant said. "That was not the perfect opportunity. At the time, an amendment worded in that way would have failed. We have to fight our wars one battle at a time, Mrs. Walker. But I admire your resilience, and I do not disagree with your cause. Its time will come."

Jubil could tell that Nelly was deciding whether or not to extend the debate.

"Thank you, Mr. President," she said respectfully.

Jubil was in awe of his wife. She had just stood her ground with the president without flinching. Once again, he saw her as an inspiration.

Grant turned his attention to Jubil. "I have been looking forward to your visit, Mr. Walker. I know you are acquainted with General Sherman, and I told him we had a meeting planned. We had a lengthy conversation about your accomplishments. I'm proud to see an Illinois farm boy doing his part to help build this great nation."

"Thank you, sir," Jubil said. "That is the highest compliment I have ever received."

"And well earned," Grant said. "I'd love to spend our time hearing tales of your adventures, but I suspect that's not why you've come. Perhaps you'd rather discuss your reasons for asking to meet with me?"

"Yes, sir, I would," Jubil said. "I'll just get straight to my point. I visited Washington earlier this year with two goals in mind: gaining the right to participate in the development of Yellowstone National Park and putting an end to the corruption in the supply situation at the Crow Agency. Walter arranged a meeting with Secretary of the Interior Delano. He is a strong supporter of the park and seemed appreciative of my efforts and open to my further involvement in its development. But when I raised the subject of corruption at the Crow Agency, he took offense. He said no such problem would exist in his administration, and my accusations branded me a troublemaker. He withdrew his support for my involvement in the park and forbade me from dealing with the Crow Agency. I've come to plead my case for you to overrule him."

"I see," Grant said. "Well, I appreciate you dispensing with nuance to explain the situation, but dealing with it may require some. I'd like to hear more about the Crow Agency."

"Yes, sir," Jubil said. "It's a bit of a lengthy tale, but I'll try to be brief."

"Take your time," Grant said congenially. He leaned forward and placed his forearms on the desk with his hands clasped, giving Jubil his full attention.

"I first became aware of the situation during the 1871 Yellowstone survey with Captain Barlow and Dr. Hayden," Jubil said. "We learned that a man named Phineas Black was extorting protection money from two men who had established businesses in the Yellowstone Basin. The same man was also supplying the Crow reservation with inferior goods at inflated prices and falsifying records for payment of goods never delivered."

He explained what had happened in his confrontation with Phineas Black and the events that had taken place after O'Brien took over. Then he came to his current problems with Lucius Black, including the harassment, assault, and kidnapping they had endured at Black's hands. He deferred mention of the gold stash for the moment but described the violent battle to free Nelly and reiterated his desire to take over the job of supplying the agency. He also explained Flynn's role in the matter and shared his own desire that Flynn remain the agent of record.

When Jubil finished his narrative, Grant leaned back in his chair and studied his guests.

"That must have been dreadful for you, my dear," Grant said to Nelly sincerely. "I'm pleased that you survived it. You must have a constitution as strong as your intelligence."

"Thank you, sir," Nelly said. "They were bad men, and they deserved their fate."

Jubil could tell that Walter had been correct. Grant felt the depth of Black's evil more deeply with Nelly sitting right in front of him.

"And you believe that Secretary Delano," Grant said to Jubil, "had prior awareness of this man's dealings."

"I can't say that for certain," Jubil said. "But word of my meeting with Delano reached Black very quickly."

Grant shifted his gaze to Walter, bringing him to attention.

"Do I have your confidence, Mr. Trumbull?" Grant said. "Can I rely on you to keep this conversation just between us?"

"Yes, sir," Walter said sincerely. "Without a doubt."

Grant nodded and returned his attention to Jubil.

"This is not the first report of this sort that I've received," Grant said to Jubil, "of corruption in the Bureau of Indian Affairs. Though it is certainly one of the most extreme. I'm sorry for the hardship this has caused you, and I'm glad to see that you have prevailed. I understand your situation now. Are you, by any chance, acquainted with Professor Othniel Charles Marsh of Yale College?"

"No, sir, not personally," Jubil said. He told Grant about his meeting with Mr. Grinnell at Fort Lincoln.

"And did he relate any specifics of the professor's concerns?" Grant said.

"He did," Jubil said. "His stories about the corruption at the Red Cloud Agency in Nebraska sounded very similar to what is happening at the Crow Agency. He said the professor was planning to communicate his concerns directly to you. I wrote to him and asked that he add my story to his, but I never heard from him. Did he write to you?"

"Yes," Grant said, nodding. "That he did. I received a passionate letter from him telling of the depravations and deceits he has witnessed. He contends that the government administration at all levels is aware of the situation, and he fervently urged me to intervene. He plans to provide me with a full report to support the accusations. If the situation warrants, there will be a change in administration, but that will take some time to happen. I see your dilemma in the meantime."

"Yes sir," Jubil said. He was a bit disappointed that Marsh had not mentioned him in his letter to Grant, but he was encouraged by the information Grant had shared.

The president appeared to be deep in thought, so Jubil remained quiet.

"Remind me, if you will," Grant said, "how you came to know Major John Wesley Powell."

"He is a friend of my family," Jubil said. "We went to the same church. My uncle accompanied him on collecting expeditions in their younger days. Then he served under Major Powell in the war." Jubil was aware that Grant had been Major Powell's commanding officer.

Grant raised his eyebrows. "May I ask what became of your uncle?"

"He died at Shiloh," Jubil said.

"I'm sorry for your loss," Grant said, then leaned back in his chair and tapped his fingers on his desk. "I think I have an idea how we can persuade Secretary Delano to agree to our wishes." Grant grinned, taking obvious pleasure in his plan. "I'll invite him to have a chat about a petition I received from a young constituent of mine from Illinois, whose uncle gave his life in the war while under my command. This young man has gone on to distinguish himself in service to his country, not on the battlefield but in the wilderness—helping us expand our great nation. I'll explain how he has also done us a service by single-handedly rooting out corruption in Indian Affairs that would have embarrassed us both greatly had it come to light. I'll remind him of his penchant for cronyism and ask his forbearance in honoring my desire to reward this young man by granting his petition. He won't be able to squirm out of that request, even when he learns the young man is that trouble-maker Jubilee Walker."

"That is very clever, sir," Walter said, showing his appreciation for Grant's strategic political thinking.

"Frankly, I don't mind the opportunity to put the secretary off his footing a bit," Grant said conspiratorially.

"Thank you, Mr. President," Jubil said. "I very much appreciate your confidence."

"You're welcome, Mr. Walker. You should be able to move forward with your plan to supply the Crow Agency. But there is still the matter of your interest in developing Yellowstone National Park."

Grant turned to Walter again. "The opinion I'm about to express is not one that I'd like known around Washington while lobbying is still under way on the matter."

"Yes, sir," Walter said.

"There is currently a bill under consideration to appropriate one hundred thousand dollars for the development of the park," Grant said, "but I do not believe that bill will pass. Despite your eagerness to show the wonders of Yellowstone to the public, there will be no funding to support such an effort anytime soon."

Grant's opinion of the fate of the Yellowstone funding bill was at odds with Delano's. Delano had been confident enough in the bill's passage that he declined Walter's offer of lobbying help. Maybe Delano was just being overconfident, or maybe he just didn't want Jubil's help with anything.

"I appreciate your candor, Mr. President," Jubil said. "I have a confidence I'd like to share with you as well. I don't know that this will have any bearing on the park funding situation, though I'd like to think it would, but the government is soon going to find itself heir to a sizeable stash of gold." He explained what the Black brothers had been up to, and how he had left the mine. He reached inside his jacket and removed an envelope. "I've drawn a crude map with directions," he said, handing the envelope to Grant. "I'm sure you'll know best how to handle this information. I don't know whether Secretary Delano knows or not, but if he does, he didn't hear it from me."

Grant took the envelope and laid it on his desk.

"Thank you for the information, Mr. Walker," Grant said with a sly grin. "This will add fuel to the fire out there. I'll handle the matter with discretion. I can't promise anything about park funding, but we'll see."

"Thank you, sir," Jubil said. "We've read reports that Custer's expedition discovered gold."

Grant nodded. "The reports in the press are exaggerated . . . but that's no surprise."

"Is there anything I can do to help?" Jubil said.

"I'm not sure there is anything any of us can do, Mr. Walker," Grant said. "It's a complicated situation." Grant became lost in thought for a moment, then came out of his reverie and changed the subject.

"One last thing about Yellowstone," he said, "I entirely trust the park's superintendent, Nathanial Langford, to decide what is done in the park and who is involved in doing it. I'll not intervene in any matters in that regard."

"I understand completely," Jubil said. "I know Mr. Langford well—we traveled in Yellowstone together—and your trust in him is well founded. I haven't told anyone about the mine before this visit with you, but now that we've spoken, I will write to Langford about it."

"Excellent," Grant said. "Well, then, have we concluded our business?"

Walter looked to Jubil and Nelly, then spoke on their behalf. "Yes, sir, I believe we have. We are grateful for your time and consideration."

"It has been a pleasure to meet you, Mr. Walker," Grant said coming around the desk to show his guests out.

"Thank you, sir," Jubil said, shaking hands with Grant one last time.

Then Grant turned his attention to Nelly.

"And it was a pleasure meeting you as well, Mrs. Walker," Grant said. "Do what you can, if you would, to improve your associates' opinion of me."

Nelly smiled.

"And you, Mr. Trumbull—see what you can do to improve your father's opinion of me."

Walter laughed.

On the carriage ride back to the hotel, Walter was exuberant about how well the meeting had gone. Jubil was pleased too, but his excitement was tempered by the weight of seeing his plans through. Nelly couldn't wait to write about her experience meeting the president. Walter reminded her to be cautious how much she revealed.

CHAPTER 21

The crossing from Hyannis to Nantucket Island was much more comfortable than the one Jubil and Nelly had experienced in the spring. The weather was fair, and the seas were light, which allowed them to stroll the deck and enjoy the salty smell of the sea breeze.

"Are we going to tell Abe and Lily everything?" Nelly said. "Or do you think that would be too much for Lily to hear?"

"We should tell them everything," Jubil said. "Your family too. I regret not being fully open with them before."

"Good," Nelly nodded. "Are you worried about their reaction?"

"I always feel like I'm pushing their tolerance of me," Jubil said, "how did Walter put it?—with the 'situations I find myself in.' I'm always concerned that their patience with me will wear out."

"They both love you, Jubil," Nelly said, giving him a hug. "That's not going to suddenly run out. We'll tell them the whole story, talk through all their concerns . . . and then we can go through the whole thing again with my parents."

Jubil grimaced.

The island was bustling, as always, and Jubil hired a carriage to take them to the Warners'. When they arrived at the elegant white house with the tall red shutters, Jubil saw, as he helped Nelly out of the carriage, that her eyes were brimming with tears—but she was smiling.

"Are you all right?" Jubil asked, surprised.

"I am," she said. "I was just suddenly overcome by a feeling of joy and gratitude for being here in this beautiful place, with these beautiful people—for being alive and well, and being loved."

As he held her for a moment, Abe stepped out the front door, followed closely by Lily.

"Hello," Abe said, waving as he and Lily came to greet them. Jubil was pleased to see no signs of distress in Lily's demeanor.

"Thank God, you're safe," Lily said.

Even though Lily had not yet heard the details of what had happened in Montana, she knew that it was something dramatic.

"We appreciated getting your messages," Abe said, pulling Jubil into a fatherly embrace, "but they were short on detail." Abe took note of Jubil's bandaged hand. "I see you didn't escape unscathed from whatever has been going on. How bad is it?"

"The bullet went clean through," Jubil said. "It's coming along pretty well now. Still sore but tolerable. On the mend."

"Will you have full use of it again?" Abe asked, examining the wrapping more closely.

"We won't know for a while yet," Jubil said. "The doc said I'll have to work at it."

"I suppose you're going to tell me that it could have been worse?" Lily said as she wrapped her arms around Jubil.

Jubil shrugged and grinned.

"Well, I'm thrilled that it wasn't."

She held him close for a moment, and he allowed himself to savor it. He still missed his mother, but Lily had eased some of that longing. He, too, experienced a moment of appreciation for his life, just as Nelly had described.

"Let's go in and get comfortable," Abe said.

They gathered around the table in the dining room, men on one side, women on the other, and Lily served coffee and cookies. Jubil began the long tale of the events that had happened since they had last seen the Warners in Council Bluffs. Abe and Lily remained silent during Jubil's narration, absorbed in the story. Jubil looked to Nelly often, inviting her to chime in, but she listened as if she had never heard the tale. When Jubil was finished, Abe and Lily sat back in their chairs, wide-eyed.

"Good Lord," Lily said. "The depths of evil in some people are beyond reason. You are both lucky to be alive."

"We are," Nelly said, reaching for Lily's hand. "We are well aware of that."

Lily squeezed Nelly's hand.

Jubil said, "I hope I haven't made you both so uncomfortable that you can't tolerate me any longer."

Lily reached over and took Jubil's hand, holding both his and Nelly's. "We're just glad you're safe," she said. Abe nodded in agreement.

Jubil was greatly relieved that Lily, and Abe as well, seemed to have finally begun to practice what Lily had always preached to Nelly—not to live in fear of loss.

"Where does all this leave you then?" Abe said.

Jubil looked over at Nelly. "I'm getting tired of hearing myself talk," he said. "Would you be willing to tell them about the meeting with President Grant?"

She looked surprised, but when she thought it over, she said, "All right," with a smile.

Jubil sat back and listened with amazement as Nelly told the story with an eye for detail that was well beyond his capabilities. She described not only the things she saw and experienced, but their symbolism and significance. She described the splendor and gravity of the White House. She painted a picture of President Grant's disarmingly common appearance and what it said about his humility, and she laughed about their little debate on the suffrage movement. Finally, she expressed her pride in Jubil for gaining the president's support. When she finished her story, Abe and Lily sat silently studying Jubil.

Abe clasped Jubil's shoulder. "We are so very proud of your dedication and determination. Your family would be too—and Luke! Well done . . . well done."

Lily beamed at him from across the table. She looked from him to Nelly and back again. "Now that this dangerous chapter of your story has ended," she said, "what happens next?"

"I've got some ideas about reviving the Council Bluffs store and financing the new store in Bozeman," Jubil said. "But all that needs to wait until we hear back from Eli. If Black has heirs, I won't be in the clear to open a store out there yet anyway—not until I've dealt with that situation."

Abe and Lily both looked shocked, that possibility not having occurred to them.

The next morning, Nelly wanted to take in the scenery, so Jubil borrowed Abe's carriage and they set off east across the island to the little village of Siasconset. There, they bought a lunch to take with them and drove north to Sankaty Head Lighthouse to enjoy a picnic. Jubil selected a spot with the same view Lily had once painted in one of her landscapes. The lighthouse, a white tower with a wide band of red around its middle, sat on the edge of a brushy bluff facing the Atlantic Ocean. A cool breeze made the air feel crisp and fresh.

"Would you like to sit on the beach?" Jubil asked.

"I'm fine in the carriage, really," Nelly said, staring out to sea as she answered. "Save Lily housework by not tracking in more sand."

"That's a lost cause out here," he said, watching her as she sat lost in thought. She was her radiantly beautiful self again. The memory of her as a dirty bedraggled prisoner haunted him, and it probably always would. The full realization of how close he had come to losing her crept in again. He would not allow himself to think about life without her—but there had been times on the way to rescue her that he had not been able to avoid it.

"It's so beautiful and peaceful here," Nelly said, taking in a deep breath of salty air.

Jubil broke out of his dark thoughts and looked out over the ocean.

"Someday I want to cross that ocean," Nelly said.

"We will," Jubil said, taking her hand. "We'll sail right out of here, straight to London. You can write pirate stories while we're at sea."

"Ooh, I like that idea," she said with a smile. She shifted in her seat to face him directly. "I'm thinking of making a change in plans. Instead of going to New York, I'd like to ask Abe and Lily if I can stay here for a while. I felt it as soon as we arrived. I saw myself sitting in Lily's studio, watching her paint, as I day-dreamed and worked on my novel. Taking walks on the beach and letting my mind wander. Helping with the housework and learning to cook seafood dishes. I understand why Lily loves this place. It feels so safe and yet adventurous. It's inspirational."

"That may be the best idea you've ever had," Jubil said sincerely. "And you've had some good ones! Lily will be thrilled—Abe too. You'll get a lot of work done here. I can't wait to read it all."

"I think Mama will be excited by the idea too," Nelly said. "She and Papa can visit. Maybe they could even move here if the carriage shop closes."

"That would be a bold move on your father's part," Jubil said. "But he might."

"I'm excited by the prospects for the future," Nelly said, then stopped and studied Jubil.

Jubil wondered what she was thinking. "Are you worried about the possibility someone may inherit the mine and come after us?" he asked.

"A little, I suppose," she said, "But we can't live looking over our shoulders all the time. I trust you to do what has to be done."

He put his arm around her as they watched the ocean roll against the shore.

"How can you afford to open a store in Bozeman?" Nelly asked.

"I've got a plan," Jubil said, "but if you don't mind, let's talk about that later with Abe and Lily. Picnics and business don't mix."

She gave him a kiss on the cheek. "I'm hungry."

They enjoyed their picnic, then drove north along the coastline past the harbor and then back to the Warner house. When they arrived, Nelly helped Jubil unharness the carriage horse, and then they went in to find Abe and Lily. Lily was in her studio, painting.

"Abe's in his office," Lily said to Jubil. "A telegram came for you this morning."

"Here it is," Abe said, entering the studio carrying an envelope. "It came shortly after you left." Abe handed the envelope to Jubil.

He opened it and read aloud.

The circuit judge arrived yesterday. No one presented a last will and testament for Lucius Black or appeared in court to claim his property, so the judge declared his estate the property of the Territory of Montana. The mercantile and the Metropolitan Hotel will be auctioned off tomorrow. The judge telegraphed the Land Office in Helena to obtain the claim for the mine, so it could be auctioned off as well. Word just came back today that no claim is on file for a mine around Cooke City for either Phineas Black or Lucius Black. It appears that they never filed a claim. Please advise whether I should take some action or return to Council Bluffs. Eli.

"Does that mean you're in the clear from further harassment?" Abe said.

"It does," Jubil said. He felt the heavy dread he had been suppressing rise and dissipate. The weight of executing his plans was still there, but he was eager to quit worrying and get started.

"How will you finance a store in Bozeman?" Abe said.

"I'm going to sell half my farm," Jubil said.

"Oh, Jubil," Nelly said, turning to look at him. "Are you sure you want to do that?"

"It's difficult to let go of it, but I may as well," Jubil said. "I'm hardly ever there, and I was ready to give it up as collateral to Jay Cooke. I'm going to keep the east eighty acres with Pete's cabin, and sell the west eighty. That should bring in enough money to not only start the store in Bozeman but repair the Council Bluffs store too. As long as the stores are pulling their weight before the savings run out, we'll be fine."

"This means that much to you?" Abe said.

"I understand your concern—I really do," Jubil said. "But this isn't just a matter of good business practice for me. If I don't put a store in Bozeman, the corruption at the Crow Agency will probably continue. I can't let that happen. I've invested too much in it already, and I would regret it forever if I didn't finish what I started. Just returning to Council Bluffs and struggling to keep that store operating is not the future I want. But I'm not going to let that store fail either—not without a fight."

Nelly looked at him with pride. "You are persistent," she said with a smile. "And I love you for it."

Jubil watched Abe and Lily silently share their thoughts with a glance.

"We hope you prove our pessimism wrong about the store in Bozeman," Abe said. "And my offer still stands to help you get the Council Bluffs store repaired."

"Thank you," Jubil said. He was very grateful to have Abe and Lily in his life, even though they would never see eye to eye on everything.

"I'm going to send Eli a telegram instructing him to bid on Black's mercantile tomorrow. If he can get it for five hundred dollars or less, it's worth it, if not then I'll make other plans."

"You're heading back to Bozeman then?" Abe asked.

"Yes. I'm going to help Eli get the new store started," Jubil said. "But on my way, I'm going to make a couple of stops. I'm going to meet Ike in Chicago and see if he'll come back to partner with me. Then I'm going to Bloomington to sell half the farm"—he turned to Nelly—"and to visit the Boswells."

"I can't wait to see them," Nelly said with a smile. She turned to Abe and Lily. "I have an idea I'd like to ask you about." She told them about her desire to stay with them for a while.

"That would be wonderful!" Lily said, her eyes aglow.

"We'd like nothing more," Abe said.

"Good," Nelly said. "I'll visit Mama and Papa for a while, then I'll be back."

"All right," Jubil said, rising from his chair. "I have some telegrams to send. We'll be on our way tomorrow."

CHAPTER 22

When the train pulled into Chicago's Union Station, Ike was standing on the platform waiting. He looked dapper in his tailored suit and white open-collared shirt. His blonde hair had grown past its usual shoulder length and was gathered loosely at the nape of his neck in a tail. Ike had always been conscious of his appearance and carried himself with composure, but something about him seemed different—a new confidence, perhaps.

As Jubil and Nelly stepped off the train, Ike and Nelly rushed to embrace one another.

"You look *so* handsome!" Nelly said, giving his long hair a little flip.

"I might say the same about you," Ike said stepping back to admire his sister. "Why have I not heard from you all summer? I haven't gotten a letter from Eli either—what's going on?"

Nelly rolled her eyes and waved him off. "It's quite a tale."

"And what happened to you?" Ike asked Jubil, looking down at his bandaged hand.

"It's quite a tale," Jubil said with a grin. "Let's have breakfast, and we'll fill you in."

"There's a place here in the station," Ike said, "if you're not too fussy."

"We're not fussy," Jubil said. "We've been eating Eli's cooking!"

Ike laughed.

"How is he doing?" Ike said as they set off for the restaurant, Nelly arm-in-arm with her brother.

"Very well," Jubil said. "He's in Bozeman, looking out for our interests there. He handled himself with distinction this summer. I'll tell you all about it when we get settled. You'll be proud of him."

"I'm already proud of him," Ike said. "But that's good to hear."

Jubil smiled. He had missed Ike's company and the close partnership they once shared, and obviously Ike had missed his sister. Jubil was hoping Ike would not choose his new life over a new version of his old one, but he would soon find out. They arrived at the restaurant, where the waiter brought them coffee and took their order.

"We're all fine now," Nelly said to Ike, "but we've had an ordeal. It all started around the time we left you here in Chicago . . ." Nelly turned to Jubil. "I'd rather you tell the story."

Jubil related the whole tale, and when he finally wound down, Ike sat shaking his head in stunned silence. He reached across the table to hold his sister's hand.

"Why is Eli still in Bozeman?" Ike said.

"There's more to the story—some good news for a change," Jubil said. He told Ike about his meeting with Grant and gaining his support for supplying the Crow Agency.

"And Eli is going to run the store in Bozeman?" Ike said.

"That's the plan," Jubil said. "We'll have help from Flynn too. Which brings us to the next part of our conversation."

Ike looked at Jubil then at his sister with suspicion.

"I won't beat around the bush, Ike," Jubil said. "I want you to come back to help me run Warner and Walker Outfitting."

Ike gave Jubil a questioning look.

"How can we afford that . . . and a new store too?" Ike said. "Did Abe agree to finance all this?"

"No," Jubil said. "He thinks my plans are too risky. But that's fine. I think they are worth the risk. I'm on my way to Bloomington to sell half my farm. That will give us some reserves to weather this bad economy and get our feet back under us."

"Are you sure you want to do that?" Ike said with concern.

There's that question again, Jubil thought.

"I'm keeping the half where the house was. I'll still have the cabin."

"Your business with the army went well then?" Ike asked, studying Jubil as Nelly studied her brother.

"Yes," Jubil said. "With the business from Fort Ellis and the Crow Agency, along with the town's business, I think the store in Bozeman is a pretty safe bet."

"What about the store in Council Bluffs?" Ike said. "You plan to fix it up and reopen just like before?" Ike said. "Business was already weak. Won't we just burn through all your reserves and have to close again?"

"That's a risk I'm willing to take," Jubil said. "I'm not ready to give up on the business where I met Abe and Luke, where Luke and I dreamed of a new kind of store. And now, I think we need to try to adapt. That's what Luke would have done—somehow. When we first met, he had a plan to adapt his father's business to the change that would come with the transcontinental railroad—but Abe thought it was too risky. So Luke and I did it together, and it worked. Our business suited the times perfectly. But the times have changed again, and we need to change with them . . . again."

Ike reached in his coat pocket and took out a piece of paper and pencil.

"You plan to sell eighty acres," Ike said, noting the figure on paper, "and the last I knew, land in McLean County was selling for forty-something an acre. We'll call it forty-five . . ." Ike's voice trailed off as he made his calculation. "That's a decent reserve," he said, looking at the total and tapping the pencil to his lips. Jubil enjoyed watching Ike's mind work.

"You know," Ike said, warming to his subject, "working with Mr. Ward has given me an appreciation for the high-quality low-cost products he has curated for his catalog—and his business is thriving in this economy. What if we were to carry some of those same products in our store? I'm sure Levi Strauss would let us sell his pants—he's already doing it with several stores. Many of the other suppliers are too."

"Hmm," Jubil said, "Like we were going to consign our custom products to other stores, but in this case our store is the consignee."

"Exactly," Ike said. "Working with Ward has shown me what is selling right now. I'm sure we could work a deal with several of those suppliers. We could offer our own custom products too, and shift the mix as the economy changes and sales dictate."

"Luke would be proud," Jubil said with a smile. "You're in, then?"

"I am!" Ike said with a laugh. "I've enjoyed my time here, but I miss painting in Lily's studio in Council Bluffs."

"Excellent!" Jubil said. "Do you mind if we tell your parents?"

"Not at all," Ike said. "I'll talk to Mr. Ward and set a date for my leaving as soon as you've sold the farm."

"I couldn't be happier," Nelly said. "I know the rest of the family will feel the same."

"I'll send a telegram after I've talked to the real estate agent about the farm," Jubil said.

Jubil and Nelly arrived in Bloomington late in the afternoon and hired a carriage for the ride downtown. The weather was mild with a hint of fall in the air as they set off, riding west past the livery, then past the McLean County Bank, where

Jubil's remaining savings were on deposit, then north toward the courthouse square. They passed Mr. Ferre's carriage shop, where Nelly's father worked. The last time Jubil had been in Bloomington was the spring of last year. He had come to ask Eli to handle the outfitting for the honeymoon trip to Colorado and to make a final plea to Eli and Mr. Boswell to reconsider their boycott of the wedding in protest of Nelly's independent nature.

The carriage drove past the lot where Jubil and Luke had once operated their Warner and Walker store, now the site of an attorney's office. Jubil imagined the store standing there once again—a square two-story wood-frame building with tall evenly-placed windows on all sides. The sign on the roof of the front porch, made by Mr. Boswell, announcing Warner and Walker Outfitters, with a slogan below—*The Journey is the Destination*—a motto they had taken from how Jubil's uncle Pete had lived his life.

"It was a beautiful store," Nelly said, hugging Jubil's arm.

He enjoyed the memory until images intruded of the building ablaze, of standing on the porch roof watching the fire chief carry Luke's lifeless body down the ladder. The ache he felt at Luke's absence had not eased much since that day.

When their carriage reached the courthouse square, Jubil asked the driver to wait while they entered the office of Weed and Toms Real Estate.

"Well, glory be!" Mr. Weed said, rising from his chair as Jubil entered. "Mr. and Mrs. Jubilee Walker! Why, I haven't seen you two in a coon's age! You're looking smart and healthy, the both of you. What brings you home?"

"I have some business," Jubil said as he shook hands with Weed. "I'm considering selling off the west eighty acres of my farm. It's been lying fallow a few years, but it could easily be cleared. I want to keep the east eighty for myself. Do you think you could find a buyer?"

Weed raised his eyebrows.

"I might already know of one," he said, beaming a wide grin. "You remember Mr. Williams—the farmer who bought your draft horse when you left the farm? Well, every time I see him, he asks if you're ready to sell yet. I'm pretty sure he'll buy it—probably pay top dollar too. I'll ride up and talk to him— you're welcome to come along. Clinch the deal on the spot."

"I remember Mr. Williams—nice fellow," Jubil said, pleased at how quick and easy the sale of his land promised to be. "We're on our way to visit with the Boswells, then I'm going to ride up to the farm and make sure everything is all right. You go ahead and talk to him. I'll come back tomorrow to see if we've got a deal."

"That's fine," Weed said. "I wouldn't take anything less than fifty dollars an acre. That's a little above average, but you've got prime land there. How does that sound?"

"That's excellent," Jubil said. "I'll be back in the morning."

"That's a stroke of luck," he said to Nelly as the carriage started toward her parents' house. "Ike will be pleased."

Nelly nodded at him distractedly. As they approached her parent's house, she looked nervous. "They're going to be so upset," she said.

"They'll just be happy you're all right," Jubil said, taking her hand.

When they reached the Boswell residence, Jubil paid the driver as Nelly gathered herself. Jubil looked at the house with its steeply gabled rooflines and elaborately carved panels along the eaves and imagined all the times he and Nelly had sat on the porch swing and talked, while Ike and Eli stirred up mischief. Those days were long gone, just like the store. He knocked on the door, and Nelly's mother rushed out to engulf Nelly in a tight embrace.

"Thank God!" she said. "We've been so worried."

Mrs. Boswell had been a second mother to Jubil, even when his own mother was still alive. She had always welcomed him into their home and cared for him as if he were one of her own children. Mr. Boswell appeared in the doorway.

"Don't squeeze the life out of her, Mattie," he said. "Jubil, hello. Come on in." He stepped out onto the porch and picked up their bags, which he set in the foyer.

"I've just made a pot of coffee," Mrs. Boswell said, ushering them into the parlor. "Would you like a cup? Are you hungry?"

"No, Mama, we're fine," Nelly said, "but the coffee sounds good. I'll help you."

Mrs. Boswell and Nelly went into the kitchen and were back with coffee before Jubil and Mr. Boswell had exhausted their conversation about the weather.

Mrs. Boswell got right to the point. "Why haven't you written?" she asked.

"I'm very sorry about that, Mama," Nelly said, glancing at her father too. "But we're here now and . . . well, I'd rather let Jubil explain."

Once again, Jubil launched into the tale of the summer's events, but this time he abbreviated greatly, leaving out many of the more disturbing details of Nelly's ordeal and the murderous rescue. By the time he finished his story, Nelly's parents were wiping tears from their eyes.

Nelly rose and went to them. She knelt and grasped one of each of their hands.

"Thank God, you're all right," Mrs. Boswell said, then she gave Nelly a worried look. "Are you *really* all right?"

"Yes, Mama," Nelly said. "I still have bad dreams once in a while, but not often."

Her father wiped his eyes with his handkerchief and nodded at her.

"We do have some good news though," Nelly said, and told her parents about their meeting with Grant and Jubil's business plans—including the news that Ike was returning to Warner and Walker and that Eli would be running the Bozeman store.

The melancholy mood in the room lifted, and the Boswells smiled knowingly at one another.

"Eli was indispensable to me this summer," Jubil said, "and he bravely helped with Nelly's rescue."

Jubil then told them of his plans to sell half his farm.

"Are you sure you want to do that?" Nelly's mother said.

Jubil laughed heartily. When the Boswells looked shocked, he cut himself off. "I'm sorry," he said. "I'm not laughing at you—it's just that *everyone* has had that same reaction! It's enough to make a fellow think he's known for making rash decisions."

At that, Nelly and her parents joined in Jubil's laughter.

"I'm going to hire a horse and ride up to the farm before dark," Jubil said, "just to make sure everything is all right. I'll spend the night at the cabin and be back early tomorrow to meet Mr. Weed."

"You can take Moses," Mr. Boswell said, referring to their carriage horse. "We won't need him until tomorrow. In fact, take the carriage. It'll be easier to tote your bag."

"If you can't stay for supper," Mrs. Boswell said, "I'll put something in a basket for you."

With that, Mrs. Boswell and Nelly were off to the kitchen again.

"How are things at the carriage shop?" Jubil said to Mr. Boswell.

"Slow," he said. "Mr. Ferre says he can hold on, but I know it's tight."

"Abe says Nantucket always needs good carpenters," Jubil said. "Warner and Walker might need one out west too. I've still got a notion to build custom carriages for Yellowstone visitors."

"Good to know a man's skills are in demand," Mr. Boswell said with a smile.

Nelly and Mrs. Boswell returned from the kitchen. Mrs. Boswell was carrying a picnic basket, which she handed over to Jubil.

"There's some fried chicken from last night in here," she said, "half of a loaf of bread and some cheese—and two slices of apple pie. It's not much, but it's better than nothing."

"Ha! Better than nothing?" Jubil said. "Your fried chicken and apple pie! I'm in heaven."

Mrs. Boswell waved him off but looked pleased by his reaction.

Jubil kissed Nelly goodbye, picked up his travel bag with his good hand, hooked the picnic basket handle on his other forearm to spare his bad hand, and headed to the stable. Slowly and carefully, he harnessed Moses to the carriage, loaded his baggage into the boot, along with a bucket of oats for the horse, and set off. He headed east, then turned north on Main Street and followed it out of town.

On the way to the farm, he passed Illinois Wesleyan University, where Major John Wesley Powell had once taught natural sciences. The summer after Jubil's mother had died, he pled his case to join the expedition Powell was leading. Powell had turned him down, but Jubil's determination to prove his worth had set him on his way to a life of adventure. Further north, he passed Illinois State Normal University, the teacher's college where the Illinois Natural History Society Museum housed many of Major Powell's collections of rocks, fossils, and shells that Powell and Jubil's uncle Pete had gathered in their younger days. Jubil had the impulse then to write to Major Powell, just to stay in touch with this man who had taught him so much about the wilderness—some of it inadvertently.

Riding past the universities rekindled an old quandary— whether he would ever be moved to pursue academic studies. Would taking such a path enhance the future for him and Nelly? He had resisted the idea in years past, but since then he had become well acquainted with many men of action who were also well-educated, and he could see more value in it now. Perhaps that was still in his future. His friend Lew Keplinger had not begun his university studies until he was twenty-seven, so Jubil still had a couple of years before he would be lagging behind his friend.

As he approached the farm, Jubil pulled Moses to a halt and studied the stone fireplace and foundation stones marking where the farmhouse and barn had once stood. He imagined them still standing. He could almost see it—his mother inside cooking while his father worked the fields and Jubil did his chores in the barn before dinner. Then he remembered that stark and unholy day after his mother had died and he was left standing all alone inside that house, wondering what he was going to do with himself.

He steered Moses to the small stable behind the cabin, which he had built using wood and timbers reclaimed after the fire. He unharnessed the horse to let him graze. He pulled the boards from the cabin door and window, and was pleased to find things inside in good order. He swept out the cabin, removed the quilt from his footlocker and made the bed, brought in firewood, fetched water from the well, washed the dishes, checked the chimney for obstructions, then laid a fire to light after sundown. Performing these small tasks in a place he loved soothed him deeply.

He brought his travel bag into the cabin and put the picnic basket inside the footlocker to keep it safe while he was gone. Then he took Moses out for a ride around the perimeter of the property for the last time. The tall prairie grass had reestablished itself everywhere, and scattered throughout this growth were a few volunteer trees, propagated by the wind and wildlife—nothing that would be too hard for the new owner to clear.

Jubil returned to the cabin and, as the sun set, lit some candles and the fire, then retrieved the picnic basket and enjoyed his feast. As he ate and watched the fire dance, he had an overwhelming sense of well-being. He could feel his family, kept alive in his memory, there with him. He knew that he would never sell this part of the farm, that he would always want to come back here.

He finished his supper, saving a piece of pie for breakfast, and stoked up the fire. He looked through the stack of dime novels lying on the shelf by the fireplace. He had once loved these books, but he had outgrown them after he started adventuring himself. He took one from the stack and smiled as he read the title—*Malaeska the Indian Wife of the White Hunter.* How many times had he read this particular adventure as a boy? He stretched out on the bed to read it again. The book held his interest for a while, but then he found his mind wandering from the familiar plot into daydreams of his own future. He put the book down and lay on his back staring at the cabin's rafters, as he had done on countless nights as a boy.

His deepest wish was to hold onto the things he already had. He was grateful for them all, and wanted only to build on them. Once the stores in Bozeman and Council Bluffs were running smoothly, he and Eli and White Dog would lead as many adventure tours as they could fit in.

Perhaps he would finally convince White Dog to visit the farm and even to live here in the cabin between tours. And if White Dog were living here, perhaps Jubil would build a house nearby for himself and Nelly. It could be a humble thing built on the foundation stones of his parents' farmhouse, or it might be a grand home that incorporated those foundation stones into its construction—maybe a huge fireplace. That sounded right. A large log home with rooms for several guests and two offices—one for him and one for Nelly—and maybe a nursery, though that still felt far in the future, if it happened at all.

As he rode these flights of fancy, his eyelids grew heavy. He rose to bank the fire, then returned to his bed. He blew out the candles, covered himself with the quilt his mother had made, and lay watching the glow of the embers in the fireplace as he drifted off to sleep.

AUTHOR'S NOTE

In the first three novels of the Jubilee Walker Series, *The Powell Expeditions*, *The Yellowstone Campaign*, and *The Northern Pacific Railroad*, I adhered closely to the historical record. As a writer of historical fiction, I am only willing to take a certain degree of liberty with history. If I am portraying a historical event or character, I take care not to alter significant aspects to fit my story.

In this novel, however, in order to navigate Jubil's story arc, as well as the arcs of the other fictional characters, I've taken some creative liberties. This book is largely framed around fictional events and people, with the addition of some historical characters and events. The reader may find it worthwhile for me to clarify what is fact and what is fiction in *The Montana Gold Mine*.

The premise of the novel is fictional: There never was a major gold strike in Montana around Cooke City, as described in the book. There were definitely gold mines around Cooke City in the 1870s, but none of them produced any vast wealth or created a major rush. It might also be worth pointing out that the location of my fictional mine is described clearly enough in the book that a determined person might seek it out today, but they would be disappointed to find nothing there but wilderness.

The part of the story that describes Lieutenant Colonel Custer's expedition into the Black Hills in the summer of 1874, to assess the amount of gold that might be found there, is historically accurate. It is true that the army was forced into the odd position of defending the Sioux against white prospectors who were encroaching on land granted to the Sioux by treaty. Jubil's observation that the area seemed destined for big trouble proved to be true, much to Custer's misfortune.

In my portrayal of events at the Crow Agency near Bozeman, I have altered the historical timeline, but the events I describe are modeled on actual events. In 1876, formal charges of fraud were filed against the agents at the Crow reservation for the same misdeeds as described in this book. But those charges were resolved without the matter ever coming to trial. My characters the Black brothers are not intended to represent any actual persons.

Yet the concerns expressed about similar activity at the Red Cloud Agency in Nebraska by the character Mr. Grinnell are a reflection of real events at the time. George Bird Grinnell was a real naturalist who traveled that summer with Custer and who was an associate of Professor Othniel Charles Marsh, who witnessed the corruption and vowed to report it directly to President Grant. His letter to Grant spurred Grant to form a commission that led to Secretary of the Interior Columbus Delano resigning in 1875. The degree of complicity Delano had in the corruption under his administration was just as unclear then as it is in this story.

Walter Trumbull and Lieutenant Doane made their first appearances in book two of my series, *The Yellowstone Campaign*. Jack Sumner made his first appearance in book one, *The Powell Expeditions*. In those books, the depictions of these characters followed the historical record, but in this book their involvement with Jubil is purely fictional.

ACKNOWLEDGEMENTS

I would like to thank my editor, Heidi Bell, for sticking with me through this whole series of books. Her patient coaching and insightful comments have helped me shape the stories and polish them beyond anything I could have done alone. Many thanks also to Regina McCaughey-Silvia for her meticulous proofreading. It is a great relief to know that she is there to save me from my own embarrassing oversights. Any shortcomings in the finished product are mine alone. Thank you to my talented granddaughter, Alyssa Kaufman, for creating the beautiful cover image, and to Alan Dino Hebel and Ian Koviak at The Book Designers for their work in creating the cover layout and interior design. To Corrine Pritchett, Hannah Robertson, Marissa DeCuir, and all the people at Books Forward, thank you for your support and efforts to bring attention to my work.

I deeply appreciate my daughter Lori Kaufman for her unflagging moral support; Rich Teegarden for his time and attention as an early reader and story advisor; Scott Lee Wilson for his artistic inspiration and philosophical insights; and other friends and family who listened to me talk about imaginary people and their problems. I am very grateful for your support.

For readers interested in a historical account of Custer's 1874 mission into the Black Hills, I offer two suggestions. For a concise overview, *Custer's Gold: The United States Cavalry Expedition of 1874* by Donald Jackson. For detailed insight and beautiful photography, *Exploring with Custer: The 1874 Black Hills Expedition* by Ernest Grafe and Paul Horsted. For a better understanding of President Grant and the charges of corruption that plagued his presidency, *Grant* by Ron Chernow. For a history of events surrounding Yellowstone National Park, *Empire of Shadows: The Epic Story of Yellowstone* by George Black.

ABOUT THE AUTHOR

Tim Piper is retired from a long career in Information Technology and has been a lifelong hobbyist musician. In his earlier days he was an avid hiker and backcountry camper, but his adventures these days are less strenuous and more comfortable. He began his education at Illinois State University as an English major, but life circumstances put him on a more pragmatic path, and he graduated with a BS in Business Admin, a degree he finds appropriately named. You can visit his website: timpiper-author.com, or follow him on Facebook: Tim Piper – Author.

www.ingramcontent.com/pod-product-compliance
Lightning Source LLC
Chambersburg PA
CBHW071545110726
47908CB00007B/1998